"Ingenuity and innovation ... nobody makes them come alive in high-tech adventures better than Dean Ing!"

— David Brin

"Strong characters and dramatic conflict point up Ing's storytelling skill."

— *Publishers Weekly*

"... An idea book ... but the characterization and action plotting offer plenty of excitement."

— Dean Lambe

"Ing is a superb describer of physical and mental combat and a brilliant creator of alternate worlds."

— *San Francisco Examiner*

Books by Dean Ing

THE BIG LIFTERS
BLOOD OF EAGLES
SINGLE COMBAT
WILD COUNTRY

DEAN ING

THE BIG LIFTERS

A TOM DOHERTY ASSOCIATES BOOK
NEW YORK

THE BIG LIFTERS

Copyright © 1988 by Dean Ing

Map and illustrations by Alan McKnight

First printing: July 1988
First mass market printing: June 1989

A Tor Book

Published by Tom Doherty Associates, Inc.
49 West 24 Street
New York, N.Y. 10010

ISBN: 0-812-54104-9   Can. ISBN: 0-812-54105-7

Library of Congress Catalog Card Number: 87-51402

Printed in the United States of America

0 9 8 7 6 5 4 3 2 1

For Joel Hughes, who surveyed those high Mojave wastes with me; and for Leik Myrabo, who'd rather fly.

ACKNOWLEDGMENTS

Wherever my capering in these pages is across thin ice, I bear all responsibility—because Fred Ullmer taught me how much fun preliminary design can be, and ought to be. Still, I would never have begun matching maglevs with sectional charts, nor existing power grids with orbital paths, had it not been for Professor Leik Myrabo's visions of future propulsion systems. The Master's Thesis of Sacheverel Eldrid, with its scramjet vehicle, preceded me as a beacon—from which I strayed at my pleasure and, from an engineering standpoint, probably at my peril.

I am also in debt to Dr. R. L. Forward for the propulsion data he furnished; and, finally, to the Lawrence Livermore National Laboratory. The LLNL, as I ended this book, released its Request for Proposals for Research In Ground-To-Orbit Laser Propulsion. They knew it all the time. . . .

SOUTHERN
CALIFORNIA

Scale of Nautical Miles

0 10 20 30 40 50 60 70 80 90 100

Plain truth is what happens
when people run out of ideas.

—Kurt Weill,
The Threepenny Opera

PROLOGUE

May, 1965

Manson Perkins knew the rules, and the tricks, of interstate hauling. Shortly after noon he crossed the New Mexico state line from Texas, taking the bumps and delays of State Highway 88 to avoid that weigh station at Clovis because he didn't have an overweight permit, wheeling back toward the west onto the main highway in early afternoon at the sun-blistered hamlet of Melrose. After a half-million miles jockeying the Peterbilt, he was tanned on his left forearm, pale under his shirt, and wiry all over. His fingers on both hands showed the marks of maintaining heavy equipment; the burn scar from his Airco welder was hidden by his denim trousers. He had lost count of the times he'd explained that pool of smooth, slick hairless skin to women.

It was already one hot sonofabitch outside, heat waves squeezing the aroma from a billion late May sage blossoms out there on the hardpan horizon, an aroma musky and mouth-wateringly pervasive that a man's nose didn't get used to. Diesel fumes weren't like that, but Perkins was smelling them now and then. Probably that goddamn fuel fitting he had replaced himself, doing his best with what he had because when you underbid the big outfits, you had to cut your expenses somehow and you weren't smart to do it by dropping your dues to the National Transport Coalition. Scary things happened to truckers who plied the highways without NTC protection.

He wished for air-conditioning because it was going to get hotter still, New Mexico blacktop soaking up the heat and feeding it back into those old retreads until, when you stopped for a walkaround, you didn't touch a tread without gloves, not unless you wanted second-degree burns. If you ever wondered what high speeds and hot blacktop did to tires on an overloaded rig, two minutes of studying any highway shoulder would give you a broad hint. Black curls of shredded rubber, flying explosively from overheated tire casings, lined highways from Maine to California, a few from automobiles but most of them big fat chunks from disintegrating rig tires. Perkins vowed he would keep it down to seventy or so. A tire change out there was murder. And later in August, when migrating tarantulas freckled the blacktop in countless numbers . . but he didn't want to think about that. Perkins had the knack of forgetting things he didn't want to think about. It hadn't killed him yet.

Caution told him to stop at Fort Sumner for a nap and to recheck the tiedowns on that bodacious load of line pipe he was hauling to a wildcatter near Albuquerque. Perkins popped a pill instead of the nap, peered into his rearviews to satisfy himself about the security of his load, and told caution to go to hell. Time was money.

The wildcatter knew about time and money; that's why he had contracted with Perkins, an independent who owned his rig and would bust his ass for a schedule bonus, and devil take the hindmost. The great advantage of an Indy was that, by doing his own maintenance, he came in with low bids. The hidden disadvantage was that while Perkins took no nonsense from straw bosses or ordinary traffic either—what five-thousand-pound Lincoln was going to argue, right or wrong, with a vehicle that weighed the same as *eighteen* Lincolns?—Perkins might not be much of a safety inspector, especially of his own work. Fuel fittings, for example. Those tiedowns, for another.

Steel line pipe is heavy stuff, fifty pounds a linear foot, and Perkins was hauling well over a thousand feet of it on the flatbed. Broad tiedown straps kept the bundle secure, cinched up so tight a man could thump it with a finger and hear a note like a bass fiddle. If it didn't sound like that, you ratcheted the strap another few notches so you wouldn't have to play pickup sticks with thirty-five tons of steel pipe. But time and dust and a hot sun will have their way with fabric strapping. If Manson Perkins had stopped at Fort Sumner and thumped that strap nearest to the cab, he would have heard only a soft *plop* like a plugged nickel hitting a pillow.

* * * *

Exercising her squint lines into the afternoon sun, Nell Peel judged that she and her grandson, Johnny, would pass Cline's Corners in a half hour, which would put them in Albuquerque an hour after that. She drove the white Peel VW microbus as she always did on these long arrow-straight stretches, flat-out, knowing the '59 bus would do that forever although Nell couldn't exceed the speed limit even if she wanted to. Without a tail wind the bus would do exactly her age, sixty-two, and because her teenage grandson knew vehicles inside out, he wasn't likely to complain that she was driving at granny-pace.

"This is a nice one, Gram," said John Wesley Peel from the passenger seat, holding up a specimen of interlocked gypsum plates to the light. The stone filtered sunlight like alabaster, a gleam the color of flesh, almost the same color as the boy's blond hair. That specimen would catch every ray when embedded in clear plastic. Unlike most rock hounds, Nell Peel felt that it was cheating to slice into a stone that the good Lord had created with ready-made beauty. Instead, and with her grandson's help, she had turned a corner of their garage into a workshop where they learned all the tricks of embedding such examples of God's handiwork. Though he might still want to be a trucker like his dead father, the boy was naturally gifted with his hands. A regular wizard with machinery, too.

Nell had explained to Johnny that she had misgivings about encasing God-made beauty in man-made plastic, but high technology was no abomination when it was used to reveal a higher way. Johnny had asked, like evangelists on TV? Well, she'd admitted, like some of them. She sold the cubes of plastic, with specimens of quartz or naturally polished agate or gypsum, as paperweights and bookends. Privately, to the boy, she claimed they were prayers of thanks for these delicately shaped natural wonders. A body simply could not understand why men craved flying to the moon, or even into vacuum, when the earth was so obviously *made* for them. Johnny had argued about that for a while, but eventually he saw it her way.

Now that her husband, Leonard, had lost interest in her outings—she knew the new TV was his toy, though he denied it—Nell thanked the Almighty every night that the boy was such a willing companion on these overnight trips to the Pecos, or Socorro, or Vaughn. Oh, he had his faults. She knew Johnny dated some suspiciously flippant girls, and cussed when fixing machinery, and his excuses on prayer meeting nights could get mighty creative; but his father, Evan, the only son of Nell and Leonard Peel, had been the same way at seventeen.

And dead at thirty-four, in Evan's own eighteen-wheeler with his wife, Ruth, by his side, in a senseless disaster that made headlines. No, not senseless, Nell amended; the good Lord had His reasons, though she suspected it must have been a judgment on Ruth somehow. She never said that to Johnny, though; it was hard enough bringing up a grandson who was half scholar and the other half daredevil, without casting shadows over the sunlit memory of his mother. Pretty little thing, and completely devoted to Evan and little Johnny, but . . . God's judgment. How else could you reconcile it?

In the rearview, which vibrated enough to make images fuzzy, Nell saw the glint of reflection from something miles behind, but catching them. She glanced at her grandson before attending to the highway, noting the way he grinned at the specimens he held. A smile to warm a grandmother's heart and rock a young girl on her heels, but not with those whiskers. "You should start shaving oftener, Johnny," she said.

"I will, if you'll learn to call me Wes," he said. "The guys call me Wes, the principal called me Wes when he handed me my diploma. Dad called me Wes," he finished with the clincher.

She sighed and turned down the corners of her mouth in that line that said more about disapproval than all the scriptures in the Book. "And everywhere that Evan went, his son is sure to go," she said, teasing him without malice, glancing at the rearview again. The glint had grown fast, so fast that she estimated its speed at seventy-five or more, and it was not a car that was moving up in the left lane. It was a big rig, with a legend cleverly painted on the bumper so it read correctly in a rearview mirror. Perkins Freight. "I suppose you still intend to follow Evan into an Autocar, like that thing right behind us."

The boy craned his neck. "It's a Peterbilt, Gram," he corrected, talking louder now because the whine of rig tires and the clatter of a big overtaking diesel was resonating the little VW bus. "Boy, he's got the hammer down, hasn't he?"

Nell opened her mouth to comment on the way he loved to use trucker jargon, and kept it open as she saw the pronghorn antelope bound onto the highway shoulder. Pronghorns knew better than this, she thought, but all of God's creatures made mistakes. All she said as she hit the brakes was a faint, dismayed, "Oh!"

Manson Perkins was already alongside the white VW van, highballing at close to eighty, when he saw the white-marked tan of a pronghorn that just seemed to come from nowhere. For one instant he thought, "Teach the damn' fool a lesson, he'll go under the chassis of my Pete,'' but he knew it didn't always work out that way, sometimes a deer leaped at just the wrong instant, and then you were picking bones out of your radiator while your coolant trickled away on thirsty desert soil. Perkins had air brakes, and he used them hard.

A big rig can stop in an astonishingly short distance if nothing interferes with the process. But the little van was already squealing its brake drums, its blunt rump skidding at a slight angle as the pronghorn turned in panic, leaping in their direction, then away to safety. Over that squeal and the lower-pitched howl of huge retreads ripping at the surface of blacktop came two reports, loud as shotgun blasts. A slowly separating retread can throw the whole tread in no time flat if it is skidding hard under a heavy load at eighty miles an hour. And when that tire goes, on the outside right rear of the trailer, all its load is transferred to the dual adjacent to it. And if *that* one is none too good to start with . . .

It had been none too good, and it got worse in a god-awful hurry. The sudden drag of those blown tires caused the trailer to whip viciously, nosing to the right, its inertia trying to whip Perkins and the cab to the left through the swivel mount. Perkins steered to straighten out, the entire rig bucking and shuddering like a skate over a washboard, and the forward tiedown parted then, and instead of slamming the barrier Perkins kept between the pipe and the rear of his cab, that line pipe began to roll sideways as it slid forward.

Nell and the boy cried out to each other, seeing long shadows a split second before the first section of pipe slithered forward, sideways and down, and then the van's windshield burst before Nell's eyes, her door springing partly open as the roof buckled within inches of her head. She screamed and ducked toward Johnny, unencumbered by seat belts that she never wore though the boy always buckled up religiously. Johnny ducked too, but lashed a corded arm out to grab the steering wheel because they were still doing at least fifty.

And now Perkins felt his rig begin to jackknife, hearing the tolling of huge dull bells as his load started to cascade off the side, and from the corner of his eye he could see lengths of line pipe hitting the highway and flipping. He had time to hope the mass of that fuckin' Kraut van would be a barrier to keep the flatbed from coming all the way around, knowing it would have to be filled with concrete to do it, but of course the van was so much tinfoil to a rig weighing forty times as much, and Perkins let up on the brakes hoping to power his rig out of this hopeless slide with the flatbed making an L to the cab as it batted the little van.

John Wesley Peel felt his grandmother's arms circle his shoulders, her foot no longer on the brake after something huge slammed them forward, and he blinked tiny shards of glass from his eyes as he tried with one arm to steer the VW bus onto the right-hand shoulder. Long gray forms the size of telephone poles, flipping like cheerleaders' batons, were slamming the bus, one of them sliding across the blacktop, and because it weighed as much as the bus, it forced the little vehicle to slew toward the shoulder. The boy knew that the entire left side of the bus was smashed in, including its top, but the trick was to ride it out without the kind of sudden stop that would catapult his unbelted grandmother through a jaggedly smashed windshield.

They might have made it but for the bent length of line pipe that flew completely over the Peterbilt, gouging into blacktop thinner than it should have been, and it was bent flat enough that Perkins's left front tire actually rode over it. There were still several hundred linear feet of pipe on the flatbed, like arrows left unspent in a quiver.

With a huge steel pipe buckling and clanging beneath its chassis and the flatbed, a tie-rod buckled and then there was no steering control left, and Manson Perkins flung his door wide as the cab began to tip, hoping to fall free. But the cab righted itself, slewing sideways, and Perkins cracked his skull

7

against the windshield before falling unconscious into the passenger footwell. The Peterbilt did what it did best, commanding the road, juggernauting over obstacles, coming to rest with a great shudder, still upright. Like many another long-hauler, Manson Perkins owed his life to that massive cab.

Though famous for its tippiness, the VW bus never actually rolled until after it stopped upright, only to be slammed again by the flatbed, now parted from its cab. The remaining pipes did what round objects do: they rolled off the flatbed, one of them standing vertical and then toppling like a felled tree, very slowly, and an undamaged VW bus might have taken this insult without its roof collapsing very far. But the roof was already creased heavily inward.

John Wesley Peel screamed "Gram!" as he saw and felt the central roof area mash downward, forcing the little vehicle onto its right side with the boy beneath and his grandmother pinned just above him. The sudden impact at his right hip nearly knocked him unconscious, but the pain kept him awake, and though he could move only his right arm in the long ensuing silence, he could see why his grandmother had not toppled onto him. In fact, he could not turn his head to avoid seeing her, so tightly were they pinned, and very close together.

Her head had been caught between the collapsed roof and the sturdy steel partition at his seat back, and while her face was turned toward him, it was not a face he had ever seen before but one that he would see again many times for as long as he lived. It did not look like a face at all. It looked like a Halloween mask lying folded on a table, two inches wide, but no Halloween mask ever had such a wealth of detail, the kinds of detail only surgeons would ever see in a well-run world.

Wes Peel, struggling against madness, thought about the way his world was run for thirty-seven minutes, until the syringe went into his free right arm. It was another fifteen minutes before they got him free, and still later before they realized how thoroughly his hip was smashed. They said he was all through with football, scholarship or no scholarship. They said he would be lucky if he ever walked again.

ONE

"Enough of this 'strange bedfellows' bullshit," said Joseph Alton Weatherby, placing one thick-fingered hand on the report before him so gently that the ash did not drop from his cigar. "Peel is killing us by inches!" Back in the 1980's, to judge by his heavy breathing, Weatherby would have slammed that hand down; but now, in April 1995, experience had taught him to use violence only as a last resort. Of the nine men surrounding the National Transport Coalition's boardroom table, not one was a stranger to violence. If you came up through the ranks of interstate trucking—and every member of the NTC Board had, including Chairman Weatherby—you had skinned your knuckles a few times. Or worse.

Antony Ciano, once called The Jersey Lily for his habit of sending bouquets to the funerals of competitors, flicked his copy of the report with a forefinger. "So find us a better source of short-haul rigs awreddy," said Ciano, who made it a point never to raise his voice because it implied loss of control. And Antony Ciano controlled a great deal in Jersey, eastern Pennsylvania and most of Delaware. "Peel's short-haul rigs are keepin' a lot of my teamsters competitive. You want to question your own figures?"

"I want," said Weatherby slowly, as a flush crept up his size nineteen neck, "to get off this treadmill to oblivion."

Two of the board members leaned back, recognizing the signs. When Joey got his rhetoric cranked up he could steal a phrase from the best. But Joey Weatherby sensed that this brisk Pittsburgh afternoon was not the time for a long filibuster. "I'm telling you guys, it's not just . . what'd you call it, Ciano? Another shakeout of old-fashioned, big-ticket rigs? There are fewer new rigs on the interstates today, for God's sake!" He waved toward a broad window and the traffic spanning the Allegheny River in the near distance, and sighed.

When Weatherby sighed, his entire two hundred and fifty pounds seemed to deflate. "Look at the figures. Peel set up a freight brokerage business that uses railroads a lot; not a fly-by-night scam, but a brokerage the independents can trust. Now Peel's Hayward plant is expanding like a goddamn cancer and our national ton-mileage is lower. Even our big triplet rigs in Wyoming and Nevada are hurting. Figure it out: Other short-haul suppliers are copying Peel, and more double-stack railroad cargoes are trundling through Cheyenne. What goes by rail doesn't go by truck. Is that a clear and present danger, or isn't it?"

Charlie Rourke, who represented most of Massachusetts, bulked like a smaller version of the barrel-chested Weatherby. Now he spoke up. "If it wasn't Peel Transit, it'd be those other manufacturers."

"The hell it would," Weatherby shot back. "A bunch of me-too marketers. John Wesley Peel is beholden to nobody, and he keeps plowing profits back into new ways to take away our piece of the action. All his high tech shit keeps him a year ahead of the others, finding more ways to undercut highway freight. It's not just a coincidence, gentlemen. Peel Transit is putting our big highway rigs out of business."

Ciano, softly, "You're talkin' vendetta, Joey."

Weatherby's thick expressive brows raised, his eyes widening as he nodded. The effect was as if he were hearing a brilliant response from a dull student. "Yeah, I am. I can even tell you why.

"First time I ever saw Wes Peel, I was fresh out of Pitt, covering an insurance case for New Empress Freight. Peel's old man drove a double-tandem semi rig out of Albuquerque, back in the days before wives rode in long-haulers. But Peel's wife rode with him. She was in the cab in, uh, 'fifty-nine it was, when his brakes failed on the old Grapevine grade south of Bakersfield."

"Whoaaa," said the West Coast man, Frank Lecano, who had spent twenty years at the wheel of the biggest rigs and now, at the top of the heap, was near retirement. "The old Grapevine had bad turnouts and sand pits, no nothin'. Blood alley," he said, and with the curiosity of an old pro, asked, "What was he haulin'?"

"Mixed load; heavy gypsum board and fertilizer. The bill of lading was doctored so it didn't say ammonium nitrate, and the driver didn't know his fertilizer was ten tons of high explosive. Hard to tell what set it off."

Lecano's "Ohhh, yeah," interrupted the chairman. "I remember. We had to route around the crater for weeks. Well, these things happen." His shrug suggested that these things had always happened and, immutable as acts of God, would always happen. In a way it was true; they would always happen as long as multiton loads of lethal cargoes jousted with ordinary traffic.

Weatherby continued, "Wes Peel was a kid then, testifying because of a long-distance phone call back to Albuquerque. His old man had mentioned to the boy that it was a no-sweat run with a load of gypsum and cowshit, and the defense couldn't shake the kid. Peel knew all the buzzwords already; he intended to be a trucker like his dad. The settlement was a whopper; punitive damages. Shit, some of that money set John Wesley Peel up in business!"

"Don't sound like a vendetta to me," said Rourke. "He wanted to be a trucker. He's building trucks." Outspread hands implied that Rourke's case was cut and dried.

"Wait," Weatherby cautioned, with one palm out, and softened it with a faint smile. "I spent good NTC money getting dope on Peel, so let me get to the payoff. Turns out that he was injured later in another accident with a rig, and still wears metal pins in his butt. His grandparents raised him after the Grapevine thing; hard-shell Christian fundamentalists, very strict. When Peel was seventeen, he was riding with his grandmother in a little van when a rig carrying oil well line pipe overtook 'em. Driver was prob'ly doing eighty or so to get his bonus pay. You know how they run flat-out on those open New Mexico stretches.

"Seems that a deer ran onto the highway, and the rig driver locked everything up and jackknifed. The line pipe mashed that little van pretty much flat. Young Peel came out of it with a broken hip, but he was pinned in the van for a half hour with his face six inches from what was left of his grandmother's head." A long pause, then, "I suspect Wes Peel did a lot of thinking in that half hour."

Lecano: "What happened to the rig driver?"

Weatherby: "Shook up a little. But that's not the point."

Rourke: "He was one of ours, Joey. That's always the point."

Weatherby, with a show of restraint, "The point I'm getting at, is that Peel started out as one of ours, and a turncoat who knows the ropes can be the worst kind of enemy. When he went into business, it was with off-road heavy equipment in Colorado. By the time he built his Hayward plant, Peel had a personal hard-on against what we do for a living. I can't prove it, but I can smell it. Ciano, you said 'vendetta.' I say we take it seriously."

Ari Pappas, whose interests spanned the Gulf Coast states, was first to raise his voice above a mutter of other responses.

"Gentlemen, this industry has a history of ignoring smoke when its pants are on fire. Our chairman may be right about Peel; I've met the man, he's a two-bottle Holy Joe, and you couldn't scare him with a SWAT team. But let's keep our hands clean, okay?"

"Spit it out, Ari," Ciano sneered. "You don't want him keepin' house in a waste drum on the Jersey flats."

Snickers, and a quick rejoinder from Weatherby, "I don't either."

Ciano: "So whose side you on, Mr. Chairman?"

"This country's side," Weatherby said. "We stay clean as we can, and we keep the nation's highway freight running in a way that doesn't get feds sniffing at our heels."

"Motion seconded," said Lecano, his eyes on Ciano's face.

"You can't get at Peel through stock holdings or a board of directors; he hasn't got any," Pappas admitted. "Maybe we could lobby for some laws that just happen to hit Peel's business harder than anybody else's."

"I think we could vote some NTC funds for that," Weatherby nodded. "And meanwhile, put out the word that the NTC is worried about Peel's rigs. Safety, reliability, all that crap. If a trucker thinks a Peel local rig might be outlawed next year, he sure as hell won't wanta buy one this year. The less profit Peel makes, the less he plows back into new ways to zing us."

"You want a few little accidents? Why didn't you say so," asked Ciano. "I got a man works on Peel stuff all the time."

"Keep your soldiers on leave," Weatherby said.

"Naw, not that kind of mechanic, a *mechanic* mechanic. Ramirez owes me," Ciano said, explaining much with tremendous economy.

"Fine, just don't graunch anybody, and I don't want to know any more about it," Weatherby cautioned. Ciano shrugged and looked out the window.

During the next hour or so, the minds of Pappas and Weatherby complemented one another, as usual: Pappas quick, Weatherby inexorably logical. Both were family men who took their religions—Greek Orthodox and Catholic—seriously. Where others might decide to break heads, these two preferred to break leases. In earlier days restraint would have been a weakness, but federal task forces against organized crime had turned this restraint into a strength. The National Transport Coalition, under Joey Weatherby's guidance, had turned legalized bullying into a fine art.

Some of the members were chafing, and the big window was splashing a golden gleam of late sunlight off the river, before Weatherby committed their voice vote results to a recorder. NTC lobbyists on Capitol Hill, and the wordsmiths who drafted proposals for trucking legislation, would briefly earn the astonishing salaries they enjoyed. No paper or computer record would be sullied with the name of John Wesley Peel, but the man's freight brokerage and his trucking equipment would soon begin to feel the pressure of a hostile NTC.

Ari Pappas lingered at his place, rummaging in his briefcase, as the others hurried out of the boardroom. Joey Weatherby noticed, and did the same.

When the two men were alone, Joey pulled a cigar humidor from a special breast pocket; chose one Haitian Crook; offered another to Pappas. They performed rituals of clipping and lighting up in silence. Then Pappas, watching his own thick blue exhalation, said, ''There's got to be a hidden agenda on this Peel business, Joey. What's the guy done to you?''

Startled, Joey coughed and then grinned. ''Swear to God, Ari, it's nothing personal. I laid it on straight. I should'a said something about Peel in 'ninety-one when I first realized how his intermodal stuff was gonna affect long-haulers. I mean, hell, that freight brokerage business of his was busting its nuts to avoid the highways.''

''But you waited until now? Yeah,'' Pappas said, putting his head to one side, ''you would. No complaints; some of these guys would've taken, uh, what my lawyers call 'precipitate action.' Lecano and Rourke are up to date, but you want to keep a friendly eye on Ciano. The day he reverts to an old mustache Pete, NTC's looking for indictments.''

"Tell me about it," Weatherby grumped. "But whattaya want from me, Tony's drivers put him here. Same as you and me." He snapped his briefcase shut and waved the boardroom lights off.

En route to the door, padding on carpet that shined the tips of their shoes, Pappas remained silent. Then, his face bathed in a dying golden light from the window, "Joey, if Peel is after our hides . . ."

"I never said that. I think he's after our business. It just happens to come wrapped in our hides."

"Whatever. But why didn't you ask for some resumes during the meeting? I have a couple of people in Atlanta who could charm a mongoose. If I said the word, they'd be happy to get jobs with Peel. Never hurts to have somebody in the other camp, drawing two salaries."

Joey Weatherby put his big meaty hand on the door and beamed. "Now, why didn't I think of that myself," he said with dry sarcasm.

Pappas, grinning back, nodded. "One day I'll learn not to underestimate you, Joey. So you know Peel's intentions for certain."

"Oh, yeah. And not just from Peel's camp," he went on, watching the door slide shut. "From inside his fuckin' tent."

If he thought about it at all, Weatherby assumed that old Ciano's accident-prone mechanic worked out of Jersey. But Joey Weatherby was not the only NTC leader with a link to the camp of John Wesley Peel.

TWO

Few of Winthorp's students during the Spring Term of 1995 recognized him as a homicidal maniac, which proves only that some maniacs are more subtle than others. With thinning dark hair carefully arranged across his scalp, small well-groomed hands, and his mother's luminous gaze, Winthorp seemed anything but a radical professor. He was fond of his splendid British diction, his three-piece suits, his campus strolls, and his glances toward the dark secret places between the knees of young women in the lecture halls of midwest Grayson University. Kosrow Nurbashi, his gaunt companion on this particular stroll, was not fond of Winthorp's dialect when speaking Persian, as both were doing now, more literary than the southern Farsi dialect. Yet it would never do to tell Professor Bruce Hassan Winthorp that he spoke the argot of a Tabriz whore. Winthorp had learned Persian from his mother.

"Your martyr was not wasted in the Elliott necessity," Winthorp told the Iranian. Another man might have said, "the Elliott assassination." Like many economists, Winthorp coined his own expressions even when—sometimes precisely because—older phrases were better understood. "Trust me in this," Winthorp added.

"Allah's warriors are too few to waste," said Kosrow Nurbashi, biting back a more caustic reply. A mullah of Nurbashi's sort, running a team of suicidal zealots in a foreign country, demanded trust utterly and at last fatally; but he did not return it. Therefore he did not entirely trust this tweedy half-English

16

intellectual, not even after the reports from Tehran which told Nurbashi more about Winthorp than Winthorp himself might know.

Possibly Winthorp knew his real father had been a Ukrainian geologist probing for Iran's oil in 1942, not the staunch British sergeant who took Sultana's babe for his own and brought mother and child back to England. Perhaps he knew why Sergeant Winthorp had taken to drink, and to beating his round-heeled wife, in 1946 after discovering how she added to her income as an exotic entertainer. Perhaps, too, the son had taken refuge in books to gain more distance from a past that one might expect of a divorced belly dancer's brat.

Sultana's later fame in English cinema had paid young Bruce's way through the Victoria University of Manchester. Secretly, she taught him the Shia way. By observing her with men, the boy learned how subtly one can take revenge on a strong but unwary opponent. His own brains brought him some fame in national economic planning, and tenure in an American university, and gradually Winthorp realized his very special position. Wary of Soviets, he never contacted them; those who scampered between superpowers tended to become very small animals maimed between very large gears. Eventually, at Grayson U., he dropped hints to certain foreign students of the Shiite persuasion. In due course Nurbashi contacted him.

Kosrow Nurbashi knew the considerable strengths, and the human weaknesses, of this middle-aged fanatic. He knew that he could not hope to find a man better trained than Winthorp to decapitate America by pinpointing Americans who most needed killing. Despite all this, Nurbashi would never completely trust a man with such a villainous accent. Raised in a culture whose every children's tale featured revenge, whose most revered figure was Ruhollah Khomeini, the mullah withheld trust as a child hoards sweetmeats. "The media say that Senator Elliott could never have become President," Nurbashi pointed out.

A snort. "Certainly not; never tractable enough for his party," Winthorp agreed. "But Adam Elliott was an astronaut before he was a politician. After the failure of the second space shuttle, he became a dervish in Congress seeking funds for orbital lifters of better design. He had charisma. He had powerful backers. He was driven by the idea that cheap cargo to orbit was the key to American wealth in the coming years." Unconsciously, the little man slowed his words as he sprinkled Americanisms, speaking with the assurance of one who was safe behind a lectern.

But Nurbashi had been harangued by coal-eyed experts before. "And to counter this mere idea, Islam sacrificed a youth?" Dependable martyrs were getting harder to find. Nurbashi's most galling secret was that he had only a few more of them to expend, and two of those needed further injections of fervor. It was not a secret to be shared with Winthorp.

"Elliott was not so mere," Winthorp objected. "People like myself have ideas in abundance. Elliott was a man like your own martyrs, a man of action. He might have put his particular idea into practice," said Winthorp.

Nurbashi made a Middle-East gesture of uncertainty with his hands. "I cannot see how that made him worth a *Farda* martyr," he grumbled.

"That is why you need me," said Winthorp. "I remember yesterday and I study the present, but I live for tomorrow. The Great Satan would plan for its tomorrows, and Allah's *Farda* servant must not do less." Winthorp's nod might have been the faintest of bows, and lessened the arrogance of his boast.

In addition, he had made a sort of pun on *Farda*. The word could mean "tomorrow," or "sometime in the future"; but it was also the name of Nurbashi's vengeance group, which took the decrees of Khomeini at face value.

The Ayatollah had called openly for the death of Saudi princes and of his "Great Satan," America itself, during his lifetime, even after the arms-for-hostages trades that shook one

American administration to its roots. After Khomeini's death, uprisings by Arabian Shiites had sparked a bloodbath of hundreds of Saudi royalty. Now, Shiites controlled Arabia's enormous oil production—fully half of the world's available supply. Now the price of Arabian crude was in line with Iran's wishes, and after a brief return to cheaper fuel, Americans were again paying dearly for gasoline. Iraq's Hussein and the Saudis had paid Khomeini's price but finally, in 1995, the Great Satan America was using its technology to recover from the blow of expensive fuel. America lived today; but with her best people erased, she might die piecemeal tomorrow—*Farda*.

They passed a bevy of American beauties on the broad stone walk before Nurbashi replied. "I accept your motive. *Farda* could work more speedily if we could research several of our . . . necessities . . . at once."

"Harold E. Kroner," murmured Winthorp instantly.

Hissing, insistent, "And, and, and?"

"Please try to be content with one name. These things take time. Would you force me to a hasty decision? It was you who said the necessity must be worth your martyrs. Of Kroner, I am now certain."

Nurbashi withdrew a small pad and pencil from his workman's jacket where an American would have produced a memocomp. "As a judge in Allah's service, I demand to know how this child of Allah commits war against Allah," he said formally. In his way, Kosrow Nurbashi maintained the ancient tradition: A public figure who questioned ordained punishment must be judged for warring against God, before his execution. Of course, Nurbashi's judgments tended to be very, very summary. The assassins, convinced that they were Allah's warriors in a *jehad*, a holy war, hoped to die so that paradise would be theirs. It all worked out neatly so long as a few barmy recruits were available and suitably worried about their chances for paradise.

Winthorp stole a glance at his watch. In ten minutes he had

an office appointment with a graduate student who was researching the swift changes in America's interstate commerce. More than enough time for Nurbashi to try, convict, and sentence a man. "Hal Kroner directs motion pictures," Winthorp said, "each of which draws huge audiences. That would be of no importance if Kroner's ideas were harmless.

"But his *Valley Forge* thrilled Americans by showing that ordinary people, with determined action, can move the world. Youth Corps volunteers tripled within the year. Kroner's *Catch A Rising Star* was picketed by minority groups, but it seems to have changed the awareness of many blacks. Their new civic pride is alarming; their neighborhood projects are sometimes called Rising Stars. You can see where this might lead."

Nurbashi made a note. "It would not offend Allah," he said, playing Heaven's advocate.

"Fellowship with the Great Satan? Reconsider," said Winthorp. "Kroner's *The Far Treasure* combines visions of great wealth with space exploration. It seems likely to win several awards this year. If Americans ever *do* make use of raw materials from the moon and asteroids, Great Satan's future is assured. This," he said slowly for emphasis, "is taken as plain fact by most economists. Hal Kroner's messages are entertaining, inspiring—and very, very dangerous."

Nurbashi nodded once. "His intent clearly favors the Great Satan," he admitted.

Winthorp permitted himself a faint smile. "Condemned by his works," he said with a lecturer's smugness. "Only Allah knows what evil the man may do next."

"Perhaps create the sort of costume epic of which you are so fond," Nurbashi said without thinking. It was one thing to drop hints that Winthorp held no secrets from the mullah. It was quite another to dangle a detail of it before him. If Sultana had become a whore-goddess to her only son in such widescreen trash, then let him ogle her cinema sisters all he liked.

From what Nurbashi could learn, the man had no other sexual activities.

"The wise master does not abuse his servant," Winthorp said, too quietly.

"I meant no abuse," Nurbashi lied, "merely to share an irony. But surely a man as learned as yourself could provide more names for *Farda* research. The farmer should know each stone in his field, whether or not he removes it."

Winthorp began to angle across spring grass toward Grayson's School of Business and Economics, making Nurbashi follow. He had met two of Nurbashi's crazies before—both dead now, with their victims. Each rated an "A" for zeal and a "C minus" for caution. The longer Nurbashi's people had to study a prospective victim, the greater the risk of exposure. *Farda*'s favorite trick was to set a human bomb on collision course with the target. This sort of holy war was hell to defend against, and took relatively little research when Allah's warrior sought to pick the locks of Heaven with a detonator.

"Let me give you an example," Winthorp said, "not a second name. Americans owe much of their remaining strength to the efficient movement of people and materials. I have been studying two men, not the richest but among the most crucial, in this commerce. Last week I might have been tempted to name one. He is an American patriot, or thinks he is; he is pro-space; and he is a persuasive leader of interstate highway truckers, which is to say that he keeps the blood pumping in Great Satan's veins."

Nurbashi's eyes gleamed. "His name?"

"Allow me to tell you *his effect*. The blood pumps through old and failing arteries today, and this man is determined to cure the problem with more patches. Let him proceed! Satan may bleed to death in time."

"It would have done no harm to begin surveillance," Nurbashi replied. "My martyrs must remain active."

Another peek at the wristwatch, this time openly. "I am a scholar, and useful to you only if I am cautious. Leave me my caution, I beg you. Shall I call the same number to reach you again?"

Nurbashi made a negative gesture; recited a telephone number with a Michigan area code; watched as Winthorp punched it into his pocket memocomp. They avoided formal leave-taking, Winthorp pacing quickly on small burnished shoes toward his office. Nurbashi remembered to walk more casually to the bicycle, and pedaled toward the Metrorail. One thing about the damned Americans, the mullah reflected: They were already profiting from British experience with expensive fuel. The Metrorail was not blazingly fast, but a cyclist could park his bike free in a special railcar and remove it fifteen minutes later at a stop twenty miles away. Great Satan had learned from the British that it made excellent economic sense. Nurbashi hated that.

Winthorp, taking a shortcut, paused as a local freight rig whirred toward a campus loading dock, towing a wide trailer. Unlike older rigs, the huge so-called kings of the road, this one could not move at highway speeds and would never tow a load farther than the nearest rail terminal. Its engine was small and quiet, geared down for twenty-ton loads in urban traffic. Laser-etched into its aluminum bumper was the bold legend: PEEL TRANSIT ASSOCIATES, HAYWARD.

Balked by a Peel truck! Winthorp smiled again at this irony and hurried around the rig. He had refused to name one man because, it now seemed certain, Joseph Alton Weatherby was part of America's problem. Probably the driver of that campus rig contributed to Joey Weatherby's National Transport Coalition, which suited Winthorp fine. But that same driver was operating a prime mover assembled in the Hayward factory of Peel Transit Associates.

Winthorp puffed up the stairs. He would assign his graduate student case studies of cargo vehicle factories which were wholly owned by one person, and which were surging into newly efficient cargo methods. Winthorp knew one of those cases would include Peel's little high tech empire in Hayward, California. Recently, the *Wall Street Journal* had connected Peel with magnetic levitation trains running hundreds of miles an hour! Oh, yes, Peel loomed as a potential danger . . .

Winthorp might never utter Joey Weatherby's name to the mullah. But given much more success in lifting America's billion-ton cargoes with high technology, one name of "necessity" would almost certainly be John Wesley Peel.

THREE

His best people agreed behind his back, with affection: No charm school could ever knock the rough edges off Wes Peel. Heavy equipment contractor at twenty-five, developer of better equipment in his forties: Wes drew top honors from the school of hard knocks. Perhaps that is why he valued good educations in the people he gathered at his sprawling Hayward factory.

This morning Wes was dressed for comfort and for action, the wide shoulders straining at a short-sleeved shirt with open collar, beltless slacks snugged against a flat belly. He wore glove-soft loafers without socks, because Wes Peel did not have to give a damn what he wore.

When he called someone on the carpet, it was Wes who wore it out. He was wearing it out now, with pauses to recheck the sheaf of papers in his hand, searchlighting the offender with intense blue eyes now and then, an old scar slanting white across a tanned forehead. If you had a silent video of those pauses, you could guess that Wes had watched a few hard-shell preachers in his time. But his pauses were rarely silent.

Wes dropped the papers on his desk as though they had suddenly burst into flame. Tall and erect despite an old hip injury, he gnawed his mustache and passed a hand through cotton-blonde hair. "Got-damnit, Tom, you guys are short-hauling me to the poorhouse!" His steady gaze challenged the shorter man to deny it.

Tom Schultheis, Ph.D. Caltech '87, felt sweat forming under his neatly trimmed, sun-bronzed hair. If it became a trickle down to his tie in this air-conditioned sanctum, Wes might start to wonder why. "Wes, I run the design shop; ask Dave Kaplan about those test expenses. But before you do, ask yourself how many ways a maglev's canard wing can fail."

Wes still had the teeth and the cheek creases for a killer smile. "Hell, that's what you phuds are for." The smile burst, then faded with the memory of those big dollar signs. "You plating those canards with gold?"

"Welded titanium, and you're lucky we only had to use up one set."

Wes swept the papers into his hands again. Those big callused hands could drive an earth mover, or assemble an intricate model with the same ease. Visualizing the hardware as he scanned the list, Wes found another item and stabbed at it. "You had to destroy three cryogenic tanks, too?"

"They're all different," Schultheis said, using his handkerchief to polish his glasses, holding the linen square for another purpose. This was the second time in five minutes that Wes had noticed something he wasn't supposed to find, and now the back of the smaller man's collar was damp. "We either test everything, or risk a malf at high speed," he said, knowing Wes's dread of high-speed malfunctions.

Wes saw the gleam of perspiration. *It's Kaplan I should bitch at, or myself*, he thought. *Tom's between a rock and a hard place but he won't try to hide behind his best friend.*

24

"Aw, shoot. Wipe your face, Tom. If I'm determined to shock the industry, guess I'm due for some shocks of my own. Maybe I'm lucky we lost the big contract."

Tom Schultheis mopped at his forehead and managed a smile. "Pity you didn't feel that way the day we lost it," he said.

"Took me a while to see that less can be more," Wes replied. Like Budd and Boeing, Wes had fought for the main contract: the magnetic levitation passenger train. And like them, he had lost to the LockLever-Santa Fe group. The others had probably fought less to get the contract for that single track maintenance vehicle. The risk was high, the profit small, and it seemed less romantic than a six-car passenger train. But Wes knew the thing could become a hovering test bed: the prototype for much faster maglevs. He fought harder for that contract, and won. The cryogenic tanks, and the high performance they implied, were still secret. The longer everyone else thought maglevs were unstable above three hundred miles an hour, the longer PTA could extend its lead in the technology.

Wes took a final glance at the folder of papers, turning to the last page. "Sorry I jumped your case, Tom. Some bunch called Exotic Salvage in San Leandro is buying up what's left of our test hardware for about one-thousandth the cost." Wes conjured images of wrinkled titanium and ruptured boron filament, treasures sacrificed on the altar of safety, and shook his head. "What do you suppose they do with the stuff?"

A pause; a swallow. "Compact the metal and send it back to wherever," Tom replied vaguely, adding, "and we get safe hardware for man-rated systems."

You're playing my song back to me, and you damn' well know it, thought Wes. "I'll spring that this afternoon when we interview that pilot, what'shisname?"

"Glenn Rogan. Spring what?"

"This month alone, I've dumped three hundred thou into tests to make sure the guy gets safe rides. So be it," he finished.

The design chief nodded, feeling the release of tension between his own shoulders. Those titanium wings, filament-wrapped tanks, and God knew how many smaller items, would be safely written off. Which was very different from their being destroyed. To abandon this dangerous topic, Schultheis said, "When do we tell Rogan about the maglev? He thinks we want him only for the Delta One program."

A wink, and the killer smile, "We let him figure it out," Wes replied. "Shouldn't take him long." Wes, who had met professional speed freaks while competing in off-road racing, knew the breed. First you hired the pilot and his silence. A test pilot already on the payroll would rather see his bonus shrink than watch another pilot walk in to test new company systems. "We can't give him the maglev details yet, but a few hints are in order, and tell Kaplan I said so. Has it occurred to you that this pilot may not be excited over Delta One? You say yourself, she won't do two hundred miles an hour."

"No dirigible has ever done *one* hundred. You bet he'll be excited," Schultheis insisted. "Big lifters are his business. Rogan's ready to leave Cyclone Crane, but you could lose him to one of the outfits developing new space shuttles. Or you could hint that Peel Transit is leaning in that direction."

"Lie to him, you mean?"

Tom tried his most charming shrug-and-grin. "Not exactly. I mean, one of these days you'll get into orbital cargo."

"Lord *Jesus*, but you're a pain," Wes burst out, slapping his desk with a pistol's report. "No, I got-damn' well never will, how many times must I tell you? The got-damn' Orient Express spaceplane might get its got-damn' cargoes down to two hundred bucks a pound one day, or it might not."

"There are cheaper ways," Tom began, then realized there was no point in talking to a self-made magnate who could talk louder.

"So you've told me, Dave Kaplan too, and someday you'll realize I've got all the challenge I need moving cargo right here on God's sweet earth, or sell your souls to Boeing or Rockwell!'' Wes closed his eyes, grimaced, then shook his head. More gently, but firmly, ''Don't start with me, Tom. I created PTA, and Peel Leasing, and Transit Brokerage, so the American public won't have to dodge fifty-ton loads on its own highways forever.''

Hand up in mock surrender, Tom nodded. Laconic, ''I've seen your motto.''

''Beg pardon?''

''In your game room.'' Visitors to Wes's showcase home near Hayward could not fail to see the framed needlepoint sampler, six feet wide, that hung on one wall near the pool table. The legend read:

> WHEN YOU SHARE THE TRAIL WITH
> AN ELEPHANT,
> AND *ANYBODY* STUMBLES, . . .
> YOU LOSE!

Wes blinked, wondering if Schultheis knew that his own sister had made that sampler, years before. Alma Schultheis had spent some good nights at Wes's place, before their alliance lost its intensity. Was Tom cramming a message in between the lines? Unlikely. Tom was only acknowledging an agenda known to top Peel employees—the private lifelong goal of John Wesley Peel: to sweep away the big rigs that had once been a mixed blessing on American highways.

And had killed the three people Wes loved most. ''It's a creed, Tom. It's what I do. Let space freaks do the other stuff.'' Wes waved a hand in friendly dismissal. ''Hey, try and collar Dave before one-thirty. If he's late as usual, it might look like we're a haphazard outfit to your man Rogan.''

His hand on the door's push plate, Schultheis stopped as if stung by Wes's final phrase. Then he nodded and walked out.

FOUR

Tom Schultheis, compulsively neat, swept crumbs onto his lunch tray and waited for his companion to finish a sliver of cheesecake. As usual, they were arguing. Had Wes Peel been the kind of man to bug the tree-shaded tables outside the Peel Transit cafeteria, he would have shaken with rage to hear them.

One old foreman at Peel Transit had dubbed them "Mutt and Jeff" because Schultheis was a foot shorter than Peel's superb stress analyst, David Kaplan, Ph.D. Stanford '85. Kaplan owned one tie nobody had ever seen and curls of his black hair hid the back of the open collar of his dress shirt. Schultheis, though younger than Kaplan, boasted a few months of seniority with Wes and seldom found it necessary to argue with anyone but Kaplan. That was because he seldom found anyone else with Kaplan's chaotic kind of brilliance. But Dave Kaplan's virtues did not include careful scheduling of everyday details.

Squinting against the pavement reflection as they strode to the executive building, Tom craned his neck to stare at his companion. "You had two weeks to look over Rogan's application, Dave. Now you've got to face Wes with a recommendation. If you know a better test pilot, trot him out."

"How the hell was I to know you were bringing this guy in without telling him about Highjump?" David held the usual resonant boom of his voice in check. "My God, you're supposed to be the cautious one!"

"Right; and I know Rogan. You know what he reads besides

Louis L'Amour? Biographies of other test pilots. Nowadays, there's no Air Force hotshot sitting on the fence like Yeager, taking the tough ones on Air Force pay. Rogan's salary demands would set your hair on end if he knew why we *really* want him, and Wes would want to know where the extra hazard was.''

David's laugh was a release of frustration. ''You think Rogan's going to strap into that thing before he knows? I can't believe I'm hearing this, Tom.''

Schultheis glanced up again in irritation. ''We'll let him in on Highjump a little at a time. Once he knows, we can offer him the rides for a reasonable bonus. Glenn Rogan's hobby is base jumping, man—he's a risk junkie. Wait and see; you won't be able to keep him out of Highjump with armed guards.''

David sighed; pointed to the manila folder in the shorter man's hand. ''If I ever saw a resume with 'hell-raiser' stenciled all over it, it's Glenn Rogan's. He doesn't seem like your sort.''

''He's not. He's just good at his work.''

''How can you be so cocksure he'll want anything to do with Highjump? If you've guessed wrong and he takes it to Wes, you and I both will be drawing unemployment. Or breaking rocks in a state quarry.''

''That's our part of the risk. Think of Rogan's risk—and then tell me who else but a hell-raiser would ride Highjump! When I was with Cyclone, Rogan never made the same mistake once. I've known the guy since 'eighty-eight. He's still parachuting from suspension bridges for the sheer hell of it, repacking his own chutes. He's alive because he's careful. That says a lot.''

Kaplan paused with his hand on the entrance push plate and grinned. ''Methodical twerp; you probably had him in mind from the first. Now we're getting down to it! Old friend of the family?''

''Not hardly,'' Schultheis grunted, using one of the many

29

southern schoolboy phrases that had dismayed his parents back in Tullahoma, Tennessee. They passed into the cool shadowed corridor which the staff called mahogany row, then waited as Wes Peel's reception office door slid aside. Kaplan beamed at the woman who sat between two computer terminals. "Are we expected, Vangie?"

He was only half joking. Evangeline Broussard, Wes's executive assistant, never knew when Wes might slip out his private back entrance without warning her. Once a week she was forced to smooth the ruffled feathers of some bird with an appointment, because Wes had ducked out. Vangie's stock excuse, delivered with languid Creole grace, was "I'm afraid Mr. Peel did not expect you, suh." With this admission, Vangie hinted that she might have been at fault; and very few men could fan a rage toward Evangeline Broussard.

Vangie was a creature of contrasts: a face almost plain, with lips too full for perfection and brows too lush for fashion; but some Caddo Indian ancestor had given her perfect skin the color of apricot flesh and her lustrous dark hair, pulled away from her face and tied with a small bow, hung to her waist. Vangie hated her full name and wore severe tweeds to work. A pencil usually peeked from above her right ear, but most men forgot her executive trappings the moment they saw her walk across a room. Vangie's calves were very long, as anyone could see, but rumor had it that her legs were her worst feature. That rumor might persist until the day she bared her calves, for Vangie always wore trousers and elegant heels.

Vangie cocked her head toward the wall clock. "Two minutes past expected," she said, "unless he's ducked outside with that cowboy."

"That cowboy," said Schultheis, "happens to be one of the best LTA men in the business, Vangie." He headed for Wes's inner office, secretly pleased with the woman's assessment.

"A cowboy riding a lighter-than-air craft is still a cowboy," Vangie said darkly.

Suddenly David Kaplan felt a surge of friendliness for a man he had never met. "You're a hopeless elitist, Vangie," he said with a mock-serious wag of his finger, and followed Tom Schultheis to the next room.

". . . ran this bitchin' Lola for half the season," said a gravelly voice Kaplan did not recognize, nor could he see its source at first. "I didn't know whatthehell I was doing in Formula cars, of course; I was just a kid. But I was third in points before the Corps accepted me. I had a choice of wheels or wings, and I chose wings."

The speaker stopped as Wes glanced past the visitor's big leather chair and stood up, waving toward the latecomers. "Glenn Rogan, meet our top stress man, Dr. David Kaplan. I believe you know Dr. Schultheis."

Glenn Rogan came up from the big chair twisting with the lazy grace of an otter. Kaplan took his hand and understood instantly, for the first time, what charisma was all about. Rogan was an inch or two taller than Tom Schultheis, with a welterweight's nose and curly blond hair cut shorter than his side-burns. He was in his midthirties, roughly Kaplan's age, with permanent squint lines and eyes like splinters of green glass. His grip was very gentle, but what Kaplan felt like an electric surge was the humming intensity of the man.

Rogan wore scuffed western boots, tan gabardine slacks with an ornate belt buckle and, much too casual for most hiring interviews, a polo shirt that showed a solid muscular belly, his throat and forearms lined by sinew. Rogan was a dynamo, his hidden rotor spinning in such perfect balance that it seemed not to be spinning at all. But brush against his terminals and *zzzzap*. The man was rigged for silent running. Dave Kaplan, smiling through his own uneasiness, said what he usually said to put applicants at ease, "I hear good things about you."

Rogan's response was unexpected; a faint sidelong jerk of his head toward Tom Schultheis with a fainter wry lifting at the corners of his mouth. To Kaplan he said, with a touch of a southwest twang, "Present company excepted?"

Wes caught it. "Tom seems to think you can do no wrong, Mr. Rogan. It's only fair to warn you that if Tom thinks a bottle's half full, David will argue that it's half empty, and vice versa." Behind the heartiness was a hint that Wes could do without the constant friendly bickering of his top people. "Tell you what; let's sneak out to the development hangar. Delta One's bulkheads are already in place." He saw silent agreement; turned and moved a hand toward the rosewood panel behind his recliner chair.

The panel slid back silently. Perhaps Rogan had expected an exit door, for he laughed to see the nicely stocked bar. Wes chose a manhattan glass, helped himself to ice and single-malt scotch, and waved a hand toward the layout. "Help yourselves."

But, "Jesus, Wes," Kaplan chuckled, shaking his head.

Schultheis declined as well, his face carefully noncommittal as he glanced at Rogan. "How about you?"

Rogan remained perfectly still for a moment. Then he gave a negative headshake. "Thanks, but I'll most likely be sittin' in a gondola sometime this afternoon. Even if it's only a mock-up." His glance toward Schultheis said that he had sidestepped a trap. Wes caught that, too, and revised his assumption about the two. They might share mutual respect, but not friendship.

Draining his glass, Wes ushered the others through a sliding rear door and claimed the driver's seat of the topless four-place Electrabout just outside. "You can take a look at our production lines another time," he said, jerking a thumb toward the massive concrete-block complex to their left. Rogan, sitting beside him, nodded agreement as Wes continued over the hum of the squat utility vehicle with its massive battery packs.

Wes drove slowly through patches of sunlight on a bright Hayward afternoon past production buildings which he owned lock, stock, and beryllium. "Local rigs come off Line Two," Wes indicated a pair of gleaming trucks on fat wheels, with only modest streamlining, and sporting enormous expanses of glass. "Ugly devils, but they don't have to be aerodynamic and they're dead reliable."

Glenn Rogan turned his head as he passed the rigs, thinking that they looked more like oversized pickup trucks than big cargo lifters. Peel might call them ugly, but the slope of their noses swept attractively down to small horizontal air scoops. A Peel Shorthauler boasted low-profile tires so wide that the full-enclosure fenders bulged, front and rear, like the haunches of some great animal poised to leap. Those through-flow radiators served a small engine, allowing the sloping nose and the excellent visibility it afforded in heavy traffic. Studying the tires, Rogan said, "Never noticed gumballs like that on a freight hauler, Mr. Peel."

"New wrinkle. A bit large for a Formula Ford," Wes laughed, "but who needs big-hauler treads at low speeds? With tires that wide you can bring the height down, and the rubber compound is soft for traction. Very efficient."

"Cog-effect tires," Rogan said. "It's sure a departure from the big interstate rigs."

"It's supposed to be," said Wes darkly, and sent a lazy one-handed wave toward the truck emerging from Line Two. To Rogan he joked, "When you own the damn factory, you outrank its trucks."

The scene ahead and to their left seemed innocent enough at first glance, as a Peel rig rolled slowly into sunshine from a short downramp at the building's mouth.

Paul Ramirez, group leader for the Line Two rollout crew, stood just inside the shadowed opening and trembled with a mixture of anticipation and self-loathing. He'd worked it out in his head for days, knowing you had to defeat several safety factors before you could send a Peel rig gliding across a downslope to ram the building opposite. The brake rider had a real errand, the emergency cable had a real flaw—and Paul Ramirez had a wife and three kids. You had to think of your family first, and old Tony Ciano knew it. You make a bad start as a wild young kid, and you let somebody like Ciano bail you out of a two-to-five stint in the slammer, knowing he could have you put back anytime he liked, and then you light out for a new start three thousand miles away hoping you'll be forgotten.

Fat chance. Well, this was the one big favor he owed Ciano and maybe he wouldn't lose his job over it, but maybe he would quit anyway. It would be a reproach to him every time he cashed a paycheck with John Wesley Peel's signature on it, a man Paul Ramirez didn't know very well but the only bigwig he'd ever met who bent over backward to be fair. Ramirez glanced outside, judging the path of the short-haul rig, and froze.

In all his midnight sweats of considering ways and means to sabotage a truck, he had never considered that the rig might strike anything but a solid wall. And Holy Mother of God, that Electrabout humming across the concrete was in the path, and you couldn't mistake the driver's shoulders or the thatch of cotton-blond hair. Paul Ramirez reached a conclusion attained by the valiant few: two-to-five of hard time beat thirty of remorse.

Dave Kaplan saw a swarthy fellow in white burst from the opening of Line Two, chasing the big rig across the slight downward slope of pavement and shouting, a shop coat flapping between his short legs as he fell and scrambled to his feet again. Kaplan gasped, "Wes, nobody's in the cab!"

"Everybody out," Wes said abruptly, still cruising toward the driverless rig at an angle to its progress. *"Now!"* He waved his free arm as if to fling Kaplan and Schultheis from the rear seats.

The Electrabout still moved at a trotting pace, slow enough for young men to vault over its open sides. The towering rig ahead, shining freshly with bright paintwork, was slowly picking up speed down the incline, and Wes accelerated sharply as Kaplan and Schultheis hit the pavement running. Wes looked at Rogan. "You had your chance," he said, aiming for an intercept point between the bulky rig and the corner of a building on their right.

If Rogan had forgotten how quickly an electric vehicle could surge forward, he was forcibly reminded. He gripped the windshield post hard and stood half-upright. "Want me to climb to the cab?"

"You won't have time," Wes warned. "These electrics are heavier than you think."

Suddenly Rogan realized that Wes Peel was right, and that the Electrabout's mass was of interest only if Wes could position it in front of the driverless rig. Within fifteen seconds, that new rig would plow into an exterior wall unless the Electrabout's rump was snug against its front bumper, braking hard. Rogan estimated the time, the distance, and made his decision plain. "You're fuckin' crazy, man; I'm punchin' out!" With that, Rogan snatched up his seat cushion and vaulted to the rear seats, then leaped hard from the rear of the vehicle, holding the cushion against the back of his head as his boots struck the pavement.

Wes judged his arc carefully, sweeping into a path parallel with the rig, the Electrabout now at its top speed of some forty miles an hour as he passed the rig's front wheels. He had time to think, *If one of those gumball tires touches my bumper, it'll climb right in here with me,* and then he was edging into position, feathering the accelerator pedal, and then his neck vertebrae popped with the slam of the rig's front bumper, harder than he'd expected, maybe hard enough to collapse the Electrabout's chassis, and another slam as he began braking. A high prefabricated wall loomed less than fifty yards ahead, some vagary of pavement surface making the rig veer toward the right, and now it was time to steer for compensation, except that you can't steer worth a damn when your tires are locked up and smoking like a chimney and squalling their own panic with six tons of Shorthauler pushing you. But which way to jump, and could he make it with that damned gimpy hip?

He didn't have to; the rig began to turn more sharply, and now Wes was sliding past the corner of the building. When his two-piece juggernaut sighed to a stop, Wes forced his shaky limbs into action again, wheeling back on tires no longer perfectly round to find Glenn Rogan. By now several men had rushed to the fallen pilot. Wes could see his design and stress men kneeling beside Rogan, who lay on his back stretched out on the pavement, his head still on that seat cushion, and as he braked Wes could see the man's chest heaving.

With laughter? "I don't think he's hurt," said Kaplan as Wes stepped from his little vehicle.

Rogan paused, held his breath until his eyes met those of

Wes Peel, and then he was guffawing again as he checked his elbows, one at a time. Subsiding at last, Rogan sat up and hugged his knees. "This was a gag; right? You set me up, and I bought it, punched out at zero altitude and fifty feet a second." He laughed again as he stood up, glancing sheepishly at the men around him, wiping the scraped skin at one elbow. "Got me a little road rash here, but . . ." He looked at the silent Wes again, then at the still-smoking wheel assemblies of the Electrabout. With a sudden furrow across his brow, squinting toward the distant driverless rig, "Whoa, you weren't kidding. Those flat spots are for real. You really got 'er stopped that way?"

Kaplan, still dry-mouthed, "You didn't see it?"

Rogan: "I was busy. Cussin', and laughin'. Mr. Peel, why'd you risk getting squashed for a truck that was gonna stop anyhow?"

Wes: "Because that wall wasn't designed to stop a truck, and right on the other side of it are thirty people doing assembly work. You want a nurse to check that arm?"

"Nah, just a scrape," said Rogan, brushing himself off. Pause. Then, "You're still nuts, you know that?"

Wes, deadpan: "Part of my mystique."

Rogan seemed on the edge of helpless laughter again as he retrieved the tattered seat cushion, tossed it into the Electrabout, and asked, "Who was it said, 'mystique equals bullshit,' Mr. Peel?"

"One of my people, most likely, when my back was turned," said Wes, and turned to the swarthy man in the shop coat. "Ramirez, you're in charge of that rollout crew?"

After two tries, the man managed a hoarse, "Yessir. My fault, Mr. Peel."

"I don't want to know whose fault it really was, but he has the choice of paying for repairs or a week off without pay." Wes knew that union rules permitted even stiffer penalties, and looked around at the abashed crew. "Fair enough?"

Paul Ramirez nodded. Wes glanced at the Electrabout with its badly flat-spotted tires, then handed its key to the shaken Ramirez. "So we walk," he shrugged to his three companions.

Presently they passed the last of the concrete structures, where freight trailers were being fitted with retractable wheels. "Line Three," said Wes. "Equipment for intermodal hauling. An old idea; we just made it work: Speeds up the changeover at railroad terminals."

Quickly, from Rogan: "How about rail sidings?"

Tom Schultheis, just as quickly: "That's where you LTA jockeys come in. If Cyclone can lift twenty tons of cut timber off a mountainside with those rotating blimps, we think a really *big* lifter could jerk a loaded cargo trailer straight from a small-town siding to a truck parked a mile away."

"I hear somebody already jerked some off-road equipment from a flatcar with a Cyclone LTA," Rogan said cagily.

"Somebody named Rogan," Schultheis replied, and smiled at Rogan's surprise. "Wes told me how much Cyclone paid the rail yard expediter to look the other way."

"A Kelley Magnum tree-harvester, I believe," Wes said, "off a siding near Tillamook, at three in the morning."

Rogan's laugh was an octave higher than his voice. "Well, I-be-damn; what *don't* you guys know?"

"We don't know if it'll work with really big lifters," said Wes. "But we intend to find out." He pointed toward the hangar, a vast white half-cylinder of fabric two hundred yards long, anchored to concrete and kept more or less rigid by air blowers. "The answer may be in there," said Wes, pointing. "The more cargo we lift off the interstate highways, the better for us all."

As he punched the six-digit door combination, Wes saw the brief silent glance between Kaplan and Schultheis. *Think I'm a monomaniac, do you? Well, maybe I am.* The door sighed open. The slightly elevated pressure in the hangar kept dust from filtering in, and they blinked against the brief rush of cool air.

Wes watched the play of emotions across the tanned features of Glenn Rogan with pride. The pilot stood, lips pursed in a silent whistle, looking up into the softly lit cavern of white fabric. "Man, oh man, oh man," he said, fists on his hips, letting his imagination complete the shape that would soon be a dirigible with the shape of a broad arrowhead: Delta One.

Light filtered through the fabric walls to reveal a half-dozen girders that hung in place like rigid wisps of gleaming black spiderweb. Rogan did not fully realize its enormous size until he noticed the tiny creature hanging in a safety harness, where one bulkhead joined to a lower straight keel beam. The beams seemed as insubstantial as thinly drawn lines on paper. The creature in the safety harness might have been an ant, but it was a man wiring strain gauges to a bonded joint. Given the man for scale, he saw that the hangar roof soared a dizzying twenty stories above the floor. Where the hangar roof arched downward on either side, it was "only" a hundred feet high —none too tall for the girders that formed the great ship's vertical stabilizers. Rogan's practiced eye followed the suspension lines to the ceiling high overhead. "You really can use this hangar as a support structure," he said, marveling. "And you've got barn swallows up there."

The other men studied the heights. "You can see a bird that far away, in this light?" Kaplan asked.

Rogan merely shrugged. Schultheis raised one eyebrow and nodded at the stress man. "It says twenty-ten vision on his application," Schultheis remarked.

Rogan walked forward then, shaking his head in awe, and laughed aloud as he stopped, the echoes muted in this enormous space. "Reminds me of the Jesus Christ plane," he grinned.

Wes: "Do we get an explanation?"

Rogan: "Sure. When the Hughes flying boat was new, engineers used to walk into the hangar and stop dead. The first thing half of 'em said was "Jee-zuss, Kee-*rist!*" He stared upward again. "And you could stack a pair of those inside this bird of yours. What are the specs?"

"Three million cubic feet of helium," Wes replied. "Less than it might be because she's fairly flat; a lifting body with wingtip rudders for better control at high speeds."

"High?" Rogan smiled. "For us helium-heads, anything over highway speed is high."

Tom Schultheis's cough was rich with meaning, but Wes waved a negligent hand. "We'll double that," he said vaguely and added a tantalizing hint, "even if you're a freeway bandit. I can't give you her gross or cargo capacity yet, but she'll carry more San Joaquin Valley lettuce across this country than any highway triple-trailer rig in one-fourth the time."

"Dear ol' goddy," said the pilot, rocking on the sloped heels of his boots, letting his eyes draw more imaginary lines. "A sure 'nough, four hundred foot, double-delta. Hell, you could play tennis in the wings!"

"Not with the aft ballonets out there," Wes replied.

"What?!" Frowning, Rogan looked to the design chief for verification. Tom nodded. Rogan put his arms out, palms flat, and rocked from side to side gently. "Won't that make this brute pretty sensitive to balance?"

"We want her sensitive," said Tom. "There's more I can't tell you yet. Just ask yourself how you'd like a computer-fed, three-point balance."

Rogan thought about that. "You'd have to fill and deflate ballonets in one hell of a hurry."

"That's what big impellers are for." Tom's gaze held perfect confidence.

"Man, oh man, oh man," said the pilot once more, turning back to the silent leviathan taking shape within ten miles of the Port of Oakland. "Well, you must have the gondola someplace."

"It's actually an airship's bridge," Wes explained. "Come on."

They spent the next half hour in a smaller fabric-covered room near one end of the hangar, a bubble within a bubble, where two meticulous white-smocked women went about the business of testing the wiring bundles that would become the central nervous system of Delta One. Schultheis noted that, even while studying the control layout and without exchanging a word, Glenn Rogan managed to captivate the younger of the two women. Schultheis was not surprised; it might have been the same if they'd sought one of the ex-NASA astronauts instead.

He forced himself away from this line of thinking. For one thing, astronauts were a cautious lot who probably would never strap into the tiny beast that Exotic Salvage was assembling, piece by surreptitious piece, in the Mojave desert. For another, Highjump would handle more like an interceptor than anything else. That meant it would land like a concrete Frisbee. *If* it landed. That question depended a lot on a mind-bending propulsion system that no one had ever tried outside of a laboratory.

FIVE

Glenn Rogan fell in love with the spacious Delta One cabin and its ample seating. He studied the layout meticulously, now and then with a suggestion for better grouping of controls. Frankly pleased with a modern control stick instead of traditional helm wheels, he was leaning back in the pilot's seat when a courier stuck her head into the cabin looking for Wes Peel.

"They always find me," Wes grumbled, and appropriated an electric scooter for the trip back to his office, pausing as he left. "When you've soaked up as much of this as you like, drop by the office."

"Can do," said Rogan absently, studying a seat adjustment as Wes left the cabin.

Clearly, the pilot was more interested in the big lifter's hardware than in friendly chitchat. "You'd think he already had the job," Schultheis muttered as he stood near the opposite end of Delta One's cabin.

Kaplan shrugged. "Doesn't he?"

The head shake was quick and definite. "Not over your objection. I told you when we first decided to try Highjump, Dave. You and I have to do a Lewis & Clark routine: equal authority, since we'll stand or fall together."

Kaplan gnawed his underlip, watching the distant pilot as he replied. "Maybe it's just that he's such a special breed of animal. Give me a little time with him alone, okay? I've got no reservations about him as a test pilot, but . . . I just need to know what makes the man tick."

"Risk, money, women and fast vehicles," said Schultheis. "But we don't have to love the bastard to depend on him."

Kaplan, squinting: "Tom, if you don't like the man . . ."

"Dead right, but I can't afford to let it matter." Schultheis turned and called down the length of the cabin. "I've got to look over some engine mount vibration work. Dave can show you around."

Rogan looked up, nodded once, and swung from his seat to kneel on the cabin floor, studying the attachments. As Schultheis left, Kaplan moved forward, struck once more by Rogan's physical grace whether walking or squatting on his heels. "If I can pry you out of here," he suggested, "you might want to see our maglev unit. It's out behind the hangar."

"I've heard rumors of that thing," Rogan replied, coming erect, looking around him. "Peel sure likes to do things different," he said.

"That's why he hires people like me and Tom—and you," said Kaplan, taking two strides to Rogan's three as they headed for a rear hangar door.

After a thoughtful silence, Rogan asked, "Something Peel said: Was it really Tom Schultheis who set this interview up?"

Kaplan, alerted by a note of caution in the man's voice: "Yes. Wes Peel thinks of himself as the great cargo innovator of the coming century. As far as he takes it, he's right." He chose the next words very carefully. "That means developing some really far-out vehicles. Tom Schultheis claims we'll need a test pilot with a feel for LTA craft and soon, uh, vehicles that may be much faster."

Rogan's head snapped around. His grin was sudden, aggressive. "Much?"

In answer, Dave ushered the pilot outside. As they stood waiting for their eyes to adjust to afternoon glare, he pointed to the long vehicle, its international orange paint gleaming brilliantly, that sat unattended over the rails of a hundred-yard railway. Though twelve feet wide and fourteen high, its great length gave it a lean, rakish look. Its windows were flush-mounted, with a sloping nose and tapered rump featuring a strut-mounted airfoil. Because the canard fins were not yet installed near its nose, it resembled locomotives which already hauled passengers across Europe and Japan at speeds near two hundred miles an hour. Those canards would be a dead giveaway to a man like Rogan. "You wouldn't believe me if I told you how much faster," said the stress man, gazing at the sleek maglev.

For a long moment, Glenn Rogan scanned the shape that squatted like an eighty-foot lancehead gleaming in the sun. "This isn't exactly my dish, Dr. Kaplan. It goes on rails, and it doesn't fly."

"If we're going to be sweating over test programs together, you'll have to learn to call me Dave. And damn' right, it flies! I can't tell you all the details yet, but, as you know, a maglev doesn't actually touch the rails. Its magnets repel the rails and other magnets accelerate the whole train. And stop it, of course."

Rogan began to walk the length of the vehicle, leaning down to peer beneath it. "Peel mentioned this thing. Talked like he owned the whole system." Rubbing his skinned forearm reflectively, the pilot muttered, "The guy's not your everyday three-piece suiter. One hell of a competitor."

"You've got that right. He competed like crazy for the prime maglev contract, but LockLever and Santa Fe had the inside track. There's nearly three hundred miles of maglev rail winding up from L. A. through the Mojave, near old high-tension power lines all the way to Vegas. Two-thirds of the track is already in place. Wes got us the contract for the maintenance unit." He slapped the stiff polymer hide of the vehicle and beamed. "We're a month ahead of schedule with levitation tests."

Rogan vented a low whistle between his teeth. "Sweet shit. *This* is a maintenance unit?"

"I know; looks more like a speed-record vehicle," Dave chuckled. "When a maglev is hauling a thousand spoiled high rollers from L.A. to Vegas in an hour, they don't want their martinis spilled. Santa Fe has sensors to report small shifts in the rail spacing. Whenever there's a minor quake or a crustal shift, they need a maintenance rig at the site fast. This is it."

"How fast?"

Dave folded his arms, grinned, and winked. "Fast."

"It'll need more clearance off the rails, then," Rogan said, squinting at retractable jacks which held the craft clear of the rail sections.

"You're too damned sharp," Dave murmured.

"They didn't let jocks sleep through *all* our classes," Rogan said wryly. "So, you'll need more power, and maybe some freedom of movement over the rails, and you've gotta know how much freedom at maximum speed," Rogan hazarded.

"I'm not going to say another word," Dave said, laughing.

Rogan started to move toward the insulated rail, then stopped. "This thing isn't energized?"

"No. When it is, it'd fry an elephant into thirty pounds of bacon in no time flat. Nobody will mind if you have ideas about safety. Wes Peel is a nut on the subject."

"Other people's safety, maybe. Not his. Man is fuckin' *crazy*," Rogan added as if to himself.

"It's my private view that all racing drivers bear watching from a safe distance," Kaplan smiled, and earned a look that could have been agreement.

Rogan passed the back of his hand a hairbreadth above the rail before gripping it with one hand to vault over between the elevated tracks. Kaplan suddenly realized that, if the rail had been energized despite all precautions, Glenn Rogan might have lost little more than the hairs on the back of his hand. It was a trick David Kaplan had never considered before. As Rogan peered up at the underside of the vehicle's rear, his gravelly voice echoed slightly. "This job is gonna have more fun rides than Disneyland. I can't see why Schultheis picked me, of all people."

"Why not you?"

Rogan duck-walked from the maglev's shadowed underhull, stood up. "Personal," he said, dismissing the subject.

Kaplan had a flash of intuition about this man who seemed to value the hands-on, physical approach to his work. Perhaps Rogan would relax more among other jocks. Without taking a run at the rail, Kaplan simply leaped sideways, scissoring his legs past the high rail to stand beside Rogan.

"Like a pro," Rogan smiled.

"Jumped my height in high school. Did seven-one and three-eighths at Cal Berkeley. That's what paid my way through the bachelor's."

"I was never much at the high jump," said Rogan, and did not understand why Kaplan laughed aloud.

"You will be," Kaplan said, savoring his private joke. Then, more soberly, "Wes worries when his companies get too big to run personally. I don't mean he pries into our lives, but the way Wes does things, we have to go a lot on personal trust. Tom Schultheis knows that. If he didn't trust you for this work, you wouldn't be here."

Rogan's laugh carried no discernible humor. "You know the Schultheis family?"

A nod. "We see his sister, Alma, at Wes's parties. I know their father—there's a character for you. Old Wolf Schultheis was an apprentice at *Zeppelinwerke*, sixty years ago. Worked with Lippisch, Bachem—those names familiar?"

"Not the last ones."

The Lippisch series of flying wings, and the rocketing ascent of the Bachem Natter interceptor, were now subjects only for archivists of Nazi secret weapons. But the brain of Wolf Schultheis was already an archive when the Americans spirited him to a huge research center in a place called Tullahoma, after the war. Dave Kaplan was one of the few people who knew how much of those archives the old man funneled into Peel Transit by way of his only son. "Well, let's just say we're close enough. My wife, Lillian, is pretty thick with Ellie—Tom's wife. Lil baby-sits for her sometimes." Finger snap of recognition: "You may have met Ellie when Tom worked for Cyclone."

Something flickered in the glass-green eyes. "I've seen her," Rogan said, and added quickly, "Schultheis lives his way and I live mine. He's conservative. I'm . . ." He waved a hand, let it drop.

"A hell-raiser," Kaplan supplied, and leaned back against the maglev hull, arms crossed, smiling. "Wait 'til you meet Boff Allington; nice guy, but he will have his jokes. And

Wes—well, he's a hellion himself. To send a rhino head-to-head against Wes is cruelty to animals. I've got no problem with any of it as long as you're all business at the controls. But you might tell me why you chose to raise hell in the private sector.''

"Wasn't my choice. It's in my file," Rogan growled.

"I'm not very good at the fine print. I know you tested a supersonic-combustion ramjet booster while you were in the Marines. What happened?''

"The scramjet test vehicle augured. Not with me," Rogan said, "with another aviator who should'a punched out and didn't. That was one jittery, hot son of a bitch; it sure held your attention at Mach five and eighty thousand feet.''

"No blot on your record, then. And after that?''

"Back to combat instructor. Shit, I know what you're after," Rogan burst out in exasperation. "Look, I like to find out exactly what my equipment can do. I've never lost a test vehicle, but I greased a few in that were pretty much used up. You remember the old Marine Harriers?''

"Vertical hover, and five hundred knots? Sure," said Kaplan. "Was it the hover feature that gave you a feel for LTA's?''

"A taste for it, anyhow, but it's not really the same. Anyway, I used to push the envelope with those things. I didn't invite anybody else to try it, but two Marine aviators bought plots tryin' to prove they could push a little farther than I could. Both instructors. I took a shit storm over it.''

"They dropped you for that?''

A slow grin spread across the tanned face, and Dave sensed the good-old-boy camaraderie that began to surface in Glenn Rogan. "Naw, not exactly. I was on my best creased-britches behavior until the 'eighty-seven war games. Our side was losin' until I did a sortie alone on the third day. I loitered up a river just over the water, sneakin' under radar coverage. Spent ten minutes and a lot of fuel hidin' out, with my ear glued to a

Blue frequency, then popped up and zapped the Blue Force command post while the Blue Commander was landing his chopper. Green won right then and there.''

"Don't tell me you were Blue, too.''

"Hell, no! But some fuckin' observer had seen me. I had that ol' Harrier nudged up under a highway bridge and over white water rapids, hovering between the girders, for maybe ten minutes where its downwash and the water noise didn't give me away.''

"Good—God,'' Dave breathed, chuckling. "Had anybody ever tried that before?''

"Guess not, and they decided nobody'd ever try it again. The actual charge was willful destruction of government property.''

"You crashed the Harrier?''

"Busted the little runnin' light off the vertical fin where it grazed the underside of the bridge. About ten bucks' worth of damage, all told,'' Rogan added. "They said I was permanently off flight status. I said bullshit, flyin' was the only thing that kept me in the Corps.'' The candid green eyes glinted at the taller man. "Sometimes I regret it. Sometimes not. I fly a Rutan, do a little base jumping when somebody finds a likely perch for a damn' fool with a steerable chute. In between, flying a Cyclone Crane can be fun when you get a crosswind up a ravine with a load of raw timber halfway to the river. Cyclone's good about hazard pay. I expect Peel to be better.''

"Maybe a little,'' Dave hedged, liking this little heller in spite of himself, feeling that Rogan deserved whatever he could negotiate. He scissored over the rail again, no hands, and jerked a thumb toward the distant low-slung buildings. "As far as I'm concerned, you can ask Wes about it today. He's a God-fearing sort, not a cardboard Christian, and he'll treat you straight. Just don't ever forget what I said about the rhino.'' Dave watched with real concern as the smaller man eyed the rail, took three running steps, and scissored over a barrier that was as high as his breastbone, no hands.

Rogan made it with a half-inch to spare. "Shavin' it close to your balls is what it's all about," he said as they began walking.

"It's the same with stress analysis," said Dave, strolling beside him.

A sharp look from Rogan, and a laconic, "Yeah, but it's *my* balls, and *you* got the razor. Sure hope you're good."

"You could ask around, but we are. Ah—you ever fly the hot stuff anymore?"

"Now and then. A Mitsui Mach Two executive jet that belongs to Cyclone, so my license is current. Not much sensation of speed except during takeoff and landing. Little fucker lands like a washtub full of hot rocks. That's the fun part," he grinned. "Let's see: and I got tutoring in math and physics at Oklahoma State because I had the hots for a degree in aero engineering and Okie State didn't want to lose their best wrestler, so numbers are like big Kansas cheerleaders, I don't like 'em a lot but they don't half scare me. And if I can get John Wesley Peel to sponsor me in an off-road racer, by God, don't think I won't. Any other burning questions from your end?"

"I guess not. You've answered the only really important question."

"Which was?"

"You're a high jumper after all," Dave said, wondering whether Glenn Rogan would ever remember the exchange— and whether, remembering, he would enjoy the double entendre.

*　　*　　*　　*

By sundown, Wes had several commitments from Glenn Rogan, including a few choice comments about experienced copilots. Wes shoved a list of applicants toward the pilot. "Any special feeling about those names?"

Rogan nodded. "Hewett. He's a Brit who's flown for years in that European blimp of Goodyear's.'" He unwittingly damned the man by adding, "He's all spit and polish, goes by the book and he'll want a twenty-page job description. And Jim Christopher; they say Chris saved a few skins when that big lifter of Piasecki's went down a few years back: Prob'ly won't come cheap, but he has good eyes and steady hands."

Wes, with his quick grin: "Is that the right stuff?"

"Aw, man," Rogan groaned. "Who knows what that is? Let's just say Chris wouldn't make me nervous."

Later, Wes decided that Rogan's only nervousness came when he learned that he would report directly to Tom Schultheis—but perhaps wariness was a better word.

Two weeks later, Wes showed Glenn Rogan his office, one of two hastily erected in the big hangar. The adjoining room, Wes told him, was reserved for Jim Christopher. Wes soon learned that Rogan had an insatiable appetite for Delta One's engineering drawings, and an unnerving habit of climbing high into her guts to study her flexible skeleton. Rogan's penchant for heights worried Wes like a hangnail, to be forgotten only when his real problems surfaced, rushing at him from three different directions.

SIX

In a way, Wes Peel escaped the deadly zeal of *Farda* as long as he did because of foul Mexican weather. Director Hal Kroner, on secret location in Mexico while filming *Sacajawea*, was delayed for weeks by ferocious canyon winds in Chihuahua's Barranca de Cobre. And until Kroner returned to civilization, Nurbashi's assassins could not find him, much less kill him. Meanwhile, by the end of April, Professor Winthorp no longer entertained the slightest doubt that John Wesley Peel must be eliminated. Still he steadfastly refused to divulge that name until Kroner was in a box; or perhaps more accurately, in several bags. By day, Winthorp lectured in public and researched other crucial Americans in private; by night he watched videotapes of harem epics and thought about his approaching summer vacation.

* * * *

In April and May, Wes often fancied that he would welcome sudden death. He agonized over the daily progress of Delta One with its gossamer framework and its enormous expanses of aluminized plastic hide. He relaxed with two double scotches the day he found Rogan inspecting a rudder fin of the monster, a giddy ten stories above the hangar's concrete floor. Wes found it hard to imagine that anybody but a cable rigger would actually *like* it up there. He said as much to Vangie Broussard over his second scotch, as they were ending a long workday.

"That's a new excuse: drinking over someone else's foolishness," Vangie replied, eyeing his glass as she filed computer disks, the fine nostrils pinched with disdain as though the disks were industrial waste. "I hope it's not catchin', Wes. You'll have me drinking over yours."

"I'll bite: What's my foolishness?"

"Liquor." She saw the defensive set of his jaw and jabbed her flow pen in his direction like a schoolmarm. "And don't twitch your face at me, Wesley Peel. This is after-hours, and on my own time I will say what I think. I'm not the only one who thinks so."

"For example?"

"Never you mind. They just don't worry about you enough to get in a flap with you about it."

Wes, studying her with a faint smile: "You do, though."

When she blushed, Vangie looked every inch a full-blooded Caddo. "Hmph. With two brothers and two sisters, I'm flap-proof."

"So I've noticed. Funny, in the three years you've been here, I never knew you were from a big family."

"Cajun Catholics. What other kind is there in Crowley, Louisiana? And you're trying to change the subject."

"Part of my charm." He grinned the killer smile.

"Or so you say. You'd charm me more without that glass in your hand," she retorted, and took her lower lip in her teeth as, with deliberate care, he set the glass down. "Oh my. That was not a come-on, Wes."

"I know it. And that's part of *your* charm; speaking your mind." He sighed and stood up, reaching for a tubular roll of plastic sheeting that stood on end behind his desk. "Well, it's time I went home where I can drink without kibitzers. Relax, Vangie; booze is only a hobby, like this sheeting. Wait 'til you see it tomorrow."

"Is that what you do up there in that big old house, between parties? Just drink and play with plastic?"

"Don't knock it. I've built life-sized manikins of all the female staff from this plastic." Straight-faced, he stroked the milky sheeting with a fingertip. "So nobody complains when I squeeze the Charmin'."

A three-beat pause before she shook her head with a knowing smile. "That is truly tacky, and I don't believe it. My ex would do that, but not you." She finished her filing and locked the storage drawer.

He lifted the roll of plastic. "Then what will I do with it, if you know so got-damn' much?"

She pursed her lips in thought, elevated her brows, then said, "You build manikins of Kaplan and Schultheis and Allington."

"Lady, have you ever got me wrong."

"Hear me out. And then you sit them down and have executive meetings and press a button and they all nod their heads and applaud."

Wes guffawed until the ceiling reverberated. "Great idea; maybe I will! It's the only way I'll ever enjoy that fantasy." Sobering: "But this sheeting is already spoken for. If I can get it stretched and heated just right, it'll be molded into a model of Delta One sometime tonight. I've spent two weeks building molds, and that's the lion's share of the job."

The dark, tilted eyes regarded him curiously. "I guess we weren't joking altogether, were we? What you do at home is put flesh on your fantasies—in miniature, as it were. No wonder you come in so often looking hung over. You stay up half the night working."

"More like playing, and this time it'll be all night, most likely."

"You can't afford that, Mister Peel, suh," she said, using her best executive assistant drawl. "You have those nabobs from Santa Fe right here in this office at ten A.M. That's," she glanced at the clock, "fifteen hours from now. You don't want to feel like somethin' the cat dragged in, not to mention how you'll look."

"Hell, that's right. But I need the model to make a point. Well, if I had four hands or a slave girl I could be through by midnight. But I don't. I guess the cat will just have to drag me—"

"You are the most exasperatin' man," she fumed, pulling the flow pen from above one ear, tossing it down. "Any ol' extra set of hands would do?" She saw him nod. "Then I'll do it, but only because I do *not* want my boss to embarrass the firm in front of the rep-tied, Brooks-Brothered Santa Fe. I've been to your parties, so I know you don't have a housekeeper; or if you do, she's taking money under false pretenses. Do you cook up there?"

He had asked Vangie out to dinner once, and she'd turned

him down. And an extra set of hands could cut hours off the job, and . . . and a lissome Creole was inviting herself up to his digs, even if she would disapprove of the stacks of magazines gathering dust in every room, and she had a dangerously vexed look that might mean withdrawal of the invitation. "Uh, well, I microwave like crazy. Got a freezer full of gourmet stuff."

She nodded and got her light wrap, talking all the while as they walked toward the parking lot. She'd help until midnight, she said, but at her age beauty sleep was an absolute requirement. He must remember her Fiero was behind his souped-up Blazer, she said, and he must not drive like it was a race. And he could shelve the "slave girl" idea, she said; any executive assistant worth spit would have made the same offer, and for the same reason.

She said so much, in fact, that Wes smiled into the Blazer's windshield, thinking about it as he led the way out of Hayward, beyond the boulevards, and up the switchbacks of Crow Canyon Road in the dusk. He had always wondered if anything could give Vangie Broussard a case of the fidgets, and now he had his answer. She might have top marks from Louisiana State; she might pop the eyes of visiting chiefs. But under that sophisticated charm fluttered the heart of a southern belle.

* * * *

Wes's shop was separated from the main house, he said, to keep its stinks and noises isolated. Vangie knew how to stretch a canvas, so she quickly mastered the art of locking a thin sheet of plastic into an oblong frame. She said nothing about the growl in her empty stomach—Wes had forgotten all about supper—and helped him arrange infrared lamps over the movable frame. Within an hour they swung the frame into position between the warm molds. Wes levered the molds together and raised a pair of crossed fingers.

He watched the sweep hand of a wall clock and a digital thermometer, then levered the male mold up and pried gently at the thin sheet which gleamed under the fluorescents, deeply contoured within the female mold.

Vangie "oohed" as the sheet popped free, then "awwed" as Wes pointed to a split. "Mold wasn't hot enough," he muttered. "Never mind. I seldom do anything right the first time."

They repeated the routine, this time with success, and Wes trundled the second set of molds into place. Vangie turned the completed piece over in her hands, marveling at the painstaking work behind the models that emerged from this high tech hobby shop. It weighed only a few grams but spanned over three feet; the flat lower half of a lilliputian Delta One, complete with a faint bulge representing its control cabin.

By midnight, cementing minor bits in place after the upper and lower shapes were joined, the two of them sat back on high stools and slapped hands gently. Wes pronounced it a failure because it weighed a few grams too much to float when filled with helium from his welding tanks. Vangie pronounced it a success because, holding it in both hands, peering at the tiny shrouded propellers and indentations of control surfaces, she could imagine it as a four-hundred foot leviathan.

"I've got goose bumps," she admitted, setting the model down carefully.

"I've got a thirst," he rejoined, reaching for a bottle that stood on a nearby workbench. "Celebration time."

He poured scotch into paper cups; touched his to hers; tossed it down. She sipped. "Congratulations," she smiled. "You haven't touched this all evening."

He stoppered the bottle, put it away. "I've been on my best behavior," he shrugged.

"I know."

He shot her a quick glance. "I didn't mean, uh—"

"I know," she repeated, more gently this time, and treated him to a winning smile. "Now, how about some supper before I run?"

A breeze from down the canyon whispered through open clerestory windows as they sat on stools at Wes's kitchen pass-through and wolfed shrimp creole with a chilled Riesling. Wes spoke around his last mouthful: "Is this stuff as good as I think? I take it you must be an expert."

"Actually it's not bad," she said, and "hmphed" to herself. "That's one thing the Calcasieus did right," she added, pointing her fork at an empty frozen food carton.

He read the label: Calcasieu Et Fils. "You know them?"

"Lord, I guess," she laughed. "Donny Calcasieu is one of those 'fils.' I left him six years ago and took my family name back."

"Couldn't get along with his plastic ladies?"

"If he'd been happy with plastic, we'd still be married." She rolled her eyes dramatically. "Divorce between Catholics; my brother Tib, that's Thibodeaux, drove a Calcasieu rig and had to quit to save his honor." A long sigh as she looked out toward the twinkle of a distant light. "It's a whole 'nother world back there, suh," she said, exaggerating the accent to lighten her nostalgia.

"I'd like to hear about it," said Wes, and looked at his watch. "But good Lord, it's past one. Ah," he hesitated, then rushed on, "you know you're welcome to one of the guest rooms, and I know you won't, and I don't know when I've enjoyed playing in the shop so much, and, and, hell, it's all your fault. Do you know what I'm trying to say?"

She took a last sip of Riesling, then slid from the stool. "You are trying," she said softly, "to say 'thanks.' And you're welcome, it was a real education. You're a man of many trivial talents, Wesley Peel," she said, smiling, taking her wrap, fishing for her car keys as she headed through his cavernous living room.

Wes sat, watching her go, thunderstruck. *What the hell!* He said as a complaint, "Trivial?"

She paused at the door and waved, still smiling. "My ballet instructor always said we mustn't let men think too well of themselves. Don't forget to bring Delta One," she said with a bewildering change of pace, and closed the door behind her.

Wes poured himself another glass of Riesling and listened to her Fiero purr its way down the canyon. He was not thinking about the model. He was thinking, *It might be a real education to see Vangie in a leotard.*

SEVEN

Santa Fe's men came expecting only to see the maglev maintenance unit, but left with a new concept in freight handling. Wes used models to illustrate the idea. If Peel Transit could develop hardware to snatch a flatcar's load in motion, was Santa Fe interested?

First they were stunned; *then* they were interested. Railroad men were always interested in any new wrinkle that made them more competitive against highway rigs. But were they interested enough to share the development costs? They were indeed. Wes saw the Santa Fe delegation puff away, and then he shared a scotch with Vangie in his office. Wes had not even hinted to the rail magnates that Delta One was nearly ready for the tests, the money already spent.

And that's good, he told himself, *because her schedule has already slipped too much. And it's damned bad too, because her test schedule will be crowding up against our maglev deadline. I could've finagled around that a year ago, but not now. If Delta One flops, I'm in hock. If the maglev flops, . . .* But he could not allow himself to pursue that one. It could mean bankruptcy, or outside control.

Huddling with his technical staff over the upcoming tests, Wes grew short-tempered when other business demanded his attention. He fumed over the brief time it took to confer with a marketing consultant firm over a new, potentially serious, problem.

As far as Wes was concerned, the marketing firm consisted of Alma Schultheis. Slender, intense, carefully tailored with bronze hair like her brother's and a weakness for bangle earrings, Alma had borrowed money from Wes to start her firm while still sleeping with him, years before. She might send hirelings to service other accounts now, but never to Wes. With her best curt nod, because she could get away with it, Alma sailed past Vangie Broussard into Wes's office one morning in May, an hour after hearing his frustration on the phone. She sat down and balanced a memocomp becomingly over crossed knees. "One of these days," she said, menacing him with a forefinger, "you'll have a seizure. If I'd known you'd have a hissy over a few rumors, I'd . . . I s'pose I'd do just what I'm doing," she finished with affection. Like her younger brother, Alma Schultheis would always cherish a few Tennessee phrases.

Nor could Wes voice a full, heartfelt blasphemy; an inhibition learned at his grandmother's knee. "Got-damnit, Alma, my local rigs have less downtime than anybody's! And Boff Allington keeps a running total of accident reports. You have to work at it to get hurt in a Peel rig," he insisted.

"But not in front of one, with an electric runabout," she replied.

"So you heard about that."

"With my brother standing by, watching you risk your neck? Lordy, I guess," she sighed. "Scared Tom half to death."

"Had to be done," he shrugged, and reached behind him toward the liquor cabinet.

"Ah-ah," Alma said. "How many have you had this morning, Wes?"

"None of your got-damn business," he muttered, bringing his hand back empty nonetheless.

Alma tried to stop the grin, then let it come, mirroring their old conspiracy but unwilling to revive it. "That's true. Well, I gave the rumor problem some thought on the way over. It's clearly hurting business. There are three ways you could fight it."

"One, find out where it started," he said, lowering himself into his chair.

"Won't help; free country," she said. "These things usually start based on fact, which isn't the case here; or with a campaign by the competition. Maybe some of those drag-knuckle NTC people. You want to hear my analysis, or don't you?"

He didn't, but said he did. What Wes really wanted was for Alma to magick a quick fix so that he could hotfoot it back to the hangar, to watch while Tom's prototype crew installed multifuel engines for Delta One's shrouded propellers.

Alma outlined his options: advertising, discounts on Peel rigs, or just ignoring the problem until it went away. She knew he did not ignore problems. She had left his bed in '88, the year before introducing him to Tom, in part because Wes Peel could not let problems alone. When juggling several problems, she knew, he would pace the floors in his home for half the night while steadily emptying a bottle.

"So I suggest a carefully worded handout to sales staff with a small·discount up front that makes lease-purchase options more attractive," Alma finished, watching the glaze over Wes's eyes. It suddenly occurred to her that Wes's thoughts were elsewhere. "Unless my baby done left me East of the Sun and West of the Moon, for two chickens in every pot in the James G. Blaine Society. And you would, too." She raised her voice a decibel. "Don't you think I'm right, Wes?"

Fingers interlaced behind his head, nodding judiciously: "I guess so."

"Gotcha!" She leaned forward, one elbow propped on his desk, chin in hand, and waited for his chagrin to wash away. "Shall I just handle this, so you can get on with whatever it is?"

He sighed. "It's my Big Lifter, Alma," he admitted.

"Oh, my very, very *dear*," she said, averting her gaze and touching her cheek with the mock embarrassment of a Tennessee girl meeting a sexual innuendo. An old game between them, which Alma always won.

Now he was chuckling helplessly. "I meant Delta One. Why the hell do I let you in here?"

"Because I'm more help than hindrance," she said, all business. "You've got Tom to worry over Delta One for you. Or is it something I should know about?"

"No, it just takes forever. We're scheduled for hover tests next week. Barring problems, our new test pilot will be matching up with a flatcar in early June." Wes gazed heavenward. "I don't have to tell you what that means."

"I'm afraid you do," she replied.

"If it works, we can unload a rail carload cheaper and faster than anybody ever dreamed. Another bullet for the freeway elephants," he added.

"Will it be fun to watch? Any marketing pizzazz in it?"

Eyes gleaming, he began to explain how it could gush barrels of pizzazz, or become a four-hundred-foot albatross around his neck. And three weeks later, thirty miles away in Sacramento River delta country, Alma saw it for herself, and met Glenn Rogan: two thrills for the price of one.

*   *   *   *

On that morning Wes drove to the test site, an isolated river delta region near San Francisco Bay, in a company van with Alma beside him. He refused to tell Alma why he kept smiling to himself on the way: because, when he'd told Vangie Broussard that Alma would tag along, Vangie—whose proper place was at the factory—had bristled without a word. And every time Wes smiled, he thought, *All that and a leotard, too . . . maybe.*

The van was packed with video recorders, telemeter equipment for the tests, and the man who knew how to talk to all of that equipment: slim, bespectacled Brian "Boff" Allington, his hairpiece slightly askew under his earphone clamp. So long as his bow tie was straight and his shirtsleeves neatly rolled on his forearms, Boff worried little about hairpieces. He had been known to doff it like a hat to a woman he disliked. Tom's wife Ellie, for example; though Alma, an old friend, was safe from Boff's darker humors.

At the moment Boff was talking by radio link with Tom Schultheis, who had arrived before dawn with several others at this remote, seldom-visited location Wes had dubbed "Delta Base." "Rajah, we copy," Boff replied smoothly to something Tom had said, and ducked to stare through the van's front window. "We should have you in sight shortly." Pause. "Bet you're only saying that because I have crullers and five gallons of coffee in here, Delta Base. Out." He leaned forward, near Wes's shoulder. "Tom says your man Rogan worked his deadly charm on the train crew at sparrowfart this morning. Crawled all over that flatcar, he did, and then rode with them on a dry run. Upset because they wouldn't let him drive the hog. Lord knows what he meant."

"Old-time jargon: a hog is a locomotive," Wes called over his shoulder. "My guess is, he's thinking about the maglev runs next month." One of Wes's best moves had been to lure

Boff Allington away from Microverse Corporation in Sunnyvale, on Tom Schultheis's advice. The son of a London electrical contractor, Allington managed to get himself sent down from Cambridge, where many of England's scientific "boffins" gathered, without a degree. His only degree, Allington would cheerfully admit, was BDIFBY: Been Doing It For Bloody Years. Programmer, circuit designer, electronic troubleshooter, Boff Allington ran PTA's computer and electronics division. In common with all of Wes's top people, he liked to deal directly with the hardware and would rather take personal charge in a crucial test than delegate it to others.

Jouncing down a road that led through a waist-high sea of grass undulating in soft summery breezes that smelled of mud and fish, they crossed miles of the Sacramento River lowlands before Alma spotted something that shone silvery bright on the horizon. "Oh, I can see it from here," she breathed, her eyes round and bright. "You call this a secret test, Wes?"

"Secret enough," he answered. "It takes a mile or so to get a diesel loco up to speed, and we had to lease an old rail spur someplace. Rogan has cruised up here at three A.M. several times on trial runs with just his copilot. Anyway, not many people out here in the flats, Alma."

"It occurs to me," Boff Allington drawled, "that you may give a new meaning to 'delta country.' " By now they were near enough to see details in the distance. The train was nowhere in sight, but the huge spade shape of a delta dirigible loomed above several vehicles, seemingly almost touching the grassy fields though its control cabin floor was fully twenty yards above the ground. As they watched, the leviathan slowly pivoted, one stubby wing dipping and then coming horizontal again, nosing around as the breeze changed direction. Allington, at his console in the van, punched a query into the keyboard and read the display. "Rogan and Christopher aren't doing it with the engines, so the brute is weathercocking on her own. Very nice, Wesley."

Wes continued at a pace that reminded his passengers of off-road racing. As they slowed and drew near, the van passed through the shadow of Delta One. It took twelve seconds by Alma's reckoning to traverse that shadow at thirty miles an hour.

Alma spoke over her shoulder. "Nice? More of your Brit understatement, Boff. Is the Matterhorn nice? Is the Grand Canyon nice?" She felt very small, letting her eyes rove across a vehicle literally acres in extent, that moved almost imperceptibly like some vast live animal floating in a sea of air. It was two hundred thousand pounds of Alumalith and high-tensile filament looming almost overhead. It was three million cubic feet of helium, and it was a dream come true for Wes Peel. Its propellers, idling inside circular shrouds, seemed tiny though they stood as high as three Kaplans, and the smoothly contoured cabin under its chin seemed no larger than a pimple. Briefly, Alma felt a chill shake her shoulders. This enormous airship was many things, but it was not "nice." Then, "There's Tom," she cried.

Alma, the eldest of two children by Wolf Schultheis and his Tennessee wife, still greeted Tom as they had as children: a full embrace, a firm kiss on the lips. As they helped themselves to coffee and doughnuts, they could hear the angry muted soprano buzzing of the engines buried in Delta One's hull, revving up in brief bursts. Two of the prop shrouds stood on gimbals, widely spaced on the craft's trailing lip. The other two, retractable for efficient cruising, lay exposed flanking the leviathan's hull ahead of its stub wings.

Dave Kaplan grinned around a mouthful of glazed jelly-center and glanced up. "Don't worry, his props are feathered," he said to Alma. "Rogan's just impatient."

She could see the featureless gleam of a helmet visor through a side window of the cabin high above. "Who's in the cabin?"

"Just Rogan," said Kaplan. "The copilot's manning the cargo bay."

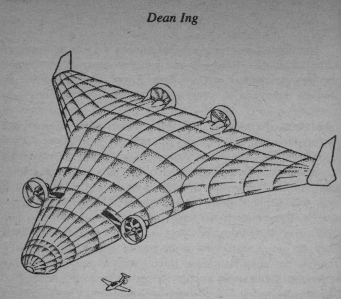

Judging from the angle of that visor, Alma had a sudden intuitive sensation of eye contact with the pilot. "With all this high tech," she murmured, "we should have some way of getting a doughnut up there."

"Not before a test," said her brother, who was listening. "Rogan claims they'll never get him on an operating table with a full stomach."

"Oh, my God," she said, and quit chewing. Not until this moment had she truly considered that a test like this might end with mangled human bodies. "But what could happen? Helium doesn't burn."

"Fuel gas does," Wes replied. "And there's a ton of it up there. Your crafty brother here decided to make the air ballonets double-walled. Some fuel gas mixtures are the same weight as air, and they burn cheap and clean, so why not start out with ballonets full of fuel gas? It lets you lift that much more cargo, and you can refill the cavity with air any time you like."

No one was a more sincere booster of Tom Schultheis than Alma. "Sneaky Tom! Maybe I could do some PR on the low-pollution angle," she said, reaching for the memocomp in her bag.

"No no no," said Wes and Tom together. Tom added a bit sheepishly, "Think of it as a trade secret. You want the truth, Alma, it was Dad's idea."

"Well, hell, so were you," Kaplan joked.

"Don't start, you two," said Wes, raising one hand like a traffic cop. "Tom, I've lost count of the ideas you say your father gave you. Do I ever get to meet the man?"

"He's coming out from Tullahoma soon to stay a few weeks," Alma began with delight, and stopped. The glance that passed between her brother and Dave Kaplan was a shared "*ohh, shit,*" but Alma could not imagine why.

"If we get through our test programs without a major foul-up, I intend to throw a wowser of a party," Wes announced. "Promise you'll bring him?"

"No problem. With all the goofy ideas you two have in common, he'll talk your arm off," Alma said, meeting her brother's warning glance with a smile. Without room for an ounce of guile in a head stuffed with ideas, Wolf Schultheis could spend an entire party sharing the technology that had occupied his life. Wes had been known to do the same. Alma had not the slightest idea what harm could come from such a meeting.

Boff Allington, walking about with his headset still in place, was speaking softly to an unseen presence. "Oh, keep your rompers on, Rogan. . . . No, she's Tom's sister; nice girl, not to be chatted up by your type. . . . And the same to you, thank-you-very-much," he chanted, laughing.

Tossing his coffee into the grass, Wes donned thin leather gloves. "We're wasting time," he said abruptly. "Boff, tell Christopher to drop me a sling; I'm going up."

Allington's jaw dropped. "Inside? During the coupling trials?"

"Wouldn't miss it for the world," Wes replied, gazing upward, feeling the hair rise on his arms and grinning with anticipation.

He waited while Allington used his headset. The first response was a growling chuff from Delta One which Wes recognized instantly. It issued from a slow movement of the big pneumatic cargo struts, and unmistakably became a mammoth sigh. *Got-damn' Rogan can make it talk*, Wes decided, watching the sling descend. He still wondered why a man who had tested hypersonic jets would enjoy herding a hundred tons of delta dirigible around.

Wes slid into the sling's seat, buckled in, and jerked a "thumbs up" at the helmeted man who peered from the hatch. Acceleration sucked his innards downward as the sling winch reeled him up, and in moments he stood on the abrasive floor covering of Delta One's cabin. He patted the shoulder of Jim Christopher, a man of his own size and coloring, as he started forward. "I can't resist this, Chris," he said.

"It's your bird," Christopher answered from his cargomaster's bubble near the entry. "Spare helmets velcroed in the seats."

Wes felt the passageway floor rise and fall in a gentle rhythm, and sought handrails as he moved forward toward the cabin. Rogan did not turn, but pointed at the copilot's seat at his right. Wes, who had not flown an aircraft for over a year, felt the same surge of pleasure he had known the first time he'd stepped into that cabin. Unlike the cramped spaces in most aircraft, Delta One's center aisle lay broad as a man was tall, and every seat had room to swing a cat. *Hell, it doesn't even smell like an aircraft*, he thought. No stink of jet fuel or scorched rubber, only a faint pleasant musk of plastic. He tried the helmet, found it only a little tight, and arranged his headset after snugging his body harness in place. Rogan glanced his way. "Let's do it," said Wes, and Rogan reached for the controls at his right.

Somewhere inside the great airship, a deep hollow *whooom* of outrushing air made way for abrupt helium expansion—a trick possible only with turbine compressors and superstrength plastic films. Delta One would have awed the Zeppelin designers of a half-century before. The pioneers of LTA flight had used stomachs of cattle to line their gas cells; spruce and duralumin for their airship frames. Starting afresh with the advances of sixty years, Wes's team had found startling new tricks. As a caterpillar spins a cocoon, they had spun a thin-wall pressure container of ten-foot diameter with superfilament and used it as a rigid bulkhead. With their lightweight compressors, helium could be recompressed within seconds and stored rather than valved overboard in emergency.

The tall grass dropped away below Wes, whose windshield sloped inward toward his feet, and he felt the great craft wheel away with all its sopranos in full voice. He blinked away the misting of pride in his eyes and coughed to free the glorious tightness in his throat.

Wes listened to the cross talk as, far below now, drivers lined their vehicles up a good two hundred yards from the arrow-straight tracks, Allington transmitting from inside the van while the others readied video monitors. Wes punched an alternate channel and heard Allington respond. "Boff, give Alma a remote headset here on Echo channel. She doesn't know where to point her Nikon."

"Rajah," was the reply. Delta One was completing her long sweep, lurking low like some enormous predator, scarcely moving now, parallel to the diesel loco.

The voice of Alma Schultheis, high and excited, entered Wes's helmet. "Wesley? Thanks for the play-by-play. Can't I get closer to the action?"

"Sure you can," Wes said laconically. "You ever see a hundred thousand pounds of cargo get bunted off a flatcar at sixty miles an hour? If it gets loose, it can go a lo-o-ong way before it runs out of inertia," he added, speaking softly. Beside him, Rogan was talking with the locomotive engineer. Wes went on, "Okay, the diesel's on its way."

Peering past Rogan's shoulder, Wes saw a plume of diesel smoke far to their left, the headset voices falling silent as they monitored the two big cargo vehicles on a glancing collision approach.

After her first howling surge, Delta One fell almost quiet, pacing the loco with ease, and by some freak of acoustics Wes heard the faint throb and whine of a railway diesel as Delta One swept in from the right to an almost parallel course very near the loco. The size of the behemoths made their speed deceptive, and in a minute or so the diesel loco was nearly abreast of them at sixty miles an hour, pulling three cars: boxcar, flatbed, boxcar. And now a great silvery beast, longer than the train, sidled directly over the track at matched velocities.

Allington, reading the Van's meters: "Zero delta vee and holding! Zero target azimuth." Now the howling coloraturas of the huge craft penetrated the diesel's drone, and on the console video monitor Wes watched four dull gray airfoiled struts swing down to flank the flatcar. The flatcar load, an oblong steel hopper containing many tons of sand, jittered slightly with the multiple vibrations of an old track and old rolling stock. Wes saw bright reflective spots, small laser alignment devices, lance from the ends of the struts. The struts moved like live things, perhaps the grasping arms of some huge preying mantis, and then slid down toward sockets near the base of the flatcar's load.

From the van: "Two locks; four!"

Jim Christopher's dry, "Four locks," verified it.

A very un-British whoop, then, "You have a cargo, Delta One. Disengage and try the downwind leg."

Wes remained silent, watching the monitor as the metal struts loosened, one a heartbeat slower than the others. He heard a grunted curse, probably from Christopher who was manipulating the struts, and then the last strut was free, the great delta rising in what Wes feared might be the start of a victory roll.

But Rogan was tending to business. With her blunt nose angled sharply upward, Delta One veered away in a maneuver that seemed in dreamlike slow motion. But at ninety feet per second, a craft of this size only seemed to move slowly. Below, so near that diesel smoke belched under his feet, Wes saw a man leaning out of the loco against the wind, watching Delta One wheel with the grace of a streamlined silver cloud.

Then the diesel began to brake as it dwindled down the track, Rogan mooching his huge craft off to loiter over a field, and Wes remembered to breathe again. He said into his mike, "Get your shots, Alma?"

"I think so. The boys are getting whiplash, pounding each other's backs."

"Premature. That's the easy part," he said, and resumed watching as Allington began talking Rogan in for a downwind run. Again the parallel course, the inexorable sidelong sweep of dirigible to train, the mantis-claw extensions. Wes could hear Alma cooing sweet nothings as she used the rest of her film roll, for the delta held position longer before locking onto the cargo and was far beyond Alma before disengaging to soar away.

They called a temporary halt as Wes conferred with his boffins on Alpha channel. Fifteen minutes later, Wes accepted Kaplan's decision: One strut lock was sticking slightly, but the hardware was new; it should operate more freely with more trials. "All the same, we should machine wider tolerances back at the plant," Wes said, and gave Allington free rein to continue.

Rogan swung Delta One back to loiter parallel to the loco and, moments later, the diesel plume signaled another run. With that wondrous surge and pounce that kept Wes grinning, Rogan again swung his silvery monster into position above the train with perfectly matched velocities. This time the struts paralleled downward quickly, finding sockets immediately.

"Zero-zero and four locks," Allington called out.

Wes seemed unaware that he was chanting, "Take it up, take it up, Lord," until he remembered to switch to Echo channel. "This is one picture you want to get," he murmured in his headset, softly to avoid splitting Rogan's concentration.

Allington again: "You have a cargo, Delta One. Up cargo, up ship!"

Rogan's hands moved swiftly as he talked to his cargomaster. Slowly, as great gushers of water ballast jetted from stubby wingtips, Wes saw the struts begin to shorten.

In his headset, a female gasp and, "Wesley, I see a slit of light under the load!"

"Not now; use your camera," he said, and dialed more zoom on the monitor. It was obvious now that the jolting sway of a freight train could not be perfectly matched by the huge stable platform hovering above it, and Wes prayed that the load would not smash against bulwarks at the end of the flatcar. Then the loco was receding underfoot and, her engines wailing in fierce four-part harmony, Delta One lifted, clearing one hundred thousand pounds of cargo from between two boxcars of a moving train.

Wes was a split-second late, because Rogan shouted it first: "Hot DAMN, we got it!" In the near distance, Wes could see tiny hats flying in the air. Down the track, a man in the loco cab was waving his cap in jubilant circles. Allington regained his calm as he talked to Rogan.

No one but Wes heard Alma Schultheis murmur, "You're a genius, Daddy." She knew her father's work on sight, but she would not have said it for Tom to hear.

Wes switched channels in time to hear Allington, with a new note of concern: "Three locks, Delta One, I say again *three* locks. Do you confirm, Chris? You have a malf on strut four. . . . Your option, old stick, just remember Dave out there in the grass. That bloody hopper is loose at one corner.''

Rogan turned to Wes for the first time. ''Mr. Peel, Chris wants to land the cargo on the road; he won't retract it into the cargo hold for fear it might tip with only three locks.''

''I heard.'' Wes realized instantly that the crew was playing it safe, preferring to ruin metal struts instead of risking damage to Delta One's cargo hold. Least risk, soonest mended. ''Hover near Kaplan, close to the grass,'' said Wes, who had started his career with heavy off-road equipment and knew better than to block even the worst farm road with fifty tons of sand.

Christopher's voice: ''Glenn, some of that wet sand has shifted aft in the hopper. Can you jolt it forward a bit?''

''I can try,'' from Rogan, who ganged the throttles forward. Wes had time to wonder, *What the hell: control failure?* Glenn Rogan swung Delta One back toward the van at a horrifying nose-down tilt, engine shrouds tilted upward to counter the effect of flight surfaces that would otherwise have smashed the huge craft into the roadway. Wes could see that the steel hopper, as big as an interstate tandem trailer, sagged away from one rear strut. Abruptly, Rogan swiveled the engine shrouds and the engines howled furiously, the high grass flattened as though pressed by an invisible sheet of glass. Delta One slowed her progress, nose still depressed, with a suddenness that had Wes's harness biting into his shoulders. The maneuver would have been simply unbelievable to men of the Zeppelin era. Then the huge craft nosed upward to the horizontal and hovered. Wes sighed, watching his monitor. The lock mechanism of the errant strut now lay level with the socket. ''You got the sand shifted,'' he said, and heard the cargomaster confirm it.

''I have alignment,'' Christopher reported. ''Cycling the lock. It's no-go.''

Without a word, Wes punched his single-point harness release and unplugged his headset, which automatically became

71

a remote, though noisy, transceiver. He ignored the handrails, racing back toward the cargomaster's bubble, then peering straight down through the open cargo hatch. "Chris," he asked, "what's the problem?"

"Can't get a good video from this angle, Mr. Peel," said Christopher, cycling the lock once more from his console.

Briefly, Delta One moved in a vagrant breeze and Wes, who did not have a safety line, grabbed for a rail. He could see Tom Schultheis with a headset, standing beside the van not fifty yards away, training binoculars on the problem. Dave Kaplan was sprinting toward the van. With a deep breath to steady his voice, Wes said, "Tom, can you see a fix?"

The engines were crooning now, holding the silvery shadow in place, letting it pivot into the wind as Schultheis stared through his binoculars. After a moment, the reply: "It's those damned Teflon shims! If we had a humongous pair of vise-grips and a hammer, I could slide a couple of shims off."

"Teflon?" Wes knew the stuff was cheesy. "Why don't I shinny down the strut and cut the got-damn' thing off?" He knelt at the mouth of the cargo bay, holding out his pocket-knife.

"No ladders on those struts," the cargomaster warned.

"Negative, Mr. Peel," in Rogan's familiar drawl. "Sorry, but she's my ship right now and," everyone on Alpha channel heard his laugh, "I know how you tempt fate."

A three-beat silence. Then, "It's your helm," Wes agreed. "But somebody can cut those shims loose."

Kaplan offered the simplest solution. "Toss that knife of yours down, Wes," he said, after using the binoculars. "I'll carve the Teflon if you can lower the ship to me."

It was Rogan's view that, when hovering absolutely still, Delta One might drop catastrophically in vagrant air currents. He did not want to risk lowering that hopper nearer than ten feet from the ground. No problem, said Kaplan; ten feet would be fine, he'd been carrying Tom Schultheis on his shoulders for years.

And that is why one of Stanford's best stress analysts strode into high grass with a knife-wielding Cal Tech designer riding his shoulders. Christopher, with caution worthy of a bank manager, jockeyed the hopper ever lower until Schultheis could place his free hand flat on its chassis, inserting the knife blade in the lock mechanism.

Rogan again: "I'm watching the grass for sudden winds. If a gust hits from starboard, we could have two men under fifty tons of sand. If I sing out, don't wait to argue."

Wes knelt at the mouth of the open hatch until the shims were removed, then hurried forward. He saw Rogan's helmet twisting this way and that, his hands never still as the great craft responded to faint stirrings in the breeze. Then, as Schultheis trotted away from the hopper with a milk-white disk in one hand, he displayed it toward the cabin. He stabbed a finger hard, twice, toward the cargo hopper, and Wes's video monitor recorded the strut's pneumatic ram as it locked into place.

Through a dozen trials, the locks performed perfectly. Wes gave the high sign for resumption of the tests, and Delta One swung away toward the distant tracks. But with the familiar giddy sway of a banked aircraft, Wes saw something else and smiled. He had caught the flicker of a hand wave toward the cabin from Alma Schultheis, and saw Rogan lazily return it.

EIGHT

If snatching a fifty-ton load from a moving flatcar was a bold success, putting it back was a triumph. Delta One maneuvered more sluggishly with her cargo, which Jim Christopher briefly retracted into the hull for the cameras before lowering it again.

Sweeping into position above the train for the replacement maneuver, Rogan took his time settling lower, the struts extending their cargo with tender care. Wes, tempted to bark a warning, manfully held his silence as the cargo hopper lowered between the boxcars; for Delta One began to move ahead, threatening to slam the forward boxcar a mighty wallop with her suspended cargo. A glancing blow from this fifty-ton maul would have taken the roof off that boxcar like an ax decapitating a dollhouse. Rogan adjusted the pitch of his props, their buzz taking on a new note for a moment, and then a relieved Allington was reporting zero-zero again. The train was far down the track, Delta One holding position while Wes stared down on the diesel loco, before Allington reported that the flatcar's special pincer grips were engaged. A moment later, one beat after Allington's cry of "Up ship!" Wes again felt gravity sucking at his guts as Rogan pulled the craft into a steep climb.

Wes traded grins and hand slaps with his pilot, then heard Allington confirm that the tests were finished. Leveling off, watching the departure of the train and toying with the controls under Rogan's tutelage, Wes determined that he would master this giant, for Delta One performed as much like a light aircraft as a dirigible. He'd been told to expect this performance. No one had warned him that the emotional experience might be as vast as Delta One herself.

Alpha channel crackled busily with a five-way conference to analyze that last-second "delta vee" velocity problem; for its size, the cargo hopper added tremendous drag to the airship. When that hopper dropped between boxcars, it no longer bulled its way through the air. Prescription: a brief thrust reversal by Rogan to keep the big delta from forging ahead.

Tom Schultheis dutifully took the blame. "I underestimated the aerodynamic drag of the load; an inflatable fairing will fix it. That's what flight tests are for," he sighed.

Wes, guiding the craft to hover within a stone's throw of his staff on the ground, gave Rogan the helm again. "I've got to look over Allington's data," he explained to the pilot as he left the cabin. The truth was that Wes needed to put some distance from Delta One, because he was sorely tempted to loop her from sheer elation.

Swaying gently to the ground in the sling, Wes saw that someone had brought two bottles of champagne, which was already foaming in paper cups. Wes stretched mightily, accepting a cup from Kaplan, and raised the libation toward Rogan.

"We can do better than that," said Alma. "Those men up there have earned some bubbly."

"Later," her brother replied. "Anyway, beer is Rogan's drink."

Alma Schultheis hefted a bottle and saw that perhaps two glasses remained. Cramming the plastic plug into the bottle, she thrust it into her big camera bag and turned to Wes. "Help me get into that sling," she said to him, and strode into the grass to stand beneath the cabin, her skirt tucked between her knees.

From the set of her shoulders, Wes knew that her heart was

set on it. *Well, it's no crazier than wanting to loop the brute*, he reflected, and buckled Alma into the sling harness.

*　　*　　*　　*

Strapped into the sling, waving toward Wes whose expression was unreadable, Alma found herself rising quickly to a foam-lined hatchway, ten yards above the undulating grass. A tall, flight-suited man with broad shoulders stood with his legs braced apart at the hatch, snubbing the cable's pendulum motion with a gloved hand. From her angle, his head was not in view and then she was busy reaching for aluminum handholds.

"Wait 'til the hatch cover is green," the man instructed, "then unstrap and use the handrails."

The hatch sighed shut and slender neon panels around the foam padding changed their glow from blood tint to the color of spring grass. Alma unstrapped her harness and turned to thank the man, who was turned half away from her. "Wes! How did you . . . ? I thought . . ." She stood openmouthed, looking the man up and down.

"You thought I was Mr. Peel," said the cargomaster with a soft basso laugh. "A lot of people do at first glance. I'm Jim Christopher," he said, holding out his hand. "Call me Chris."

Alma introduced herself, smiling with residual embarrassment. Straw-blond hair, mustache, big lean shoulders: the hallmarks of Wes Peel. When you described one, you described the other, yet all the details were different. Christopher's nose was broad, his forehead unscarred. Wes spoke in a light baritone, but Christopher's voice reminded her of a good radio announcer—or of the Oakland *Tribune*'s Reese Masefield, one of Wes's few close friends.

Followed by Christopher, she moved forward using handrails though her footing seemed as solid as the floor of a bank vault. At Christopher's gesture, she chose the copilot's seat. Glenn Rogan snapped his helmet visor up then, and Alma decided that his eyes might very well be lit by green neon. "Welcome aboard," he said with a frank, smiling appraisal.

He wore cowboy boots. His watchband, peeking from the sleeve of his flight suit, could have doubled as chain mail. He had sideburns like wool, a voice like Oklahoma sod in a mixmaster, and he probably stomped to country-western music, and Alma Schultheis forgave him everything for those eyes, and for his mastery of this silver giant her menfolk had designed. "They said beer was your preference, but we'll just have to make do," she said, aware that she was blushing as she pulled the big bottle from her bag.

Rogan suggested that she harness up to be on the safe side, drinking from the bottle, handing it back to Christopher. He watched as Alma drank, and studied her face for a long moment. "You're a Schultheis, all right. I never knew he had a little sister."

"Big sister," she corrected. In her business, Alma had grown adept at reading poker faces. This one, under its deep tan, was hiding a pair of deuces. "Is that a problem?"

"Guess not, if Tom hasn't bitched to you about Glenn Rogan. That's me," he said, extending his hand with a flat meaningful look toward Jim Christopher.

Christopher took the hint. "My flight station's aft for these tests," he said with a half-salute, and headed back into the bowels of Delta One.

Alma shook hands gravely and gave Rogan her name, adding, "You'll never believe I don't do this all the time."

"Never," he agreed, then changed expression and swung his throat mike into position. He spoke with the men below for perhaps a minute before swinging the mike away again. "Mr. Peel says it's time for you to go. I'll have to punch this ol' cow down the river a ways and then across the bay to the plant."

"My father built Zeps, so I've been a helium-head groupie from the cradle, Mr. Rogan. Why can't I ride with you?"

" 'Cause it's an experimental, that's why.' '

"That's not the reason."

He grinned. "Nope."

"Give me that headset," she demanded. In a moment, she had Wes Peel at the other end. She also had the Nikon around her neck and intended to use it for possible public relations flackery, she said, and listened a moment. Well, then she had stowed away, she said, and listened again. Then she insisted that, dammit, this was a ride to tell her father about and she did not intend to be cheated out of it by her little brother or, for that matter, the devil himself.

In the end, it was Glenn Rogan who heard Wes's grudging permission. "If she's made up her mind, that's that," Wes said, still too pleased with the morning's triumph to deny her. "You filed two flight plans, right?"

"Right. Plan A if we had problems, down through Contra Costa County after dark. Plan B is across to Berkeley in broad-ass daylight, then down the bay so ever'body and his dog sees us. You still want me to open her up? Got us a passenger," Rogan warned.

"Let's just say all deliberate speed, since we're running on Plan B."

"Life is Plan B, Mr. Peel," Rogan drawled with a wiggle of eyebrows that made Alma laugh, and then he palmed the throttles ganged at his right. The engine song was faint, muted from inside the cabin. Swinging the throat mike away, Rogan reached for the champagne bottle again as he nosed the great airship toward the southwest, her nose high to gain more lift. Alma judged that he had consumed a few swallows of the stuff at most, and after one more swig he waved the rest away.

Alma was aiming the Nikon past him, trying to compose a shot with the pilot and nearby mountain peaks, when he spoke again. "The way you talk to Peel, you and him go back a ways."

"Ten years. I was three years out of Mizzou U. with a

marketing job in San Francisco when I met Wes. We were what my fey, light-footed boss called 'a number' for a while. Long enough for me to start my own business in Oakland. With Wes's help.'' She turned toward him calmly. ''Tom doesn't know about the number, or the loan, which I paid back. I introduced him to Wes in 'eighty-nine. I would just as soon Tom never heard about, ah, the full connection. He's . . . he's my brother,'' she said, the lift of her shoulders speaking volumes.

''But you've told me, and I'm a terrible blabbermouth.'' She did not reply except for her steady gaze, with spots of color on her cheeks. Rogan saw the spots; nodded. ''Real, up-front lady. I like it,'' he said with a show of strong teeth.

''You like all ladies,'' she accused, silently begging him to deny it.

''That's been said—by folks who don't know me. I look at all ladies, maybe. I like a few. And while we're swappin' secrets like strangers on a ship—which we are, by God!—let me tell you something, Alma. About your old 'number' with Peel? Tom Schultheis is good at math; he knows numbers he never talks about. There's lots of numbers in this world. Tom got me this job, and *that* was a three-headscratch puzzler, I can tell you. If he'd thought it would ever put you and me, uh . . .''

''One and one?''

He laughed. ''Yeah. Well, I'd still be liftin' logs across the Tillamook burn for Cyclone Crane, I expect.''

Her jaw fell open, very slowly, her mouth forming a silent ''ah'' while old memories flashed past. ''You were the ex-Marine.'' He nodded, and she searched for subtle phrases before abandoning the effort. ''Would you believe I don't care? I love my brother. I don't have to love every mistake he makes.'' It was not necessary for her to identify Tom's wife, Ellie, as one of those mistakes.

''Just remember, Miz Alma,'' he grinned slyly, ''your brother signs my checks. I like you, but we'd best make our number about this big.'' His thumb and forefinger calipered a space the thickness of cardboard. At the moment, they were banking like a sailplane above San Francisco Bay while two private aircraft flew alongside, drinking in this awesome bird of passage. He nodded his head toward a nearby Cessna. "If that bozo gets in our wake, he's gonna be sayin' hello to his tail wheel. We don't know just how fast ol' Bossy here can head for the barn, and Peel wants me to switch her rump a little. Somethin' for the late evening news. Don't let the noise bother you.''

With that, he palmed the throttles forward to a detent and, with the surging soprano buzz muted by a helium-filled hull, the airship gained speed. Soon the rising note of windsong became steady. Alma did not know how fast a little Cessna could fly, but it was not keeping pace with Delta One as the silver giant fled southward over the bay.

Rogan looked across at Alma, laid his hand out, palm up. She took it without hesitation, feeling the vibrant hum of the man, frightened of it, drawn to it. She laughed aloud. "This is going to be a ride to remember,'' she said. *Especially if ours turns out to be an irrational number.*

NINE

Being the first precept of Farda: *All precepts must be memorized, for memory is the sheath of the martyr's essential weapons—joyous faith, joyous fury.*

Director Hal Kroner knew that the fun part was over, now

that he was back in Southern California. Now it would be party time, where the wheeling and dealing must be done after *Sacajawea* was edited and in the can. And partying required some highly illegal party favors, like it or not. He spent his first few days at home with the telephone, seldom glancing past his alarm-equipped fence toward the street. That is why he never counted the number of times that tan muscle car thrummed past.

Kroner had a connection or two in San Fernando, but instead, he drove the Mercedes northeast to his Antelope Valley supplier. He did not notice the sand-tinted Camaro that picked him up two blocks after the automatic gate slid shut on the electronically monitored acre he called home. After months on a wild Mexican location, he enjoyed the drive up Route 14, a thoroughly domesticated canyon with a nice tame highway. He would certainly have noticed if that Camaro had followed him onto the dirt road near Agua Dulce, but the Camaro stopped at the sign near the highway. The sign was, perhaps, an omen: It said, DEAD END.

Being the ninth precept of Farda: *The beetle knows only how to fly, but the spider knows how to hide and also to wait.*

Kroner's supplier, an actress in the old days, offered him a free toot but Kroner declined with a smile as he wrote out a four-figure check for her "consultation." He rarely used the stuff anyhow, even the best Bolivian coke; but the select few guests for his home screening of the rough-edited film would expect nose-candy, and toot sweets they would get. Kroner walked back to his car, clapped his brightly banded Borsalino jauntily over his bald spot and listened as his black Mercedes convertible harrumphed in its throat. He dropped the wrappered, hollowed-out loaf of Malt-O-Bran containing the baggieful of powder on the seat beside him. *Give us this day our daily jones,* he thought. *The things we do for popularity! There was a time when a black Merc ragtop was all it took to prove you don't need the money you do need . . .*

He was doing fifty on the narrow lane, considering a right turn toward the Angeles Forest Highway, before he saw the slight figure that stepped from bushes near the main road. For an instant, as long as it took him to hit his right-turn flasher, Hal Kroner thought of giving the kid a lift.

But Kroner had spent thirty years developing visual nuances, and the swarthy youth with the big nose did not act like a hitchhiker. Instead, he stepped squarely into the gravel path so that, if Kroner turned right, he must either stop or run the kid down. The kid, at closer range perhaps not quite a kid at that, held a backpack out like a shield, smiling over it into Kroner's eyes, for all the world as if the bulging pack were protection against a heavy automobile.

Kroner saw the sand-colored Camaro then, and realized just how vulnerable he was to anyone who might want to inspect that loaf of bread, and blasted hard on the horn as he twisted the wheel hard left while still fifty feet from the kid. The kid leaped like a gazelle from that horn blast, and then Kroner had the Merc spewing gravel as he accelerated onto macadam. Kroner had time for only one glance in his rearview before the next turn, but it was enough; the youth was alone.

Being the twelfth precept of Farda: *It is fitting that Satan's weapons be turned against him.*

The highway shoulder was soft and the brush-choked ravines were hundreds of feet deep along here, Kroner noted. No point in letting his famed imagination put him over the edge. He sighed and flexed his hands, easing up on the pedal, laughing at himself. Neither lawmen nor cokejackers, he decided, operated as lone youths with backpacks. Maybe the Camaro didn't even belong to the kid.

On the other hand, maybe it did. Two minutes later it appeared behind Kroner so quickly, growing larger in his rearview so fast, that he did not even spot it until it swung into the left lane, drawing abreast. Kroner, feeling the sudden invisible fist of terror squeezing at his guts, first thought of tossing the expensive loaf of bread out. Then he was braking hard to avoid the Camaro as it veered sideways, its driver twisting the wheel hard with both hands, its right front fender slamming with an unbelievable thunderpeal of noise just behind the Merc's left front wheel. Kroner had time to think, *Crazy bastard's trying to bunt me into the ravine,* before his Michelins lost traction on the shoulder. Then he could only pray that, however long he spun, his horizon would not begin to tilt.

After six century-long seconds, Kroner realized that he was not moving, his Merc on firm roadbed near the shoulder and pointing back the way he had come. His foot was frozen on the brake and an oncoming beer truck, swerving to miss a sand-tan Camaro that slid sideways down the centerline, gave a despairing blat of its horn as it tipped in the effort to avoid the black Mercedes. His mouth agape as the truck slid past, Kroner stared into the horrified face of the truck driver, who had always stacked his load two cases higher than the company permitted and had never paid the price yet. He was paying it now.

It seemed to Kroner as though the world was suddenly soundless, but his eyes were still at work. The Camaro stopped, the beer truck rolled onto its side, and countless silvery cartridges scattered from the truck's ruptured cargo box, spraying thin gouts of Coors into a fine hot June day. Kroner, on knees of aspic, stepped from the Merc intending to run toward the truck's cab but nearly fell. He caught himself on the Merc's open door and saw the youth from the Camaro. The Camaro was two hundred yards away, but with no other cars in sight, the youth had halved that distance, sprinting up the highway toward Kroner while hugging that damned backpack to his breast with both arms and grinning like he was coming in his pants.

In a burst of intuition, Kroner realized that the youth wanted him dead and might be capable of doing it in several ways.

Kroner fell back into his convertible and mashed on the accelerator, aiming the Merc's hood ornament to shave the back of the truck's cargo container which leaned like an old barn roof in the road. A hole appeared near the center of his windshield but Kroner did not hear the long-barreled .38 revolver, nor see the young man who stood on the centerline, chest heaving as he aimed again after firing each round.

Being the third precept of Farda: *The death of Allah's enemy is success, whether or not accompanied by martyrdom. Martyrdom is the ultimate reward, imsh'Allah, if God wills.*

Kroner made it around the truck and had time to feel a tug of guilt that he could not help its driver, before his intelligent self-interest took over. Help would reach the truck driver within moments. Kroner had demanded much from many an actor, but now it occurred to him that he had never seen the real, no-shit, genuine glint of suicidal glee in a man's face until he saw that kid, pounding toward him with his arms clasped over that goddamned pack so that his hips undulated like a woman's as he ran. Because the kid had run away from that fast Camaro toward him, Kroner could still outrun this whole problem.

Except that now his Merc was swerving, fiendishly sensitive to any movement of its steering, and soon even at thirty miles an hour he felt as if he were driving hard over railroad ties, and while Kroner had not heard those gunshots he knew that one of his rear tires was as flat as an ingenue's kiss on the forty-third take. Shedding pieces of rubber, he *blub-thump, blub-thumped* away from the wreck as fast as three good wheels would carry him.

They carried him several miles, and Kroner could see a cluster of buildings in the valley, before the tan Camaro rounded a bend behind him. Smoke poured from its right front wheel well, but even with half a tread worn off against buckled metal the Camaro was catching up at a hell of a pace.

The kid had sideswiped him once, and might do it again,

and Hal Kroner was a man who kept himself fit. In the gimpy Mercedes he was helpless; on foot he might outdistance the kid, but only if he stopped *right now*. Kroner stabbed the brake pedal as he pulled over. Without hesitation, he grabbed the Malt-O-Bran wrapper and flung the loaf into the ravine, hoping no one saw it, wondering if he could ever find it again. He started down the ravine on foot with the Borsalino cocked crazily on his head, cursing his soft Bally moccasins, exulting in the knowledge that the crazy little fucker in the Camaro could not very well follow him down through heavy brush in a car no matter how much power it had, unless he was—crazy.

He heard a deep squall of brakes, oddly muffled in the ravine, and then saw a prow the color of sand emerge against the sky, and heard the growl of a Chevy 350 urging the Camaro along the shoulder until it was nearly above him. Then, because Hal Kroner was a very good director, he made his intuitive calculations of time and motion and stopped flailing at bushes.

He was a hundred feet down the ravine, exchanging stares with a wild-eyed nut who couldn't aim a handgun and drive, too. If the kid left the car, Kroner could flee for miles. Even if the kid was sufficiently out of his gourd to drive the Camaro down the steep side of the ravine, he would not be able to steer it worth a damn. Assuming the kid *did* send his Camaro over the side, there would be time for Kroner to simply dart sideways, out of its path.

For the first and only time, Hal Kroner spoke to the youth. "Looks like a wrap, kid," he called, grinning. He was thinking, *I'd never film something this beserk. Who'd believe it*, when the youth made his decision.

The Camaro kicked sideways like a shying stallion and began its slide down the brushy slope toward Kroner, bucking and bellowing as it came, the youth steering for Kroner without effect, seeing that Hal Kroner was too quick on his feet. Kroner backtracked for a few yards and then paused, grinning, estimating that the kid couldn't steer and couldn't aim a blunderbuss, much less a handgun, the way the Camaro was pitching and slamming as it neared Kroner's level.

Kroner figured the kid had another three hundred feet to descend whether he liked it or not and, instead of flipping off the Camaro driver, he doffed his Borsalino in triumph, holding it by its crown and flourishing it like an Italian. He was still holding the hat out when the kid released the steering wheel, reached into the seat beside him, and brought up that backpack in both hands. Kroner, twenty feet away, was smiling.

Being the second precept of Farda: *Death is the war-horse a martyr rides into paradise. Greet it with loving joy.*

The youth was smiling too, as he slapped the trigger plate that lay just beneath the pack flap.

Thirty pounds of plastic explosive can do strange things. It blew some of the Camaro's chassis three feet down into hardpan, with the lower half of the driver. It distributed the remainder of the youth in a roughly hemispherical pattern with most of the car's bodywork, the right-hand door whirling into Kroner like a runaway saw blade, carrying all but his head and upper torso some two hundred feet. And as the shock wave moved outward it carried Kroner's Borsalino, an unresisting leaf on a hammering wall of wind, another hundred feet where it landed in scrub, intact, atop another piece of discarded garbage. But for the bright band of color on the hat, Los Angeles County deputies would never have seen it, and the Malt-O-Bran loaf beneath it with Kroner's fingerprints.

TEN

On a late June night, Reese Masefield leaned against an open window in Wes Peel's game room and swirled his snifter of Drambuie, combining work with pleasure. As long as Masefield made his deadlines for the *Tribune* and kept the Oakland paper in contention for Pulitzers, his hours were his own affair. Solidly built, with densely matted dark hair and deliberate movements, Masefield had an introvert's smile and his slow measured speech seemed out of place in an investigative journalist. He would have passed as a senior accountant, or an insurance executive. It was only when you noticed the deepset brown eyes that never seemed to rest, and the hairline scars on his nose and chin, that you remembered Reese Masefield was a man whose enemies had found him more than once.

"I know the *Trib* would be interested in your maglev unit, Wes. And if they aren't, I am." Masefield lifted his chin against a cooling breeze from nearby hills and turned away from the window. "It isn't every day I get to watch a locomotive fly. I'm still browned because you didn't tip me off before you sent that damn' dirigible of yours across the bay last month."

Wes slid his magnifying goggles up until they perched on his forehead and placed a tiny replica of a cargo container on the green baize of his pool table before answering. "Sorry, Reese; I got outvoted."

"I never knew any other votes counted," Masefield replied. "Something new?"

"We were getting some bad press on our local haulers at the time—all lies, but it hurt sales and we're still feeling it. My top staff were getting paranoid about the press, and I let 'em have their way." Wes stood up and arched his back against cramping muscles. "Matter of fact, they weren't too happy when I said I was inviting you out to the Mojave in July."

"So when have I ever been unfair to you in print? Discounting the Baja Run back in 'eighty-one, of course." They had first met while contending for the same cheap scotch in a Mexican cantina after a younger, less cautious Wes managed to flip his off-road racer. Masefield's interview, widely copied in the states, had left room for doubt that John Wesley Peel had all his marbles sacked. On their second meeting years later, Wes quoted the most damning passage verbatim, then congratulated Masefield on his expose of highway maintenance kickbacks. Both men favored scotch, both knew change was essential to improvements; and neither would yield an inch in the search for those improvements. After Wes's move to the Bay area, their friendship became inevitable.

"I've got no complaints, Reese; got you a ringside seat for the maglev runs, haven't I?"

"Not if it still depends on a vote," Masefield said with that disarming shy smile. "I know who's worried: Kaplan and Schultheis. Those two won't give me the time of day. You'd think I was . . ." he paused and added in mock distaste, "a journalist or something. I get more about your doings from Miz Mahler than I get from them." Masefield knew Alma Schultheis from the days when she was closer to Wes, and knew how old Wolf Schultheis had named his children: the daughter for Alma Mahler, the son for Thomas Mann.

"Aw, hell. Well, call direct to me then," Wes suggested.

"And Vangie Broussard may deflect my calls."

Wes, chuckling: "Maybe I'm better protected than I thought."

"Or maybe just more isolated."

Wes studied his friend's face for a moment, then dismissed

an unspoken thought with a shrug. "Well, what haven't you been able to find out?"

"Nothing big. A few things I really didn't want to ask you personally. Like, was there any substance to those rumors on your local rigs? And why the secrecy on your maglev trials next month?"

Wes nodded and reached for the scotch, then reconsidered and poured himself an inch of Drambuie. He still thought Vangie's complaint overdone, but lately he was tapering off as a matter of principle. "Public safety records can tell you there's absolutely no basis for a recall of any Peel rigs. The National Trucking Coalition's drumbeaters will try to tell you different. A few bills making the rounds on Capitol Hill would restrict us unfairly, but nobody expects 'em to pass. The plain fact is, the NTC is running scared so they're trying to nick us."

"Make sure they don't nick your carotid artery. Those people used to play very hard ball," Masefield said, "even after the Hoffa days. They're a lot bigger than Peel Transit, Wes. I know what you're up to, of course." He nodded toward the "YOU LOSE" sampler hung on the wall. "If the NTC knows too, you'd better watch your back."

"I do. Now, about the secrecy with our maglev unit. When you're pushing any performance envelope, there's a chance of a major malfunction. With these rumors about our equipment safety I couldn't afford coverage of a major malf on network TV. I can give you one thing for the record: If Allington's computer simulations are right, our maglev may be a little faster than anybody thinks.

"We have to match the passenger maglev's max of two hundred and fifty miles an hour. But ten years from now, people will want to commute along major corridors at three hundred, maybe faster. Perishable cargo, too. Bay Area to San Diego; the Bos–Wash corridor; the dogleg routes from Chicago to KayCee and Dallas–Houston–Austin. Air corridors can't absorb the volume of traffic, but maglevs can do it with clean electricity and no bottlenecks at terminals.'' His eyes shone with an inner vision.

''And Peel Transit will be ready,'' Masefield said for him, miming a toast. ''Won't that put your big deltas out of business?''

Wes sniffed at his glass thoughtfully. ''Off the record?''

''Absolutely. For deep background, as they say.''

''I *want* 'em out of business, eventually. The big lifters are a transfer mode between railroads and local rigs. They erase the last advantage of long-haul trucking, and they'll be a stopgap for fast western freight until somebody has the guts to put fifty billion dollars into a maglev route through the Sierra and Rockies. Of course, it'll take a lot of deltas. But Boeing built a lot of 747's,'' he grinned.

Masefield glanced out toward the twinkle of distant lights, and the horizon glow of cities along the bay. He imagined a phalanx of the huge craft hovering like modular clouds on the outskirts of Hayward, and vented a long, low whistle. Then, ''If it all works, you *will* be bigger than the NTC. My God, Wes, Hayward will be the new Detroit!''

''Yeah; if. But without a fast link between railheads, we're still stuck with eighteen-wheel kings of the road. Look, I don't expect to make *all* the big rigs obsolete. They'll always have a few advantages in special cases. If Delta One can't haul lettuce over the mountains to Denver or El Paso better than a long-hauler, she won't complete the links the railroads need. More deep background: I'm staying conspicuously at the plant, but my hotshots are spread from the Mojave to Arizona this week, setting up tests or performing them.''

Masefield absorbed this with a nod and a pause. Then, ''Isn't it pretty chancy to crowd so many different kinds of tests into a few months?''

''Lord God, tell me about it!'' Wes rolled his eyes and grimaced. ''That was a mistake, but we're committed now.

While Schultheis and Kaplan are training a maglev crew up near the Nevada border, Glenn Rogan will be skipping Delta One over peaks in Arizona tomorrow. Mountain wind is a killer; they're trying some . . . let's say, some powerplant mods, to see if a fully-loaded delta can be boosted past the rough spots.''

Now Masefield was laughing. ''You have a way of understating it. I've flown a puddle jumper through the Rockies, and every cloud has a rock and a cyclone in it.''

''It's worse for a dirigible,'' Wes replied. ''Ever read about the *Shenandoah* on her way through Arizona? Winds in Dos Cabezas Pass got-damn' near tied a seven-hundred-foot dirigible in a knot.''

''Folklore, to me,'' said Masefield. ''That was a long time ago.''

''Seventy years; but God assembles the same winds today,'' Wes answered. ''We've got some tricks to change Delta One's pressure height and aerodynamic lift to get over the rocks, but 'til now it's just been theory.'' He swirled the liqueur; inhaled. ''I'll give you details when it's all over, but 'til then, I haven't told you a thing. Maybe that's what my boffins were afraid you'd uncover, and they don't trust you like I do.''

''Could be.'' Masefield strolled to the pool table, gazed at Wes's handiwork, then flopped into a couch which hissed faintly as its air cooling unit sensed his warm body on a sticky summer night. ''I sure haven't done much uncovering lately. That Berkeley jocks-at-stud thing turned out to be somebody's imagination. And I wasted a lot of time down south trying to make sense out of the Kroner mess.'' Headshake: ''We'll never know, I guess.''

Wes hauled the squat Drambuie bottle to the couch, set it at Masefield's feet as a silent offer, and leaned back to favor his hip. ''The movie director? Guess I read about it; got problems of my own. Blew himself up in a ravine, didn't he?''

''Got blown up, anyway. He was involved in a truck ac-

cident, and drove away, and a few miles off they found his
Mercedes with a shredded tire and a bullet hole through the
windshield. Okay, so somebody was after him; caught him,
probably. Whoever it was, drove a heavy metal Chevy coupe
off the road into the ravine. Halfway down, the Chevy made
a report to the nation. Blew the driver into the kind of pieces
that don't give you an ID. Hal Kroner was cut in two, but you
could recognize him. Cops figured the guy forced Kroner into
the Chevy at gunpoint. Kroner tries to jump him, the car goes
into the ravine, one of them has a shitload of explosives, and
bouncing down the ravine sets it off. By some freak of shock
waves, the upper part of Kroner is left ten yards away and the
rest of him goes for an over-the-fence homer.

"And get this: down the ravine, past Kroner's body, they
find this snap-brim hat of Kroner's in a bush, without a blem-
ish, sitting on a loaf of bread which has Hal Kroner's prints
all over the wrapper. Here's the kicker: The bread loaf is
hollowed out. It's got three ounces of cocaine inside." Reese
Masefield's hands went out in an elaborate shrug as if offering
the scenario for examination.

Wes leaned back, eyes closed as if asleep, for thirty seconds
while he took up the game they had played for years, ever
since they began swapping paperback mysteries by the handful.
Then he opened his eyes, nodding. "I got it. The director
parks, runs off with the coke, and leaves his hat on it so he
can find it. *Then* the gun toter catches him. Kroner doesn't
like staring down a gun barrel and tells the other guy where
he put the dope, and the other guy's already on something like
PCP that makes him weird, so down they go toward the stash,
in the nut's car. Blooey. Do I get the cigar?"

"Well, you had to be there, I guess. I got a batch of reports
and went out north of L.A. and looked around. No trouble
finding the spot; there's a naked oval on the hillside and a big
hole in the middle of it. Took a hell of a lot more than a few

sticks of dynamite to do that, Wes. All they found of the upper part of the driver were a few little pieces the flies found first. His lower body was—well, it took experts to be sure it had been a man.

"But it didn't do that to Kroner. He looked like somebody had come at him with a dull scythe at a thousand miles an hour. I don't think Hal Kroner was in the Chevy when it blew, I think he was running from it. Or toward it, maybe. And I don't see how the driver could've been on angel dust or whatever, because he handled himself well enough to chase Kroner down."

"Then it doesn't make any sense," Wes said.

"In a way, you're right. It was plain crazy to drive a car down that ravine. But if he saw Kroner down there, and if he *was* a fruitcake bent on taking Kroner, then he might go for it."

Wes reached for the bottle, pouring a half-inch into his glass, and saw Masefield looking curiously at the small potion. "I promised somebody," Wes shrugged in explanation. Then, "Maybe the explosives weren't Kroner's. He got caught after he stashed the cocaine, tried to run for it, and the nut came down in the Chevy and set off the explosives."

"Possibly. I told you it was a fucking mess, didn't I? There's not enough to hang a responsible byline on, so I let it go." For perhaps a minute they sat and tasted the night breeze through the room. Then Masefield said, in afterthought, "The nut had to be a small-time freelancer. I just can't believe big-time drug people would hire a man who drives down ravines and keeps explosives wired in his lap so they can go off by accident."

"Of course not," said Wes. "He wasn't a druggie, either."

Slitting his eyes, chewing his lip reflectively, Masefield regarded Wes through a slow count of ten. "Solid deduction?"

"Naw, just a guess. You say the gunman did everything

like a man in control of himself, but he deliberately drove down the ravine after Kroner; practically suicide. Well, given one suicidal move . . . *why not two*?''

''Namely?''

''The explosives.''

''Sonofabitch! Why didn't I think of that?''

''You don't read enough detective stories.''

Nodding, assembling the pieces for himself, Masefield emptied his glass and leaned back. ''So maybe the guy didn't give a good shit about Kroner's drugs. He was a . . . a frustrated actor bent on suicide. Hell, they're all bonkers anyway. Or the twin brother of the kook who assassinated Senator Elliott with a handshake and a few pounds of plastique taped to his chest,'' he went on, making an Olympian intuitive leap without much conviction, and laughed suddenly. ''Oh, bullshit, I'm reaching now. This guy had a gun, too. Why not the twin brother of John Wilkes Booth?''

''Why not? Booth was a political assassin. So was that foreign student who killed Elliott. Why *not* your gunman?''

After a thoughtful pause, Masefield reached for the bottle again. ''Forget I mentioned it. It just won't play from Kroner's end, Wes. You never saw a less political man than Hal Kroner. He had a lot of things to say, but no bandwagons to push. Sorry.''

Neither Wes nor Masefield thought of the biggest bandwagon of all, bigger than any single politician or any political party, which Hal Kroner had pushed relentlessly all his life: the United States of America.

They were still arguing scenarios, and Wes had nearly succeeded in forgetting his anxiety over an overdue phone call, when he heard the buzz of his scrambler phone. He reached it in three seconds flat. Glenn Rogan was calling from the moorage at Globe, Arizona.

ELEVEN

North of the Superstition Wilderness, in central Arizona, Lake Roosevelt lies in the lap of mountains reaching nearly eight thousand feet above sea level. Many regions in the west were just as remote, with winds equally treacherous to test the mettle of Delta One. But none of those other wild areas boasted a mountaintop site capable of firing a half-*billion*-watt, free-electron laser beam.

Arizona State University operated the site, built before a lackadaisical Congress castrated the Strategic Defense Initiative. Now the laser's chief use was as an emergency standby, to energize satellite accumulators. Fed by high-tension lines that stretched upward from nearby Roosevelt Dam, the laser could gulp so much power that it could not be operated at full intensity while citizens in Phoenix, sixty miles distant, drew peak loads from the power grid. Peak load times spanned early morning and late afternoon hours. At any other time, given sufficient reason and a check to cover the costs, ASU's ground-based laser could be used for industrial research.

The proportion of the check that paid for electricity alone was astonishingly *small*. No laser could use a half-billion watts for even one full minute, even with the liquid spray radiators which ASU built to cool the brute. Besides, the laser-energized rockets spread across Delta One's underhull had their own heat problems; Tom Schultheis estimated that twenty seconds were more than enough. The thrust chambers needed no oxygen; the liquid hydrogen fuel was vaporized only too well with the ravening energy from God's own wall plug below, focused into the chambers by Delta One's beam catcher mirrors.

The test profile called for brief bursts of thrust, first for a tenth of a second, escalating finally to twenty seconds. After each firing, the crew waited for those thrust chambers to reach a stable temperature again. When you're trailing an exhaust plume of incandescent hydrogen, you want to be *certain* you know what all those numbers mean.

Aboard Delta One with Rogan and Christopher, Boff Allington monitored hundreds of readouts between each gargantuan zap. Jim Christopher, doubling as flight engineer, climbed down past the protective armor of carbon filament and eyeballed each thrust chamber just outside the hull, because the forward face of each chamber held an almost perfectly transparent, synthetic sapphire the width of a cantaloupe. Crystal windows of this kind had been lab-synthesized for years. Until now, no one knew whether they could pass a high-energy laser and function as the front end of a big rocket chamber at the same time. Schultheis knew the old adage was often true. Scaleup equals screwup.

Glenn Rogan did not have to ask why Schultheis had ignored ordinary turbines when he chose Delta One's high-altitude boost engines; by now, he knew. Nothing else would serve for their ultimate purpose with Highjump. For the record, those laser rockets were compact and their hydrogen exhaust became clean water vapor, reason enough to convince Wes Peel of their advantages on Delta One. Laser rockets had shown great promise, but when laboratory funds of the Strategic Defense Initiative were chopped, several promising propulsion systems went into mothballs. Two years back, Tom Schultheis had assembled a pile of unclassified papers on laser propulsion. And among the authors of those papers were a few people willing to quote numbers the way other men argued baseball statistics. Now those numbers would be checked by the engineer's prime maxim: One test is worth a thousand expert opinions.

Navigating with excellent radar, the crew needed only two nights to assure that Delta One's Fresnel "beam-catcher" lenses and those laser rockets could boost the huge craft over a two-mile peak with room to spare. When he first saw the cost estimate, Wes had been certain someone had misplaced a decimal point. The actual cost for electricity came to less than three hundred dollars for the twenty-second burst. There was no mistake. A rocket fed by external beamed energy was incredibly cheap.

At the time Wes had thought: *Bloody shame they can't fly airplanes this way. Clean, cheap, efficient.* But of course an airplane would need that power continuously for many minutes. And one of the big NASA shuttles, attempting such a far-out scheme, would need upwards of a *hundred* billion watts. No way, with existing technology. Merely drawing that power would have caused urban blackouts from Phoenix to Seattle.

Far beneath these surface thoughts, Wes felt in his bones that man should not intrude into Heaven. His grandmother had fed him that notion from childhood, had ingrained it so deeply in him that Wes rarely gave it much thought. Wes Peel would remake, re-*form*, American transportation—but he would not invade Heaven with his changes.

* * * *

When Wes answered his phone on that June night, he did not care that Reese Masefield could hear his end of the link. Faintly fuzzy from the scrambler unit, a familiar gravelly voice: "Glenn Rogan, Mr. Peel. We got a sweet ship here."

Wes felt a wave of relief sweep through his body. "I never doubted it," he lied. "Those college boys didn't shoot a hole in you by mistake?"

"Nope. That's what those little alignment lasers are for.

Damn' good thing the thrust chambers aren't any bigger if we're gonna kick her in the ass like this. But man, with a three-second wallop she can put her nose up and climb shit-hot.''

Wes grinned at the pilot's cavalier way of making a postflight report. ''You think you can clear peaks in Colorado some-day?''

Suddenly Rogan was the cool professional again. ''Not with only a three-sec boost, and that's as far as we took her tonight. Boff says the thermoclines across those crystal windows could do funny things after a long jolt. It may turn out that turbo packs will work better; ask me tomorrow night. Ah, you said to call you directly, but you might pass the word to Schultheis: so far, so good.''

''I'll try to call him. Tom's out near Barstow with the mag-lev; I thought you knew.''

If Rogan knew otherwise, he kept it to himself. ''He's mis-sin' a great ride here, tell him that.'' With the enthusiasm of a youth, he added, ''You really ought to give this a try yourself, Mr. Peel. Hell of a ride.''

''I intend to,'' Wes replied with a chuckle, then sobered. ''Think you'll run on schedule tomorrow?''

''Yep, if we don't get a malf during the short snorts. We're scheduled to leapfrog Aztec Peak after a long boost, sometime after twenty-two hundred hours our time. Takes a while to get her moored here at Globe but I'll call you, soon as we've buttoned her down.'' Pause, and a cackle of sheer high spirits before, ''God *damn*, a rocket-powered dirigible! That's a first in anybody's logbook, Mr. Peel.''

''Just don't bend it,'' Wes replied with an unconscious head-shake, wondering if Rogan's ego involvement could affect his judgment. How could the man be ruthlessly professional and still a hell-raising cowboy? It suddenly occurred to Wes that, in his racing days, he had kept the same strict compartments in his own mind. In the work compartment you focused on the job; nothing else existed for you. In the play compartment you defocused wildly because, if you didn't, you risked stomach ulcers and neuroses. You could go from work to play with an abruptness that bewildered most people.

Rogan's, "We'll stick to the profile," was professionally cautious, as near a promise as anyone could ask. The test results, he added, would be sent to the plant by modem the next morning.

Wes replaced his handset gently, feeling as though he were full of helium. "Reese, I've got another call to make. May take a while." The hint was unmistakable.

"Your hours are worse than mine," said the journalist, rising, seeking his summer-weight jacket. "Thanks for the background stuff." He stopped at the front door as Wes was reading from his memocomp display and punching interminable numbers into the phone. "That was good news, I take it."

"Couldn't be better," Wes replied, realized he had hit a wrong digit, and said a word he rarely used. Reese Masefield made an exaggerated comic pantomime of tiptoeing out, but Wes did not notice.

*　　*　　*　　*

Without cellular radiophone relays along Interstate 15 through the Mojave, Wes could not have made his call to the maintenance unit's garage building near Barstow. And without forwarding modules, Tom Schultheis could not have diverted that call to a very different location ninety miles to the east.

That location was a secondhand, prefabricated shed bought cheaply by Exotic Salvage and painted the dull colors of desert rock. From the shed, Tom could have seen the moon-glint on the very tips of high-tension lines that marched across Clark Mountain on their way from Hoover Dam to Los Angeles. The maglev route followed those power lines, which dropped off their highest elevation on the mountain's flank and proceeded due east almost to Nevada. The shed could not be seen from the maglev route. You could hide a lot of stuff in plain sight out here, but behind a nearby butte you were twice hidden.

And inside the shed, beneath its reflective mylar blanket, Highjump was *thrice* hidden, on the off chance that some desert prospector might wander by when the shed was unlocked. Dave Kaplan, bleary-eyed with fatigue, blinked at the phone's buzz. "Who could it be at this hour?"

"Only one person," said Schultheis, and tossed him a bag of fasteners while hurrying to the wall telephone.

"Shut off that damn' power plant before you answer," Kaplan called, and saw his friend slap the kill-switch. The muffled engine wheezed into silence and, as a battery relay clicked, the shed's fluorescents flickered. Kaplan tore open the hardware packet and cursed as he wriggled back into the innards of Highjump. He could hear Schultheis easily across a shed that was no larger than a small aircraft hangar.

"Maintenance building," was the first lie as Schultheis picked up the handset. It would not be his last. "Hello, Wes, it's Tom." Pause. "Nobody but me. I was just going over some spec sheets. What's the good word?"

A longer pause, so long that Dave Kaplan began removing flathead titanium screws from a bracket while he listened. Highjump had a lot of brackets, and Kaplan had installed every last one with screws a quarter of an inch longer than necessary. That meant roughly two pounds more mass than Highjump needed, and Kaplan had no choice but to undo his mistake. This was one delta craft that could not afford an extra ounce.

Schultheis again, "That's great. I'll tell Dave; he was worried about those sapphire ports. . . . What? Well, we'll be done here by Friday, but there's a certain stress analyst who thinks he's a trout fisherman. . . . No, the Kern River over in Tulare County somewhere." After the next pause, a great show of patience. "Wes, if anything goes wrong, it'll happen before the weekend and we'll fly back as soon as we know. I'll be back in my office Monday, okay?"

He returned muttering and then, taking up a powered screwdriver, "Wes just heard from Delta One. They're right on track; going to try the Aztec Peak profile tomorrow night."

Wedged beneath an insulated sphere that nestled between sturdy diagonal braces, Kaplan jerked his head around. "What does Wes know about the profile?"

"Only that they'll boost over Aztec peak. The crystal ports look okay, and they have the readouts."

As usual, Schultheis avoided even mentioning the name "Rogan" when he could. Kaplan groaned as he shifted toward another set of brackets. "Jesus, my eyes won't even focus anymore. How am I going to help you with that plasma coating?"

"Your brain won't focus either; we aren't scheduled to spray that leading edge coat until this weekend while we're supposed to be fishing. You'll be okay by then."

A grunt, and several deep breaths while Kaplan wormed his way further into the bowels of the little craft, now brushing against the cockpit module that would house Glenn Rogan one day soon. "You know what I just realized?"

"Don't make me guess," said Schultheis, who was just as bone weary as Dave Kaplan midway through their second night without sleep. He tried not to think of the next morning, when they would have to show up back at Barstow for another full workday.

"Monday, we've got to face Wes looking like we've been relaxing on the Kern River all weekend; and I don't know how I'm going to manage that."

But Dave Kaplan was spared that problem. Within twenty-four hours he would be on a chartered plane headed toward Globe, Arizona, to investigate the failure of Delta One.

TWELVE

Wes was at home the following night, with a special weekend guest, when that second call came, as brief and as stunning as a lightning strike. Wes made fast decisions and three phone calls.

For Kaplan and Schultheis, the next few hours were one long peal of thunder: the conspirators driving back to Barstow, groggy from lack of sleep; speculating fruitlessly why a Delta One thrust chamber had exploded in flight; flying to meet Wes in Las Vegas with a faster aircraft; and finally a kind of nirvana after climbing into the twin Piper behind Wes and the charter pilot.

Sunrise was creeping into Arizona's parched interior as the Piper banked into its final approach leg. Wes felt the pilot's hand on his shoulder, tentative at first, then more insistent. He jerked upright from a fitful dream to a worse reality. "I'm awake," he said over the hissing of turboprops.

The charter pilot, a windburned woman in her fifties, tossed him an appraising glance. "You people sleep like dead men," she said, then pointed with her chin. "Nobody's asleep down there, though."

Wes reached back and shook Dave Kaplan's leg, pointing ahead as both sleepers sat erect. "Looks like the word is out," Wes said. The town of Globe lay miles to the west, a dawn sun heliographing saffron winks from windows in the taller structures.

"I spotted an ABC logo on a Bell chopper," said the pilot, getting her gear-down signals, lining up the Piper neatly.

"That's all we needed," Wes grumbled. He said no more for a moment, reflecting that the pilot had no more special loyalty to Peel Transit than would a taxi driver. For a moment before the Piper dropped further, they could see the scatter of small aircraft around Delta One, and Wes thought of jackals sitting around a dying elephant—or a dead one. Hopefully: "No obvious damage from here. Can you taxi us all the way?"

"Why not? Everybody else in the world did," cracked the pilot, attending to her flareout, letting the Piper settle gently. The others peered anxiously ahead and said nothing.

Before the craft braked to a stop, Wes could see the impact jacks of Delta One anchored rigidly in the hard, burnt-ochre earth to one side of the taxi strip. Another Schultheis idea: With a properly designed gimbal mount and a cartridge-powered stake driver, a dirigible could anchor its own moorage platform. No sign of the crew, but plenty of the wrong kind of sign: media, come to sniff for hints of carrion. One fat-tired little three-wheel vehicle, then another, puttered toward the Piper with cargo panniers full of video equipment. "If we don't know anything, we can't say anything," Schultheis said quickly.

"One of us will have to make optimistic noises," Wes replied. "Otherwise you know damn' well what they'll speculate in print. I probably shouldn't do it myself. Dave, it's yours. Make it brief, and offhand."

"Gotcha. And I smile like hell," Kaplan replied, unfolding his legs. Their pilot only stared in awe at Delta One.

They met a pair of hand-held microphones and a score of rapid-fire questions, and they smiled. They identified themselves and they smiled some more, striding the hundred yards to the long shadow of Delta One as more reporters met them. Wes claimed they would issue a statement when they knew more. He saw Boff Allington walking toward him, and Allington's smile seemed almost genuine as they shook hands.

"If this gasbag traveled as fast as bad news," Allington remarked, "she'd need a titanium hull."

And now, because microphones were very near, Wes's smile became the grin of a man biting off a hangnail. He had already seen the tight-stretched plastic sheeting, bigger than a bedsheet, taped under the hull to hide the thrust chambers. "This is great news," he insisted, propelling Allington toward the big delta. "Everything went according to the test schedule, didn't it?" Nodding his head ever so faintly at Allington: *"Didn't it?"*

"Why bless me, of course. Just having my little sarcasm," Allington said, hurrying to the tubular ladder near the lowered cargo pallet between sturdy jack pads. Responding automatically to a shift in the breeze, Delta One nosed a few degrees to the north, tip rudders moving like live things. The behemoth still seemed to be flying at her moorage.

Behind them, Kaplan paused to scan every square yard of Delta One's surfaces, ignoring reporters from a half-dozen aircraft and three choppers, nodding to himself as Wes and the others ascended the ladder. Finally, with one foot on the ladder, Kaplan turned, standing tall as a giraffe among the jackals.

"If this isn't an unscheduled emergency," one voice demanded, "what do you call it?"

"We call it peripheral testing," said Kaplan, the babble around him ceasing instantly. He knew damned well that plastic mask was the center of their curiosity, so he dismissed it immediately, pointing at it. "We don't intend to show our competition all of Peel Transit's high-performance secrets, so don't ask." Of course there was no real competition to Delta One yet. "Mr. Peel wanted to prove Delta One could navigate the Rockies, at night, in treacherous winds and at very high speeds. And that, ladies and gentlemen, is exactly what she did, two nights running."

Another voice: "How do you explain the mayday call last night?"

Kaplan repeated the question, buying time to assemble his reply. Then: "My fault, I'm afraid. The structure is my job, and I wasn't sure Delta One could take an airspeed of over a hundred and fifty knots. If the instruments showed a gust beyond that speed, the flight crew was to declare an emergency and land as soon as possible." He paused, looked at the enormous span of hull above him, and waved a hand. "Do you see any fins torn off? Wrinkles in the hull? Me, neither. I was overcautious; she did it. Now if you'll excuse me, we have a long inspection to do, to *prove* I was wrong." A beatific smile. "Mr. Peel was right. Delta One *is* capable of world-record speeds for lighter-than-air craft. One thing we do know: She proved it last night." And with that, he climbed the ladder while a dozen reporters sprinted for their microwave links.

It was Rogan who pointed out that network crews might use tiny lasers against the hull to eavesdrop on a conversation, and Jim Christopher who suggested idling a pair of Delta One's big hummers so their vibration would make hash of a microlaser audio pickup. "We got here from Aztec Peak. Why don't we just fly the fuck outa here while we talk," Rogan wanted to know.

"Not just yet," said Dave, glancing toward Wes, getting a nod. He glanced at Christopher. "Did you lose any helium?"

"A little," Christopher admitted. "Hunk of shrapnel the size of my thumb. There must be pieces of lab-grown sapphire scattered all over Aztec Peak. I bonded patches on both holes, so we have full buoyancy again."

Wes: "Did anybody call that laser-boost expert at Rensselaer?"

Schultheis: "Lake? Not without your say-so, Wes. Besides,

Lake knows we're up to something like this; he'll want more answers than we have.'' He turned to Allington. ''Boff, did you get a printout on the strain gauges? We don't know how far this sets us back, yet.''

Allington produced a hard copy, a finger-thick sheaf of numbers that kept a running tally of stresses and instrument readings throughout the test series. With Wes and Kaplan kibitzing, Allington punched up the animated video on his data-reduction display. Christopher and Rogan remained silent and alert while the others fed scenarios into the data processor. They found one scenario that matched the facts after ten minutes. They tried for another half hour without finding another. It was clear that the ferociously cold hydrogen feed line to chamber four was the culprit. A simple re-routing would have prevented the uneven heating near that sapphire port.

Allington yawned as he returned to the MLF mode—most likely failure, sometimes aptly called malf mode—and paused. ''Sorry. We've been up all night, y'know.''

Wes nodded, studying Rogan who, except for the stubble on his face, seemed fresh as unlaid eggs. ''Glenn, tell me your impressions.''

Rogan lit an unfiltered cigarette and drawled, ''We finished the short snorts, up to fifteen sec—there's enough beam scatter off those Fresnel lenses to ruin your night vision without a visor, by the way. Each time we'd take another vector. The laser alignment was perfect. So we line up on the one-oh-two-degree bearing at about two thousand meters, heading for Aztec Peak where we gonna be marmalade if we can't jump 'er. I get a hundred-ten percent out of the props. Chris asks for the big zap; the full twenty sec. They send it. Gawwww, *damn*!

''I feel the jolt come on like dialing turbo boost on a sprint car, I put the wheel in my gut, and for seventeen seconds it was fuckin' Highjump time.'' His left hand described an arc, and he did not seem to notice Schultheis flinch at the forbidden word.

"Seventeen-point-six-three," Allington injected. "But who's counting?"

"Well, at point-six-three the shit hits the air conditioner. We're not quite over the peak but our inertia is takin' us there; I feel this *wump* and a hell of a shudder, fire-warning lights, loss of power, and Chris terminates the boost while he's playin' video games with extinguisher buttons. I'm committed to the maneuver, thinkin' about those fuckin' hydrogen tanks and chewin' washers outa my shorts, because I can see the damnedest light you *ever* saw reflecting off Aztec Peak. And that light is coming from under Delta One's hull!"

The pilot paused, flicking at his cigarette ash, and Wes glanced toward his design chief, who had the pallor and rigidity of marble. "For God's sake drop the other shoe, Rogan," he urged.

"Right. We clear the peak, but a piece of that polished carbon armor is tearin' away and we can all hear it, and I reverse the props and hit the air brakes hopin' that debris doesn't feed itself to one of our props."

"It tried," Christopher said with his gentle smile. "There's a scar at the portside aft shroud. You had the props reversed so the slipstream blew the debris aside."

"Did somethin' right," Rogan said with a shrug. "But you know those magnesium compression tubes, Kaplan? When that thrust chamber blew, a piece of mag got in the way of the laser for just about a jiffy. And we had a flash bulb that wouldn't quit, buddy."

"You had a got-damned magnesium flare under the hull," Wes exclaimed.

"And hydrogen inside with us," said Rogan. He saw Kaplan stare at his cigarette and grinned. "Don't worry, I purged that propellant tank soon as I could. Anyhow, some of the carbon armor was still hangin' in there, insulating us from the burning mag. Chris grabs this fuckin' fire hatchet, runs aft, shinnies down into the slipstream, and beats the shit outa that mag tube at its base.''

"Thank God, that alloy's cheesy and brittle," said Kaplan.

Rogan, his face reddening in a second: "Then why the fuck was it out there?"

"Because it's good for compression loads," Kaplan said mildly. "But I should never, *ever*, allow mag alloys anywhere near a high-energy laser target. I just didn't think, Rogan."

Wes put up a restraining hand. "Okay. We were lucky, and we have Boff's printouts. Meanwhile, we don't know whether Delta One is airworthy."

Christopher: "Of course we know, Mr. Peel. We've got strain gauges bonded on every girder in the ship. Boff had the data reduced before we landed."

Wes, venting his frustration: "Well, tell me!"

"A little yielding where that carbon insulation was torn away," said Allington quietly, reproachfully. "No structural failure."

"Then why is Delta One stuck here?"

"We landed her here to assess the damage," said Rogan. "We stayed here because he told me to." Rogan's nod was toward Tom Schultheis.

"Hell," Schultheis breathed, running a hand through his hair. "That's right. In the event of any failure of the boost system," he explained to Wes, and dry-washed his face with both hands. "I was too tired to think straight when you called, Wes."

Wes Peel sat back, staring at his design chief for a long moment, then began to shake almost imperceptibly. The others needed some time to realize he was laughing, the laugh of a man too drained by worry to put much energy into it. "Never forget what orders you give," he said at last, and clapped a gentle hand on the smaller man's arm. "So there's no reason why we can't up-ship for Hayward right now?"

"Just confirm a flight plan and retract the anchor jacks," Christopher said.

"Then do it," said Wes. "Those media people will get the message loud and clear. Just be sure when you wave, you don't do it with one finger."

"Seconded," said Kaplan quickly, glancing at Schultheis. "Anyone disagree?"

No one did. "What are we waiting for," Wes snapped, shrugging into a seat harness as he reached for a headset. "Patch me into a cellular link, Chris. Vangie Broussard will be watching the store alone." No one noticed that the number Wes dialed was his own home, where he knew Vangie was waiting.

THIRTEEN

On both coasts the trials of Delta One were featured prominently by media but, in the Midwest, it was not on the front page above the fold. Winthorp often smirked to his classes that headlines are about things it's either too late to do much about, or things no serious person cares to think much about. Tonight, Winthorp had very serious things to think about; that brief anonymous message left on his answering machine, for one. It had been only the audio portion of a television ad, chosen for its brash commercialism. Nurbashi's idea of humor, and always the coded command for a return call. It was Winthorp's pleasure to wait, to exercise what small controls he had.

Alone in the study of his tidy bungalow, submerged cozily amid the cushions of a very expensive and comfortable chair, Winthorp read three newspapers that evening, as was his custom: the U. S. edition of the Manchester *Guardian*, the *Wall Street Journal*, and the local daily. He had cut two unrelated items from the other papers before he saw, on page six of the local paper, the picture two columns wide.

In the AP color photo, Delta One seemed poised forever in a steep upward bank, her stubby wings spanning the sky, thick masses of cloud for a distant backdrop. The picture might have been taken anywhere. The caption read, "Peel Transit Dirigible streaks for coast after secret tests in Arizona. AP"

The head, just below, asked: "WORLD RECORD SPEED FOR PEEL DIRIGIBLE?"

Winthorp pursed his lips and read:

"GLOBE (AP)—Executives of a high tech industrial firm announced today that their new dirigible broke existing speed records in high-speed runs over central Arizona last night.

"John Wesley Peel of Peel Transit Associates, a Hayward, California, firm, flew into central Arizona at dawn this morning with the airship's designers to inspect the craft after secretive night tests. Unveiled recently over San Francisco Bay, the hybrid airship has provoked much speculation among aerospace pundits, and derision in some quarters.

"But Peel spokesman Dr. David Kaplan said the 400-foot, helium-filled monster, 'Delta One,' exceeded design speeds of 170 miles an hour, and would undergo thorough inspection near Globe before flying again. Later in the day, Delta One outran network helicopters after filing a flight plan for Hayward.

"Peel, the maverick industrialist whose California plant manufactures cargo trucks and is a subcontractor for Santa

Fe's superspeed magnetic railway, had no comment. Informed sources say that Peel's Delta One is the first of a class of hybrid cargo vehicles intended to compete with other modes of high-speed freight.''

Nodding in agreement with himself, humming an old nursery tune, Winthorp cut out the article for his files and knew that his decision was irrevocable. He scribbled a date on the newsprint, then pressed the stud which brought his chair erect, depositing him on his feet before the massive file cabinet that dominated the center of the room. He withdrew keys from his vest pocket, chose one, and unlocked the cabinet with the precision of a man who enjoys doing small things well. The contents of those drawers were exactly what anyone might expect of an Econ professor: teaching records; his stock portfolio; fat subdivisions labeled Communication, Education, Foods, and so on, the pillars supporting Great Satan.

The late Senator Adam Elliott was not the only subject in the government file, but he was there, all right. The late Harold Kroner was not the only figure with a subfile under Entertainment, either. Winthorp flicked his way through manila tabs in the Transport section, withdrew one, and carefully centered the picture of Delta One in the file, then paused, tapping the file with a forefinger. He returned to his chair and began to review the Transport file, shuffling quickly past the material on J. A. Weatherby and others. The Peel sheaf was not thick, but some of those snippets from *Fortune* and *Business Week* yielded hints about the habits of John Wesley Peel.

Winthorp read slowly, thoughtfully, with the same care that national security spooks used in assembling a scenario. Peel was not a family man, but his home and his parties there had impressed more than one scribbler. He was a man of decidedly irregular habits. He had spent a night in a Colorado jail once, after flattening the driver of a pickup in an argument over highway manners. During the past few years Peel had developed a smoother way of collecting media spotlights with attractive stunts, rather like that fellow Hughes of an earlier generation. It might bring Peel the same kind of following. Once famous, Hughes had become fanatically shy of the public; a difficult man to find, much less to kill. The party-tossing Peel just might recede the same way.

No point in waiting until Peel retired from the target area of public scrutiny. Hal Kroner had been dealt with—however sloppy the job—and Winthorp had no doubt why he was expected to make that telephone call. Nurbashi would be pressing for another name. But the film director had been taken out very quickly and when you used the same weapon too often in a brief period, you made an obvious pattern. Nurbashi seemed to care little about that, but Winthorp cared very much. The problem was in exercising some control over a mullah who made a fetish of control. The solution? Well, one solution was to beg more time in researching a name, which might buy an extra week if you could avoid the pious arrogance of Kosrow Nurbashi. Perhaps more than a week if one could play the mullah's scratchy records back to him.

Winthorp closed the file folder, sat back with closed eyes, and in the utter seclusion of his womblike chair, sucked lightly on his left thumb while, with his right thumb and forefinger, he pulled gently at an earlobe. Somewhere in the wisdom of the Middle East was an epigram to cover it, and Nurbashi was an addict of epigrams.

What was that old wheeze his mother always quoted, to justify her languid pace? Supposedly from the Holy Koran, but not to be found there. Ah, yes: *Haste is child of the devil, brother of delay, father of failure and a stranger to wisdom.* One way or another, to save his own skin if nothing else, Winthorp would keep Nurbashi's eager loonies from giving the game away with too-frequent repetitions of their trips to paradise.

Besides, it made him feel exultant whenever he managed to

manipulate Kosrow Nurbashi. Smiling to himself, Winthorp sat up and levered the chair's tray-sized desk module into place before him. He ran a code tape through his memocomp and then began to punch a Michigan area code into his phone.

FOURTEEN

Holding a grocery sack in each arm, Wes followed Vangie Broussard into the kitchen of her condo with a twinge of delicious guilt he might never outgrow. Across the pass-through, he admired her high-ceilinged living room made somehow mysterious by its hanging planters with lush foliage. The summer dusk flung a splash of subtle color through big windows, washing the room in gold. Magazines neatly stacked, couch and chairs nicely matched, a budgeted elegance: a Vangie room. "I like it," he murmured, helping her sort the groceries.

"You'll have a while to poke around in it," she replied; "jambalaya from scratch takes time. Now shoo, scat! I need elbow room for this," she added, softening her gentle push with a smile.

He scatted, kneeling to inspect her record albums: Les Baxter, Maysa, vintage Brazil 66, Almeida guitar. Not too esoteric, but lush, tropical: Vangie music. Wes moved near the windows and stood beside long drapes to scan the scene below. "Those buildings with the manicured lawns," he said, "Mills College?"

"That's right," said Vangie, pausing to study the way he held that drape aside. "Don't tell me you're a wanted man on the campus."

He turned away, chuckling. "Not that I know of. Just a feeling I've had, this past week. Ever get the sensation of being watched?"

"When I don't, I'll know I'm slipping," she said. "You have that little whittler on you, the one Boff claims you fix dirigibles with?"

"I'm not worried about getting mugged, if that's what you—"

"What *are* you talking about, Wes? I just decided you could stand across the pass-through and dice the celery and peppers for me, if you have a knife sharper than my cutlery. I never got the knack of sharpening a knife."

He pulled the scarred old article from his pocket, grinning foolishly, and drew a cutting board to him. He took the vegetables from her, noting her quizzical half-smile. "What's wrong?"

"I do believe you're afraid somebody will spot you here, Wesley Peel. And I'm not sure whether I'm flattered or déclassé." She resumed operating on the shrimp, with the adroitness of long practice, and her expression was not far from a frown.

"Why do women always infer the wrong things from a man's behavior?"

She arched one brow. "You mean, why can't a woman be more like a man?"

"*Vive l' difference*," he said in his best Albuquerque French. "I meant that my jitters aren't on your account. For that matter, it was you who claimed we ought to keep our winks and nudges out of sight at the plant. I agree, by the way." He paused, gestured with the knife toward her big windows. "But you're right about one thing: I feel . . . spotted. Not here especially, and not because of you."

He was gratified to see Vangie's frown lines disappear as they proceeded with their tasks. It was no wonder he felt watched, said Vangie, with all the media attention he was getting. In the weeks since Delta One's notoriety in Arizona, he'd given interviews to *Aviation Week*, the U. S. Naval Institute, the *Wall Street Journal*, and to his utter astonishment, *People* magazine. He agreed without much conviction that perhaps this was the source of his uneasiness, then set to work sharpening her kitchen knives as Vangie busied herself over the jambalaya. From time to time he studied the graceful lines of Vangie's throat, the curve of her insteps, the swell of her hips—and managed to nick himself, which robbed him of the erection he'd been kindling just for practice.

"Penny for your thoughts," said Vangie as she handed him a corkscrew for the burgundy, and could not understand why Wes burst out laughing as he glanced at the implement.

"Thinking about the maglev trials," he lied. "With a little luck, we're going to have a lot of folks absolutely hornswoggled. You know about the canards we're fitting on the maintenance unit in Barstow?"

She looked at him sharply, then gave a noncommittal shrug. "I know it's supposed to be a big secret. Don't ask me why."

He explained, holding nothing back. If he couldn't share company secrets with the woman who kept the place shipshape . . . "We're not sure how fast she'll go ultimately," he finished. "Front end drag and instability is why maglevs can't go faster, and the cure is to borrow from the agile aircraft programs. We let a computer operate those titanium canards, and—well, we'll got-damn' well *fly* the sucker. No human being could do it, not even Glenn Rogan."

"I'll bet he thinks he can," she said darkly.

"You don't like him any better than Tom Schultheis does," Wes observed, "but for my sake, be nice to him. He's okay, Vangie; he won't spit on your shoes."

"He won't get close enough," she replied.

"Tell you what. Dance with him just once, at the party. You might even like him."

"What party?"

"Big blowout at my place, after the Mojave trials. Catering, a clown to keep everybody's kids from under—you know. You'd *better* know, I'll send fifty invitations and I'll probably have my, um, executive assistant take care of the details on company time. It's business. Some press people, a few from the Department of Transportation."

"That gives me, what, fifteen days? Thanks for not telling me during the trials, ten days from now. Lordy, the things I do to further my career," she sighed, and he saw she was teasing.

Now Vangie was ladling rich, steam-clouded masses of spicy yellow rice and creole stew together, and Wes helped her place everything on her transparent glass tabletop. She whisked her apron off, tossed it aside, then skipped toward her bedroom with a "Just a sec." It was nearly full dark now, and from the shadowed bedroom she called, "Changing into my hotsy-totsies, dear. Hope you won't mind."

It took more than a sec, but it also took his breath away. He turned with his hands on the back of her chair, inhaled, and held it, suddenly dry-mouthed. He had seen those flesh-tan sling pumps before, but not matched to stockings of exactly the shade to make it seem as if those delicate spike heels were extensions of Vangie's legs. He had seen the yellow scarf, too, but now Vangie was tying it at her waist, accentuating the swoop of the short skirt of natural suede which ended above her knees. He had certainly never seen that blouse before, gleaming silky golden with its high collar to frame her throat and some of its buttons left enticingly unfastened. And after three evenings of love-making at his place, he knew that Vangie Broussard's legs were stunning. But he had never seen all of Vangie's charms framed with such . . . well . . . lecherous intent.

She made her expression innocent, trying not to laugh, her hands out as if she were holding a watermelon to him, then performed a perfect pirouette. "Shall we dine, suh?"

Deciding that leotards were sexless by comparison, he said, "I think I may be full already."

"You're getting there," she murmured, with the briefest of glances at his tumescence. "But mama always taught me not to play at the table, so watch yoah mannuhs."

That primly proper delivery of hers, he thought, somehow heightened his desire. And she got-damn' well knew it. "If you don't sit down in this chair, I may have my dessert right here on the floor."

"Good heavens," she giggled. "I hadn't even thought about dessert."

"The hell you haven't," he growled. "Sit."

She did, with a propriety that had to be exaggerated, the long hair loose, brushing his cheek as she pivoted in front of her chair. Laughter bubbled just beneath Vangie's surface, not at Wes, but with him. He backed to his side of the table, looking her over with frank ambition, fumbling with his chair, then sitting. "The wine, the sourdough, butter, napkins," she recited, checking the table. "Is everything here?"

"A couple too many," he admitting, smirking.

"What's wrong?"

"These placemats."

"They're my favorites," Vangie pouted.

"They obscure my view through the glass," he said, and leered as she removed her placemat. "I think it's the color of those pantyhose that makes it perfect."

"These are not pantyhose, as you may just possibly verify by-and-by," she said. "And you dassn't drop your napkin if you're a gentleman, suh. Will you pour now?"

"If I'm not very careful, yes," he said, making her whoop with merriment as he reached for the wine. Burgundy had been a good choice, he decided; anything less full-bodied would have been inappropriate for jambalaya—and for Vangie Broussard.

*   *   *   *

Zahra Aram, a darkly attractive young woman with a narrow chin and nervous hands, kept her sunglasses on, and the floppy hat that hid most of her face, until dark. She found it necessary to cruise repeatedly past the ranked condominiums until she found the right parking space. Zahra had found one spot for the Toyota panel van earlier, and spent ten minutes verifying that an E. Broussard occupied the front-facing, third-floor condo, the same one that lit up two minutes after Peel entered the structure. But because a broad-leaved sycamore spread its foliage between her van and those high windows, she had to abandon that position. A microlaser audio pickup yields only frustration when leaves are constantly moving into the beam.

Zahra saw that she could hold an unimpeded line of sight from this new position, locked the van, and moved into its cargo compartment. She cranked up the ceiling hatch a necessary three inches, working in near darkness with only a red six-watt bulb to help her position the beam transceiver. She had learned to use the equipment in Dearborn with reluctance, and only because Golam Razmara demanded it, but the truth was that Zahra was beginning to love this work. It was a truth she would not have shared with Golam because, she knew, like many men from the Middle East, Golam treated a woman more like an equal when he wanted something she did not want to give. Zahra's tactics, perforce, were those of an old-fashioned girl.

Zahra would be a fool to tell Golam how she became aroused, listening to the intimate conversations of a man she had never met, would doubtless never meet. She had managed it first in a rented Ford parked off Crow Canyon Road. She had found no way to do it on Peel Transit property, but by now Zahra knew a few things about the relationship between John Wesley Peel and the leggy Broussard woman, a statuesque creature who could have passed for an Iranian herself. Zahra did not have to monitor the audio pickup constantly because the cassette machine recorded everything, and those cassettes would soon be in Dearborn, Michigan, by express mail. No, Zahra Aram used the headphones because she liked listening. She liked it so much, she felt a moistness between her legs when she did it. And presently, aiming the wire-thin beam against an unobtrusive corner of a big window, she was doing it again.

Zahra needed some time to conclude that the drapes and a stack of pillows were damping a dinner conversation to audio mush. The cassette dutifully recorded that mush, but Zahra was betting that she herself enjoyed the experience more than Golam would—Golam and his friends, and another man she had never met, one who gave her gooseflesh merely from the way Golam spoke of him. A Shiite herself, Zahra knew that religious leanings came in all weights, from gossamer to very, very heavy. Golam himself, she felt, lacked the fiery zeal of a few of his friends; and in this delusion, Zahra took comfort.

In a way, Zahra felt it was too bad she would never meet this Peel fellow; but in every way she was satisfied that Golam did not intend her to meet that crazy mullah, Kosrow Nurbashi.

* * * *

Wes allowed himself two medium helpings, taking more wine than he might have as an antidote for the cayenne in that wondrous jambalaya. He refused a third, leaning back, patting his stomach and trying to avoid looking down through that glass tabletop because looking tended to make his fingers tremble. "Just let me digest awhile," he explained; "maybe listen to a record."

"I have a speaker setup in the bedroom," she said.

"This woman is trying to destroy me! Nothing would suit me better, Vangie, but you've stuffed me like a turkey. Remember, you never go swimming for an hour after a heavy meal?" She nodded. "That goes for beddy-bye, too. I mean, uh, what if I got a cramp at the wrong moment?"

"That might depend on where you got it," she said, and sipped demurely.

"Shameless hussy."

"In the dining room, no; I hate a messy carpet. In the bedroom—yes," she agreed happily.

"In the bedroom you won't be blushing?"

"I might, but you won't care," she promised.

"I've just realized a great truth: Provocation is the enemy of digestion," he said.

Vangie laughed then, and pointed a finger at him as she arose. "I'll bet you didn't know what I play. Musically, I mean," she added, and retrieved an astonishing device from her coat closet. He was captivated instantly.

Wes had never heard of a National guitar, a huge instrument not of wood, but of metal plated with pure nickel. In a less subdued light, he realized, the damned thing's mirror sheen would send you groping for sunglasses. He was further amazed to learn that it was over sixty years old, heavy as an armload of hymnbooks, a piece of technology far ahead of its time. Under Vangie's fingers the thing resounded wonderfully with no amplifier but the thin cone of spun aluminum inside. Vangie's percussive effects, he decided, would have literally shredded a wooden guitar. Lounging on her couch, listening to her renditions of some familiar pieces with "Jolé Blon" for lagniappe, Wes found it almost possible to ignore the nearness of those long trained legs, one foot tapping daintily to the rhythms of Cajun and Bossa Nova music.

And then she caught him gazing at her with distinctly unmusical intent, and asked, "Any requests, big fella?"

He stood up; reached a hand out, not caring that it trembled. "Yes, let's see how the bedroom speakers sound."

Vangie purred that they could make their own music. They moved slowly into her big-windowed bedroom hand in hand, chuckling together, Vangie's head on Wes's shoulder as lovers stroll through a park, and Vangie snapped on a night-light because, as she had told him at his place, when engaged in serious affairs, a woman wants to see what she's doing.

Once, when she had tossed his shirt from the bed and he was kissing away the imprint of a frilled garter—for those stockings were *certainly* not pantyhose—he wondered aloud why Vangie had chosen to be so much more daring on this night.

"I suppose because I'm at home here," she whispered, loosening his belt. "Or maybe I'm just changeable."

"I love it," he whispered back, proving it with his hands and his mouth, her musician's fingers massaging his scalp strongly, urgently. Neither of them noticed the tiny beam that eventually moved to the corner of one bedroom window, and perhaps neither would have cared much. They spoke little in any case, for the next half hour, although Vangie cried out twice during that time.

Eventually, as they lay with fingertips touching, their breathing normal again, Wes studied her face in the dim light. Amazing, he thought, that each curve of her lips and chin could be precisely expressed in equations, yet their sum remained inexpressible. All the equations on earth could not break a man's heart with loveliness. She saw his smile lift the corners of his mouth and turned her head slightly, closing her eyes.

And something about that movement, and the faint play of tiny muscles in her face, was deeply disturbing. "Problem?"

"No problem," she said, and made herself smile.

"Liar," he said gently.

Now she was regarding him again, seriously. "Certainly no problem with us tonight," she insisted. "Believe that, my dear. Whatever may happen in the future."

"No problem except guilt, maybe?" He saw the instant flicker of . . . something; admission? sadness? . . . in her eyes, which she quickly forced away, and he continued, "That's my line, Vangie. Early teaching, but I seem to have overcome it."

"All right, Wes, guilt. Please, let me deal with it." She lifted a languid arm; traced the heavy vein up his forearm with a fingertip caress. Then she deflected his thoughts with, "Now tell me more about that whopper of a party you're going to toss. And do you still toss it if the maglev trials are disappointing?"

It was, he reflected, the damnedest setting for shoptalk he could imagine. And it did not last longer than it took Vangie to brush all the tangles from that ebony mass of hair, and to bring tiny aperitif glasses full of Drambuie into the bedroom, and by her outrageous applications of drops of liqueur here and there, each of which needed to be licked away.

But the shoptalk did last long enough for Zahra Aram, fifty yards away in a sweltering panel van, to become moist with her secret success. The tape cassettes, in their own way, were a smashing success back in Michigan.

FIFTEEN

"You've got a strong sense of the spectacular, Mr. Peel," said Patrick Sage, marketing exec of Santa Fe Industries, nodding toward the lancelike maglev a hundred yards away. "Maybe even overdeveloped." His delivery matched the morning air of the Mojave, dry and cool. The two men watched as the maglev unit, slung beneath Delta One, settled evenly between energized rails outside the Barstow maintenance hangar.

"She only weighs fifty tons. Why take two days to piggyback her out here by rail when we can do it in two hours?" Wes said it loud enough to be overheard by the handful of

Santa Fe men, all properly suited for a boardroom, all looking very much out of place here on the cutting edge of a bone-dry desert in mid-July. Pat Sage moved and gestured like a handball yuppie but had the squint lines of a more seasoned man. Wes made a private guess that Sage would be driven out of that suit coat and tie before lunch.

But Pat Sage was not all that conservative in his ideas. "Five years from now, maybe we'll have a maglev spur from Hayward. Beat your time with that gasbag," he said slyly, watching Wes for a reaction.

"I hope so," Wes winked back, then unlatched a handset from his belt. The maglev hovered now in its cradle of rails. "Boff, how does the console look in there?"

Allington's reply from the maglev chirped in the speaker, "All systems up and green, Wesley. As soon as Rogan turns the helm over to Chris, he can come down here and replace me in this thing. I'm checking the instrument feed circuits; won't be long."

What Allington did not say was this: Part of his checkout, in the minutes prior to boarding by the Santa Fe test engineer, involved remote controls of the maglev. Allington's slave relays lay hidden behind the maglev console panels, a necessary feature only for Highjump. The remote console, no larger than a keyboard, sat in Delta One's cabin, for now. When the sleek orange maglev inched forward, then back, the newly attached canard winglets jittering noisily, Wes assumed it was Allington who operated those controls.

"Tell Rogan not to leave without me," Wes said jauntily into his handset, smiling, not seeing the sudden concern sweep across Sage's face. "I've never ridden this sucker, and today's the day."

Pat Sage migrated quickly toward his own people and spoke to Santa Fe's contracts man. At the edge of his vision, while replacing the handset, Wes saw razor-cut gray heads swivel in his direction; heard two murmured responses. Then Sage,

a little louder now, "Isn't there some way? It's his own skin."
More murmurs. Finally, from Sage, louder still, "I know that,
Mr. Burridge, but you can bet your debentures *he* doesn't."

Stan Burridge, with a sigh that strained his vest, made a
command decision, not loud, but one that would carry as far
as it needed to. "Then tell him, Patrick. Without waving small
print in his face, if possible. But wave it if you have to; we
still go by the book."

How simple it would be, Wes fumed, if you could just go
head-to-head with prime contractors, yell like hell if you had
to. But men like Burridge always seemed to have a man like
Sage handy, senior enough to know his onions but junior
enough to know his place, running interference. Wes was
thinking it before Sage returned to his side, and he kept thinking it as they strolled toward Delta One's moorage pylon.

He was sorry to run back and forth like a messenger boy,
said Pat Sage, but that was better than watching an argument
get out of hand. It was very simple, said Sage. The railroads
were bound by union contracts like Gulliver by Lilliputians.
Santa Fe's test engineer would sit at that console, and a brakeman would sit at his portal near the rear foil, and only because
Glenn Rogan's papers had been rushed through, Rogan would
ride beside the engineer as engineer-trainee. Given advance
notice, they could have put through papers making Wes a
fireman-trainee. Yes, *fireman*, Mr. Peel, don't tell Santy Fee
that was idiotic; Santy Fee knew. Of course there wasn't any
firebox in a maglev, and if there ever *was* any fire, by God,
the union would be apoplectic. Even though that same union
was still trying to find some way to require firemen on maglevs.
Maybe they could install a wood stove next to the helium
tanks, said Sage, tongue firmly in cheek.

And no, they couldn't bend union rules if they wanted to
run a railroad. Mr. Allington's checking of controls was ac-
ceptable, but when the duly appointed engineer and brakeman
signed on, even Allington must leave. Nope again, John Wes-

ley Peel couldn't wander in masquerading as a brakeman-trainee, either. The contract, in case the subcontractor had forgotten—that's you, Mr. Peel—specifically denied dead-heading by unauthorized persons—that's also you, Mr. Peel —and Stan Burridge Himself would, as always, stand on the perquisites of the prime contractor—that's us, Mr. Peel. Santy Fee was not Santy Claus.

Wes, craning his neck to watch Rogan nose the big delta toward her moorage, vented a sigh audible over Delta One's props. "Sage, off the record, how old are you?"

Pat Sage, now four hundred yards from executive country, became another man with his grin and his, "None of your damn' business. Why?"

"I suspect that however old we get, we never cease to entertain dumb ideas. For example, every now and then I dicker with the notion of going public with a stock issue, get me a board of directors, let 'em turn gray in the front office while I play." Pause, then a slow headshake. "But I wouldn't have any more got-damn control than I have this morning, would I?"

Pat Sage, not quite smiling, looked Wes in the eye. "No more than a toad in a blender. And if you got nasty about it, some number-crunching glorified accountant would push the 'puree' button on you." A companionable silence as they watched Delta One's modified cargo platform lever downward, with Glenn Rogan standing on it. Then, "Peel? We still off the record?"

"Sure."

"I'm a number-cruncher myself. I'm good at it, but I know my limitations. You don't; maybe that means you don't have any." Sage stared with envy at Wes's open shirt, glanced lazily over his shoulder, tugged to loosen his tie. "Whenever a man like you gets to the top, a thousand men like me point him out as a dinosaur from the old days, not real corporate material, out of control, maybe a little crazy." He ticked off on his fingers: "Hughes, Getty, Onassis, Northrop. I mean," he laughed, a cackle like Rogan's, and waved toward Delta One. "Imagine NASA gluing that thing together in less than ten years! Shit, imagine NASA putting up a real fleet of second-generation orbiters, no matter that the Russkies are almost there, while every manager is busy guarding his family jewels from fifty different people. *Any* top-heavy management outfit has the same problem. But you dinosaurs, you're top-heavy with teeth: overachievers, risk freaks. So long as a few of you are roaming the corporate jungle pounding new paths, Peel, this country's got a fighting chance."

Wes, always uncomfortable with this kind of praise, turned it aside with, "I just realized what really killed off all the dinosaurs."

"I give up."

"Top management," Wes grunted. He met Sage's grin and handclasp, then glanced toward the distant gray heads. "I should put it more diplomatically, but how would you like a good job?"

"I've got one, so I didn't hear that. There are a few of us bean-counters who can watch the track ahead while we watch our backs too. I'm where I ought to be. And so are you."

In Sage's frank gaze, Wes saw a commitment to excellence, even excellence of a sort very different from Sage's own. *I'm glad he turned me down. We need him where he is*, Wes thought. Aloud he said, "Well, how about a ride to the test site? Couple of spare seats in Delta One."

"I thought you'd never ask," Sage replied, letting his eyes rove across the monster with that mixture of fondness and awe which, for Wes, was the only proper flattery.

Rogan hopped down from the platform, strode to Wes, and waited only long enough to shake Pat Sage's hand. "Sorry you can't come along," he said to them both.

"What the hell," Wes grumbled, then essayed a lopsided grin. "How's it feel to be a trainee?"

" 'Bout like you'd expect," Rogan shrugged, and left them standing there.

"At least I'll get the ride I wanted," Sage chuckled. "You understand, I'm only going because I had to sweet-talk you out of a rage. For the record," he added, waving toward Burridge Himself.

"And so you could worm your way into my confidence and find out what I'm planning for next year," Wes countered.

"Naturally. My God, Peel, it would make my career if I could tell old Burridge what you'll be doing in orbital freight ten years from now!"

Wes frowned his disbelief. "I doubt the hell out of that, 'cause I won't be doing anything in that field. Ever. Somebody's putting you on, Sage. Where'd you get such an idea?"

Blank look, then a shrug. "Uh—the people you hire, I guess. Their resumes were in your proposal to us: Rogan, Schultheis, Kaplan, that Brit import. I'm sure you play boardroom games like that. You know; take a look at the staff in the wheelhouse, and guess where the boat is headed."

"Um," was all Wes said as he motioned Patrick Sage onto the cargo platform of Delta One. But he thought about that all the way to the test site.

*   *   *   *

Jim Christopher waited only until Allington was aboard, then nudged Delta One eastward a thousand feet above the desert, above the two parallel sets of maglev rails. His passengers watched black limousines crawl toward Interstate 15 far below. Patrick Sage had the gift of remembering names on first acquaintance: Tom and Alma Schultheis, Dave Kaplan, Brian Allington, Reese Masefield.

Allington busied himself at his own console, announcing presently that the maglev was underway. "If I know Rogan, he'll beat us to Coyote Dry Lake."

"If I know a Santa Fe test engineer with forty years of

seniority, no he won't either," Sage replied with a chuckle, as Alma readied her Nikon and peered at the maglev rails gleaming below. "We've set up a dummy load and misaligned a track segment for your maintenance unit to play with before the acceptance runs."

"Nobody tells me anything," Alma sighed, tossing a vexed look at Wes. "What's going to happen?"

"Nothing very exciting before lunch," said Dave Kaplan, "but it's all vital."

"Vital stuff is boring stuff," she said.

Reese Masefield, fingering the Hasselblad in his lap, burst out laughing and nodded agreement, earning wry expressions from Wes and Pat Sage.

Presently the shadow of Delta One ghosted over Coyote Dry Lake ahead of them. Christopher loitered the big craft southward, bringing her about so that his passengers could watch the "vital" stuff. Sure enough, Santa Fe had erected bleachers with a sunshade for its nabobs. Nearby, near the rails, a slender maglev passenger car lay on its side. "One of our old prototype cars," Sage told Alma Schultheis. "It shouldn't ever derail that badly, but it's possible." Two choppers with network markings identified the scatter of press people already scurrying for high bleacher seats. Soon, the bright orange dart of the maglev slid into view along its right-of-way between towers of the old Los Angeles power line. Wes patched himself into the circuit with Allington, listening to the cross talk with Rogan.

Santa Fe's brakeman, with his alignment display, found the misaligned rail segment—to no one's surprise, nearest the bleachers—and soon the sleek orange maintenance unit squatted on pneumatic rams for the rail adjustment. It was not soon enough for Alma and Masefield, who quickly pronounced it dishwater-dull. No matter that Wes and Sage composed a cheering section; no matter that the maglev's deployed boom snatched that "derailed" passenger car up and oriented it over the adjacent rails an hour later: It had no pizzazz, said Alma, and the hell with it, added Masefield. They persuaded Jim Christopher to circle the area, locating the hamlet of Manix and, on their westward swing, the Calico Mountains archaeological dig.

The maintenance unit had towed the old prototype passenger car out of sight to Barstow, and Delta One's people were casting aspersions on the sandwiches in their box lunches— "I never believed in rubber chickens," said Kaplan, " 'til I tasted rubber-chicken salad,"—when Wes noticed Tom Schultheis respond to some silent gesture from the direction of Allington's console. The others chatted comfortably, a background noise that might mask a quiet conversation. Wes moved his headset an inch and leaned back.

"Got a drag coefficient for you, Thomas. Not good enough by half, I think."

Tom Schultheis glanced at the console, grimaced, then asked, "On the way out, or coupled with that car?" They spoke so quietly that Wes was certain they did not expect to be overheard.

"With the car."

A long exhalation. "You wouldn't believe the cruddy drag figures on long trains, Boff. Relax; run the program again on the speed trials when it isn't towing that brick of Santa Fe's."

Allington again: "What do you have to see?"

Thoughtful pause. Then, almost inaudible: "Point-four-three to meet Santa Fe's velocity on nominal power."

"Piece of cake, then. But for *your personal* target velocity?"

Wes almost missed it, Tom's fingers making a three and then a one before Allington sat back, pursing his lips for a silent whistle. "That would be good for a racing car," Allington observed.

Tom patted Allington's shoulder, said, "Not if I designed it," in a slightly louder voice, then poised motionless.

Wes could not be sure without looking, and he forced himself to avoid that look; but he felt certain that Tom Schultheis was suddenly aware that he was being overheard. After a slow count of ten, Schultheis moved forward again to his seat.

It was another twenty seconds before Schultheis announced, "Mr. Sage, according to our data, we ought to challenge your best loco to a race sometime."

Pat Sage smiled around a mouthful of sandwich. "Brave talk before the trial," he murmured.

"My personal target velocity is over three hundred miles an hour," Tom said jauntily, and reached for a cookie.

Wes listened to them banter, and wondered if Tom Schultheis had made his boast to dispose of that phrase. *Personal target velocity; why would Boff consider it any more personal for Tom than for me?* Far back in his experience lurked a simple drag calculation. Why not just ask Tom? Wes didn't know why—and then he did. Tom had taken too much time thinking it over before his announcement. Maybe time enough to think it all out, maybe time to rehearse his phrasing. *Unless my memory's slipping, a drag coefficient of point-three-one implies a top speed of more than three hundred.* A *lot* more. And even though the cabin air conditioner was going full tilt, Tom Schultheis was sweating.

* * * *

Alma and Reese Masefield claimed seats by open windows when the speed trials began. Delta One wafted her enormous bulk lower, ". . . So you'll get a better impression of her speed," Wes explained. He did not add that press photographers in those bleachers would see Delta One in their viewfinders, like it or not. On her first run, the long lance of international orange came flying out from Barstow trailing a faint rooster tail of dust.

"Now this is more like it," Alma crowed, her Nikon whirring and clicking. Below, a faint hiss of air signaled the maglev's distant passage, gliding smoothly across the desert. The sleek craft stopped near the first bend, several miles to the northeast.

On its return, backing toward Barstow though the vehicle was obviously designed to run nose-first, it seemed to be moving even faster. "Rogan reports two hundred twenty feet per sec," Allington announced.

"Can you patch him into the cabin speakers?" asked Wes, then remembered Pat Sage. "Never mind, Boff." On their scrambled channel, Rogan and Allington might voice concerns best kept from the Santa Fe's ears. When Alma complained, her brother promised subsequent numbers in miles per hour.

Tom Schultheis moved, perhaps too casually, to stand at Allington's shoulder for the succeeding runs. On that next run, the maglev's dust trail was now obvious, the hiss of its passage more pronounced, dopplering up and then diminishing through open cabin windows. "A shade over two hundred and fifty," Tom called forward. "That's *miles an hour*, Sis," he added. "Mr. Sage, you've bought yourselves a maintenance unit."

Applause resounded in Delta One's cabin. Wes called back, "Boff, did you get the drag coefficient?"

A two-beat silence. Then, "Oh-point-three, give or take," Tom Schultheis replied. He added quickly, "It won't look that good when the canards are really working."

As they spoke, the maglev reappeared, reversing toward Barstow. Its dust trail was even more pronounced because it battered the desert air harder while moving backward. Boff Allington began to chuckle as he attended to his console and cross talk in his headset. "Santa Fe's engineer is happy as a clam, Wesley," he said. "He's never backed up at two hundred miles an hour."

"Well, that's what we came for," Pat Sage exclaimed, slapping his knees happily, and turning to Wes. "Can you get me down to my people? Mr. Burridge will want his debriefing. I needn't tell you how pleased I am."

"There's one more test," Wes said.

"But you've already passed!"

Still smiling at Sage, Wes called, "Tom, what's the record for maglevs?"

Kaplan, who had seemed lost in thought and his memocomp for most of the day, supplied the answer. "In Alma's terms, um, about two-eighty-five. That's where nose buffeting gets pretty savage on all previous maglevs."

Wes, still looking toward Sage: "Does your engineer follow his test profiles religiously?"

"You bet he does," Sage laughed.

"Tom Schultheis wrote this profile with my blessing," said Wes. "Your man will run at the best speed he's comfortable with."

Sage stood, a bit unsteadily, peering far down the rail toward a filament of orange on a sand-colored background. "I know something about that buffeting problem," he said. "It's risky as hell, Peel."

"That's what those canards are for," Tom Schultheis said evenly, leaning on Allington's seat back.

"Overachievers and risk freaks, you said," Wes quoted to the Santa Fe man, and pointed toward the southwest. "Well, here comes the payoff."

The orange filament grew. It became a dart, then a lance-head, and this time from their view aloft its dust trail became two small and clearly separate tornadoes, arrow wakes trailing behind. Masefield muttered, "Holy Jesus," manning his camera as the mighty lancehead flashed below them trailing its twin cyclones. Several tiny figures leaped from the bleachers, perhaps in panic, and the others swiveled abruptly as the maglev passed. Wes heard it, a faintly howling thunder that had been only a hiss before, and called to Allington: "Gimme a number!"

"She's still accelerating," Schultheis called back.

"Rogan reports they're heading for the turnaround at Hal-

loran Springs,'' Allington called. ''Arf a mo', she's slowing. . . . Rogan reports the engineer is worried about a steady
vibration. Rogan thinks it's just the canards doing their job.''

''The speed, dammit, the speed,'' Wes demanded, display-
ing crossed fingers on both hands.

Allington smiled at his display, then cocked an eyebrow
upward toward Tom Schultheis. ''You tell them, Thomas; they
know what a liar I am.''

Schultheis raised a fist in triumph, his voice husky. ''Three
hundred and twenty. Mr. Sage, we'll race anything on rails.''

An instant's silence, then a cheering pandemonium, and
Patrick Sage's voice rang as loud as any.

An hour later, after a turnaround and a return run that bet-
tered three hundred miles an hour, the maglev hovered sta-
tionary near the now-deserted bleachers. Wes Peel pocketed
a document that was as good as money in the bank and bade
the Santa Fe men good-bye before lifting toward Hayward in
Delta One. He understood that Glenn Rogan would ride the
maglev back to the Barstow facility. What he did not understand was that, thanks to careful misdirections that were not
quite lies, the Santa Fe test engineer signed off where he had
boarded, twenty miles from Barstow. Perhaps the good man
thought that Delta One would carry that maglev away as freight.
He certainly thought, and said with confidence, that those
canards had raised the potential of maglevs a notch.

He was wrong; the canards amounted to a quantum leap.
Glenn Rogan, with the innocent brakeman still aft at his post,
waited until Delta One had disappeared from his horizon before
backing northeastward to the end of that laser-straight rail
section. The brakeman, moments later, quit watching from his
window and, with eyes clenched shut, started praying as that
vibration hummed louder. That is why he was not watching
his console and could not tell the Santa Fe what Rogan told
Tom Schultheis later that night. Not bad for a maintenance
unit, not too shabby even for a rocket sled. Yes, it gobbled

power, but when Rogan throttled back near the end of that straight stretch his fifty-ton lancehead became an orange lightning bolt shooting toward Barstow at nearly five hundred and eighty miles an hour. At that speed, Rogan admitted, she did want to ''hunt'' a bit between her rails. Tom Schultheis would have to do something about that.

SIXTEEN

Kosrow Nurbashi had not kept a hit team in place through naiveté, and he knew how Great Satan infected young men even while they denied it. In an Iranian village, surrounded by the faithful, they would not dream of doubting a mullah's inspired decisions. Here, he had exactly three dedicated lunatics left, and instead of replacements from home, only excuses. Well, he would use what he had and then return, beat thornbushes for new recruits if he had to.

And those recruits, on American soil, would doubtless begin to show the same American infection as the present crop. They might refrain from questioning an order aloud, but Nurbashi sensed unspoken questions. It was therefore essential to justify some of his orders—without seeming to. He justified placing Majid Hashemi's holy suicide ahead of Golam Razmara's with a lie, claiming that Golam was not ready.

Golam was as ready as any to perform the Peel necessity, fired with holy ardor, stoked with faith. But Golam had another talent. He charmed unquestioning allegiance from a slip of a girl, Zahra Aram. Zahra's surveillance work bordered on the magical though she had the distressingly expensive habit of flying back to be near Golam after each mission. It was the price extracted by old-fashioned girls.

Nurbashi paid without complaint. Thanks to her findings, he could send any of his three remaining zealots to dispatch John Wesley Peel with an excellent chance of success. He would not send Golam Razmara on any suicide mission so long as the girl performed her task so well. It was an irony rich enough to delight Nurbashi: Golam's success with the girl denied him the right to blow himself to paradise—for now. Nurbashi gave the Peel sanction to homely little Majid Hashemi instead, in a ceremony worthy of Allah's greatest warriors; gave him a thorough private briefing, gave him a fistful of cash, and finally the keys to a Buick.

The only visitor to this ceremony was a man known to Farda's young members as "Hassan," except that twice that night, Golam heard the mullah call him Winthorp. Golam did not give it much thought at the time, but he got the distinct impression that Hassan Winthorp was some sort of half-caste academic.

The following night in Lansing, doling out snippets of that meeting to Zahra though he would never divulge the holy ceremony to a mere woman, Golam toyed with her black tresses and looked wise. "Yes, Hassan Winthorp is without doubt an academic," he repeated, lowering lashes as long and as beautiful as Zahra's own.

Zahra, who did not much care at the moment, faked interest for the same reason she faked orgasms. "From the university?"

"Not from ours," he replied. "But I would know that above-it-all smirk anywhere."

"Perhaps a gynecologist," she said, and gathered from Golam's reaction that hers must have been strictly a woman's joke. Golam was in no mood for jokes anyhow. Zahra gathered that his funk grew from the mullah's choice of another young man, Majid Hashemi, for some unspecified holy task. Zahra might have forgotten the entire conversation if Hashemi's name had not cropped up soon afterward in American newspapers.

Majid Hashemi drove to California because, with American chemical trace sensors now so commonplace, a vest sewn full of plastique slabs was hard to get past airport security. The day before the maglev trials, Majid learned that the Buick's air conditioner was broken while crossing the Great Salt Lake Desert on U. S. 80, licked sweat from his luxurious mustache across most of Nevada, and damned near drove off the shoulder several times while studying Nevada billboards. A small, slight fellow with an outsized nose and rabbit teeth which that mustache could not entirely hide, Majid had never enjoyed Golam Razmara's luck with women and, until now, he had always found himself shy in their presence. Those billboards seemed to offer the near certainty of luck with games of chance, and with the kind of statuesque bimbo Majid imagined in his version of paradise. Somehow, thought Majid, he did not think he would be shy now. Something about the certainty of imminent death gave him confidence, a plan for the evening, and a monumental hard-on.

Perhaps Allah had guided the Buick's prow to Reno, to give Majid a foretaste of the houris allotted to holy martyrs, and with Divine help Majid might win enough cash to rent the commercial lady of his choice. A foretaste of paradise, so to speak.

Majid drove around Reno until he found a casino the size of the Pyramid of Gizeh. He lost half of his two thousand dollars in an enormous pile of masonry called the MGM Grand in the expectation that Allah would guide his hand. But Majid lost Allah somewhere between the crap tables and the slots, and bitterly reproached Him for the lesson while lying alone in a fever of fury in a cheap motel near the edge of town.

The next day, as the maglev trials began near Barstow, Majid pointed his big nose past Truckee and Sacramento and, as the summer evening waned, managed to get himself magnificently lost somewhere between Walnut Creek and Castro Valley, California. Twisting the Buick down a steep blacktop toward Hayward, he spotted a street sign and realized, for the first time, that he had just traversed Crow Canyon Road. Instead of seeking another motel, Majid felt the lure of kismet. It was beyond belief that his bumbling up Crow Canyon had been pure chance.

Majid retraced the winding road upward between stands of eucalyptus, studied cryptic notes he had taken in Michigan, and parked off the road near the acreage of John Wesley Peel with his hood up for protective coloration. From the trunk, he drew a deceptively heavy little black silk vest, inserted fresh batteries in the detonator's plastic holder, and donned a light jacket over the vest. Then he knelt, guessing at the direction, and prayed.

The high fence and the automatic gate did not keep little Majid from monkeying over and across fifty yards of unkempt lawn in the friendly darkness, to the base of windows above the grassy berm. The lights said that someone was home, and Majid trembled with the expectation of luck he had missed in Reno. He had committed pictures of Wes Peel to memory. As he pressed the doorbell, Majid wondered what he would say if one of Peel's servants opened the door. His command of English was fair, but which words should he use? Car trouble; yes, that was it. And by the way, if he could please speak to the owner of this fine place . . .

But the lights had lied. Wes kept no servants, and while Vangie Broussard had waked in Wes's bedroom that morning, she had spent her day at the Hayward plant. Vangie was still there, helping Wes and his staff celebrate after Delta One whispered to her home moorage at dusk. If Majid had seen the evening papers, he might possibly have guessed at that celebration.

Majid scuttled back to the Buick, put the vest away, and found a motel in Hayward, feeling only slight anguish after he bought a newspaper. One thing Nurbashi had promised him was that, *if* Peel's latest gamble triumphed, the man intended to throw a pasha's party. That event was the one for which Majid Hashemi had been dispatched in the first place.

SEVENTEEN

The major sensation of Wes Peel's party, until the gobbets of human meat started flying, was the sight of Vangie Broussard's legs. "She claims that you insisted on that dress. Now every woman on these five acres hates her when it's *you* they should be hating. You ought to be ashamed, Wes," said Alma, watching Vangie move among guests who strolled between the house and the pool. It was dusk, and nearly everything on Wes's property was well-lit, including some of the early arrivals.

Wes saw Alma's envious glance and grinned. "Oh, I *am* ashamed. But how else were we ever going to learn whether the lady had legs?"

"The usual way, and you may as well not lie to me about her. I've known you too long, my dear."

He accepted the congratulations of a syndicated science writer who had just walked in, recommended the diorama he'd arranged in his shop, pointed him toward the booze, and turned to Alma again. "I admit nothing, and I hope nothing shows."

"Nothing obvious," she admitted.

"Not as obvious as you and Rogan, anyhow."

She arched her brows to manufacture a look that was part

innocence, part challenge. "Are we being a little paternal, Sire?"

"Nope. Blessings on you both. But unless I misread some signs, it's Tom's blessing you need."

He was startled by the sudden narrowing of her eyes, the twitch at her jaw. Alma grasped the sleeve of his suede shirt —Vangie had chosen it and the matching slacks despite his complaint that they made him look half Daniel Boone, half Truman Capote—and pulled him toward privacy, a burst of castor bush foliage near the pool. "Listen, if it weren't for sweet little hotpants Ellie, Glenn would have my brother's blessing. If I told her not to jump in your pool, Ellie would do it to spite me. So I don't know how you'll manage it, but if you don't keep my sister-in-law away from my man, I'm going to bless her with a champagne bottle."

Wes stared, realized his mouth was gaping, and fitted it against his glassful of ginger ale. The sip gave him time to resolve a small nagging mystery. "Isn't that Rogan's responsibility?"

"He's avoiding her. He would have avoided her at another party a long time ago if he'd known she was married. Not that *she* knows it when she gets a tankful. And she's tanking up tonight."

"And Tom knows about . . . whatever happened?"

"He caught them. Among the coats tossed on a bed. You want the, you should pardon the expression, blow-by . . . ?"

"Good God, spare me!" *And yet Tom brought Glenn Rogan to us*, he thought. *That's dedication.* Wes assumed that the dedication was to Wes himself, and scanned the pool area. He saw Rogan, thumb-stoppering a squat bottle of Anchor Steam, in earnest conversation with Tom and an old fellow who was built like Rogan's bottle. "I'll dragoon another singleton and tell him who Ellie is," Wes promised.

"Just don't tell him *what* she is," Alma bit the words off.

"We like to keep it in the family—and you're practically family yourself."

Wes nodded. Jim Christopher was a romantic figure, of sorts; perhaps he could pair Chris with Ellie. Surely, if Chris knew who the bosomy, curvaceous little Ellie was, he wouldn't end up among the fur coats with her. "I've thought of somebody. Hey, wasn't your father coming tonight?"

In answer, Alma jabbed a finger toward the green phosphorescence of the lighted pool, where Reese Masefield was swimming in borrowed trunks. "Across the pool, with Tom and my man. But first things first, Wes. Please?" She watched him move off in search of that safe singleton, saw her father's stubby fingers weaving an obbligato to his words, and smiled grimly. At least old Wolf did not know Ellie's weakness.

At the poolside, distant from the ebb and flow of other guests, Glenn Rogan sat with one booted foot on the diving board, the other stretched out, and took up the thread as old Wolf Schultheis finished. "Hell of a risk to the hardware, just for a dead-stick landing," Rogan said, taking the younger Schultheis in with his gaze. "I'm all for it, though. It's my butt in Highjump, and I'll have a chance to see if I *could* pitch her over and fall clear, or climb out if I had to. There's no ejection seat, you know." He said it almost apologetically.

"No room, and too big a weight penalty," Tom put in, answering the old man's sudden look of concern.

Wolf Schultheis let the silence extend a few moments. By now, Rogan was used to the slow careful phrases. Highjump, he knew, was as much the work of this short, balding, barrel-shaped German as of anyone else, so this was one old codger he didn't want to rush. The old man's voice, when he finally used it, was deep, with the softness of one who had nothing left to prove in this world. Bifocals bounced perilously atop his head whenever he nodded, and from time to time he pushed them back with a forefinger. "Den I think maybe you will want first-stage separation at de highest velocity you can get, Thomas. Give Mr. Rogan more time to test his options.''

"Can't do it, Dad," Tom said, palms out. "Without second-stage boost, there's too much drag on the bird for a high-velocity separation.''

"I accept your word," said old Wolf, and was silent again for ten seconds. Then, "Maybe you can try a liddle second-stage boost," he said, smiling shyly, his thumb and forefinger a half-inch apart.

Tom laughed at the extravagance of the idea. "God love you, Dad, you don't ask for much!" A three-beat pause. More seriously then, "It means purging the system, a real dry-run for the big jump, and getting some fuel stored ahead of time. But we might manage it. Maybe we ought to.''

"With just the few guys we have?" Rogan shifted his weight, and his leg brushed that of Tom Schultheis. Tom did not move away as he would have done a month previously; conspiracy had taken its toll on Tom's outlook. "And I don't think you can afford to bring anybody else into this little shebang. Not this late in the game," Rogan added.

They argued the logistics of high tech conspiracy as equals, gazing at the brownian movement of guests in proper suits, in slacks, and a few in the trendy lederhosen. Masefield climbed dripping from the pool nearby, donned a huge bath towel, and sloshed away toward the house. He saw the small figure scurrying from Wes's driveway in the black suit with the shiny lapels, and assumed the man was part of the catering staff—which was precisely what Majid Hashemi had hoped with his rented tuxedo.

Masefield emerged fully dressed, ruffling damp hair and smiling, from a guest bedroom as Wes finished making his plea to Jim Christopher near the dining room. "Just look for the little brunette with the cleavage and maybe one martini too many," Wes was saying. "Basically a nice girl, Chris.''

"If she's Tom's wife, I'll treat her that way," Christopher smiled.

Wes had time to reflect, *Tom's now using Rogan's name, and Chris is on first name terms with them all. Getting to be a friendly bunch,* and then he saw Vangie with the refreshed Masefield. The journalist's smile faded as Vangie spoke. "You're no longer one of the great unwashed," Wes said to Masefield as he approached.

"What's this about a prowler?" Masefield said, not smiling.

"Wes thinks it was some freelancer trying to get a scoop after the maglev runs," Vangie went on. "I thought you might know if they did things like that."

"The tabloids are capable of anything," Masefield admitted ruefully. "Did they get into the house?"

"No inside alarms," Wes said, faintly peevish that Vangie had mentioned it. "Just a silent telltale at the front fence, and it was two nights ago, for God's sake. I shouldn't tell you these things, Vangie," he grumped.

"You can't know everything in this world, suh," she said charmingly. "You don't even know how many people might be jealous of Peel Transit, now."

Wes: "And you do?"

Something fled past her eyes before she donned her most ravishing smile. "Maybe I'm a better guesser than you are."

"My guess is, it was some kid after those Satsuma plums in your yard," Masefield said. "But I'll keep an eye open for any known *paparazzi*."

"Or any unknown thugs," Vangie put in, clearly working on some private agenda.

Masefield made a helpless gesture. "Vangie, half these people are unknown to me." He met the gaze of Jim Christopher, who had paused nearby to collect a plateful of hors d'oeuvres. The two exchanged nods. If the delta pilot was listening, he gave no sign. "Just let me know if you see anybody that I ought to, um, interview,'' Masefield added to Vangie. "I could spot a phony very nicely on that footing.''

"Much ado about nothing,'' Wes predicted, and moved toward a fast-dwindling plate of bacon-wrapped escargot. "Vangie, could you wheedle some more of this stuff from the caterer?'' She went one way, Wes another, steering Christopher by an elbow. "I'll point Ellie Schultheis out, and you can stuff her with that fish food,'' he said to Christopher.

Masefield stood alone, munching an escargot that would have cost three dollars at Scandia, replaying that conversation. Whatever Vangie Broussard was worried about, it wasn't some camera-toting dipshit with a deadline. At last he sighed and moved toward the front door. The shoulder holster was in Oakland, but his snub-nosed little .32 Colt revolver lay in its usual under-dash clip in his Thunderbird. It was probably dumb, and he already regretted it, but the Colt would fit against his kidney if he wore his coat. A sport coat on a night like this! The things a man did for friendship . . .

Majid Hashemi, standing in a darkened bathroom at the end of the west wing of the sprawling house, had been watching past the crack in the door, ready to shut it. He saw two people carrying trays and collecting dinnerware: a stocky woman in starched burgundy and a heavy man all in white. The kitchen was evidently to the right somewhere. He saw a half-dozen others, including a delectable little brunette sipping from cocktail glasses in both hands, before he realized that his formal attire needed only one thing to be perfect. He took off the rented coat; stuffed the coat into the toilet tank; neatly rolled the starched sleeves of his shirt halfway to his elbows. If he could find the kitchen, and simply took a tray of food and mingled with the guests, perhaps no one would think to ask why.

Majid knelt and prayed, then took a deep breath and marched out of the bathroom, hell-bent on paradise.

Near the pool, Rogan belched, tipped up his Anchor Steam, waved it toward David Kaplan who was dancing with his wife on Wes's seldom-used handball court. "Maybe Kaplan has some ideas," he said.

A finger snap from the younger Schultheis. "Fishing! Wes will buy it; we'll claim we didn't get to go because of that laserboost failure on Delta One. Dad, how long since you helped fuel a jet?"

"Not since we fired the last Natter at Waldsee," Wolf Schultheis replied, looking into the sky, remembering another age and another battle against time. A battle he had lost; but some battles were well-lost, and some wars were fought without bullets. A bass chuckle: "Dere will not be any strafing of our site dis time, I trust."

"Don't bet on it," Rogan said cheerfully. "If there is, it'll come from the guy heading for us now."

Wes had only pointed Ellie Schultheis out to Christopher before hurrying outside in search of a man he had long intended to meet. He beamed now, approaching the trio that lounged between his diving board and his big pool filter, wondering how he had missed them at their entry. He would never have suspected that Tom Schultheis might be delaying an introduction. "Hello, all. Tom, is this the Zeppelin builder?"

Tom Schultheis made the introductions. "I am honored to meet de builder of Delta One," said Wolf Schultheis with a straightening of the shoulders, the slightest bow of his big round head. "And now, alzo of de world's fastest locomotive," he added.

"You can say that again," Rogan grinned, his gaze flickering to Tom Schultheis, who seemed to be silently counting to ten.

Wes and the old man plunged almost instantly into comparisons of dirigibles old and new, searching not for agreement but, in the manner of enthusiasts everywhere, for some point of contention to explore. Wes did not notice the fidgets of the younger Schultheis, who had harbored misgivings about this meeting since Alma first arranged it. As much as he wanted to hear every word, Tom Schultheis felt an increasing temptation to try censoring his father's end of it. And that, he knew, would not only be obvious; it would also offend his father deeply.

He escaped the dilemma by excusing himself, noting that Rogan seemed to be searching for someone—probably Alma, or anybody with an extra beer. A moment later, Rogan wandered off to widen his search.

Wes blundered into the contention area with Wolf Schultheis after the old man broached the subject of Delta One's laserboost experiment. "De only thing between Peel Transit and cheap asteroid mining," said the German, "is bigger lasers."

"There's a guy named Lake working up a paper on that from our flight data," Wes said, "and more power to him, if you'll pardon the pun. But I made a bargain with the good Lord: If He doesn't stop me down here, I won't poke my machines in His eye up there." Wes realized it sounded idiotic, and hoped the old man would take it as a joke.

But: "Avoiding de future on *religious* grounds, Mr. Peel?"

"Transport on earth is my religion, Mr. Schultheis. I just haven't got time to spread myself so thin." *It would sound even stupider to admit I'm stuck with a promise I made to Gram, thirty years ago. And I could eventually lose my best men if Patrick Sage is right, but got-damnitall,* . . . "That doesn't mean I'd turn down a honeymoon suite in an orbiting Hilton," Wes went on, grinning. "I'm not against them; I just don't build them."

"And if you do not pioneer de inexpensive boosters, you must plan on paying for dat honeymoon in rubles, and you will not have even dat choice for many years," Wolf Schultheis said wryly.

"Oh, I dunno. I seem to be wavering about honeymoons, lately." Wes's smile was reflective as he swung his gimpy hip onto the edge of the pool filter housing and glanced toward the house.

Inside, Jim Christopher was plying Ellie Schultheis with food, and keeping her entertained. For someone that small, she seemed to have huge appetites for canapes, for martinis, and if her liquid gaze was to be trusted, for men. "I'd say a hot-air balloon reminds me more of a ripe pear than a condom," he replied to her latest suggestion, hoping to steer the discussion elsewhere.

Ellie lowered her lashes demurely to her glass and sipped, wondering just how broad a hint this wide-shouldered specimen needed. She'd show the big oaf a pair of ripe pears! She inhaled, her breasts riding dangerously high in their lace chalices. She saw him looking, all right, and smiled up at him, trying to focus on his mouth. When you looked at their mouths, they got the idea in a hurry. "Caught you peeking," she purred, very slowly, to avoid slurring. "Big tall men like you have *lots* of advantages." Her big eyes challenged him to enumerate a few.

"Have a banana," he offered helplessly, lifting a skewered slice of fruit from his plate.

As Ellie was batting her eyes and admitting she didn't mind if she did, Majid Hashemi turned away from the congressman and the TV anchorwoman, who had taken tiny smoke-fragrant morsels of meat from the tray he held. He had tried one himself before leaving the kitchen. He heard the legislator admit that barbecued pork was among his minor vices, looked down at the loathsomely tasty meat, and swallowed hard. No matter. Even the sin of eating pork would soon be cleansed from him. Hashemi tried to smile, avoided the lurch of the science writer, and froze. From Hashemi's angle, the tall man's mustache was barely visible. Blond, slim-hipped, wide of shoulder, the man stood a pace away from an opened sliding door that led to the patio. Hashemi did not care in the slightest that a dozen people were in that room, nor that an obviously drunk woman looked up at the man, murmuring something intimate.

Hashemi balanced the tray in his left hand—pork was not really food—and moved his right hand down to his vest pocket as he stepped near. He was breathing quickly, lightly, and his eyes dilated as he stepped up to his quarry for this final, shattering intimacy. In a transport of joy he asked formally, "Mr. Peel?"

"No, but it's a common mistake," said Jim Christopher, turning, smilingly grateful for any interruption. Christopher saw a look in the little waiter's face that was beyond earthly pleasure; saw it falter as the swarthy little fellow's eyes swept his face. Disturbed, Christopher glanced away and, by chance, saw Wes a hundred feet away. "That's Mr. Peel on the other side of the pool. Uh . . . why don't we take you to him?" He grasped the little man's right wrist, the one with fingers halfway into a vest pocket, hoping he could guide Ellie Schultheis outside in the process.

Majid Hashemi's hand flew from his vest. No, this was not his quarry, and he had come within a finger of martyring himself to no purpose! In consternation that bordered panic, Hashemi dropped the tray and bolted through the open doorway into the night, toward the distant pool, slamming the drunken woman out of his way with his left forearm as he ran. Christopher's plate flew into the air with a scatter of food.

Ellie Schultheis did not even bleat, caroming from the door facing to fall on her knees. Christopher snarled, "Clumsy idiot, what's the . . . ?" And then, reaching for Ellie's arms, he remembered what he had overheard between Wes, Vangie, and the *Tribune* man. Thugs or phonies? The shirt-sleeved little waiter seemed too insignificantly small to count, but no waiter in his right mind ever behaved that way and, if a phony, perhaps a thug as well. And he was looking for Wes Peel.

This reflection took perhaps two precious seconds before

Christopher, in the act of raising Ellie Schultheis by her elbows, saw Masefield turn toward the commotion. "Masefield! Mayday! Nail the waiter," he bawled.

Reese Masefield, at that moment, was nursing a scotch and water, admitting to Vangie that he felt a bit foolish about his surveillance. They stood near the well-lit table-tennis arena with Alma, watching a surprisingly even contest between Rogan and Pat Sage, and as he turned toward the shout, Masefield saw a black-vested little man dart from between guests in Wes Peel's direction.

Masefield delayed an instant too long before reacting; realized, even as he dropped his glass and reached toward his kidney, that he must not risk a shot in this throng and that such a little fellow could not be all *that* dangerous; and then he ran to head the little man off.

Hashemi scarcely heard the sudden buzzing commotion among the people he passed because now he recognized John Wesley Peel, and Peel had not even turned his head, and if Hashemi ran along the near side of the pool, the one man who was sprinting toward him would find a thirty-foot expanse of water in his way. Majid Hashemi, a dozen steps from paradise, began to laugh.

Masefield wondered later why he was unable to shout anything more useful than, *"Wes!"* The little waiter was now across the pool, streaking unimpeded along the tiles, and Masefield grabbed the metal folding chair without much hope of doing anything with it. He hurled the chair as he would hurl a discus, seeing as he lost his balance that even if it cleared the pool, its trajectory was much too low to strike the man. Masefield shouted his friend's name again as he fell on his back.

Wes, fascinated with Wolf Schultheis's firsthand account of a 1932 Lippisch tailless glider with canards, glanced around only when he heard his name. He saw the flicker of a folding chair as it scissored shut in midair; saw the little man racing toward him; blinked at the slashing clatter of the chair on poolside tiles, twenty feet from where he stood.

Hashemi's footing was only adequate, but nothing human could stop him now, and he could round the edge of the pool in four more steps. He managed only one of them. The metal chair, sliding on tiles still wet from Masefield's emergence a half hour before, skidded directly underfoot and Hashemi's next step was onto the flat, spinning chair. He cried out, arms flailing, and kept his balance just enough to leap across the edge of the pool toward Wes Peel. Hashemi knew that he would hit the water. But his right hand was already flashing into his vest pocket.

Wes saw the little man lose his balance, saw him vault across the corner of the pool, and did not want this diminutive drunk to get him or old Wolf Schultheis soaking wet. Wes lunged forward, bearing the old man down with him onto the lawn, hoping that the pool filter would be their splash barrier.

A sound of a small body cannonballing into water, and almost simultaneously, a bucking concussion through turf. The explosion of six pounds of plastique underwater was curiously muffled, a resounding *kaTHUMPaaaa* that blew the filter housing from its mounts and beyond Wes's heaving shoulders. The rounded inner wall of the pool formed a reflector even while it split into slabs, and a thousand gallons of water lofted toward the guests.

Fifty pounds or so of Majid Hashemi were mixed with the deluge, a splatter of flesh and fragments of cloth falling in a fan-shaped pattern as far as Wes's patio. Wes rolled to his feet, helped old Wolf Schultheis up with ringing ears and a muttered apology, and turned toward his guests. A few of them, drenched and half-blinded by the underwater flash, were just beginning to realize the nature of the stringy stuff plastered on their clothes and in their food. The stuff of martyrdom and, imsh'Allah, of paradise lost.

EIGHTEEN

Because Alameda County deputies were not fools, they alerted Treasury agents in the Alcohol, Tobacco and Firearms division. Because Reese Masefield was no fool either, he phoned the briefest of reports into the *Trib* and stayed into the night, long after the other guests made their statements and fled their living nightmare past Sheriff's men and the plastic tape that now ringed the Peel acreage.

Vangie stayed as well, paying off the caterers, seeking ashtrays to empty. And, Masefield felt certain, waiting for the authorities to leave. The prowler story was now on tape, but it wasn't the whole story. He knew one of the T-men slightly, the gaunt one who left attaché cases full of electronic equipment to others, and made do with a video-modem memocomp that any reporter would die for. Shortly after midnight, he waited with Wes while the T-man plugged his gadget into Wes's phone to send a set of images over the wires. While the T-man waited, Wes stared at that very special memocomp. "Whose fingerprints?" he asked.

"Don't know yet," sighed the T-man, lighting a Camel. "They were all over a credit card in a tux jacket somebody stuffed into your toilet tank. Frigging bathroom floor's all wet since the float was held down," he said, and fired blue smoke from his nostrils. "We'll see if the credit card belongs to those arms we fished out of the soup in the bottom of your pool."

Wes, astonished: "I didn't realize there was that much of the guy left."

"Lower legs, too. Water does funny things to inhibit blast effects," said the T-man. "I'd make a guess the suspect had the stuff taped around his middle, and that his head was still above water when that French C-4 went off; no mug shots for this guy. Gonna be a lot of jays hopping around on your lawn for stuff we don't find."

"Not so loud," Wes frowned, nodding toward the next room. "The lady's had a rough day."

"Uh . . . sorry." The man favored Vangie with a thoughtful glance. "Your secretary, you said?"

"Exec assistant," Wes corrected.

The T-man pursed his lips, let his eyebrows rise and fall. "Help like that is hard to find. You oughta remind her just how lucky everybody was, tonight. From the look of her, you'd think somebody died."

"Somebody did," Masefield reminded him. "Whose credit card?"

A slow smile from the T-man. "No can do, Masefield. I didn't let any other reporters past the warning strip. You're here because you tripped the suspect, and according to my notes, you suspected something was going down. So did the woman," he added, nodding toward Vangie, who sat staring into space in the next room.

"So did Jim Christopher," Wes put in, mystified.

The T-man conferred with his memocomp's offline notes. "Yeah, he heard you two and the Broussard woman talking. Be glad he did, Mr. Peel. If all your friends didn't have a healthy dose of paranoia, we might be collecting you and that old fella in a bag, right now." He looked Wes up and down with a faint smile. "Hell of a note; your pool is a total loss, Mr. Peel, but the lens effect at the deep end kept you bone-dry. You, ah—you pretty good with explosives?"

"Not that good," Wes answered, ignoring the innuendo. "The stuff was French?"

"According to our instruments and the gas traces. Not much

help without taggant chips. The French will sell breeder re-actors to Iraq, or plastique to the IRA.''

Masefield jerked slightly, then looked away.

A chiming tone announced that somewhere, someone was finished feeding data back to that nifty memocomp. The T-man disengaged the instrument, excused himself, and strode outside with it to confer with two waiting men, one still strolling Wes's grounds with flashlight, throwaway gloves, and a body bag.

Masefield nudged Wes with an elbow and nodded toward Vangie. ''I could drop her off on my way home, but I need to talk to you.''

''So does she. Damned if I know why. You two keeping something from me, Reese?''

A pained expression: ''Get serious. I'm putting some twos together. Remember Adam Elliott? Remember Hal Kroner? I wonder if—''

''Mr. Peel?'' The T-man again, standing at the sliding door, motioned Wes outside. ''Just you, please.''

Wes sighed, unfolded his arms, and saw Vangie looking his way. He gave her his best smile and an ''OK'' hand sign; she gave no indication that she saw either, grayish patches of exhaustion showing below her eyes, and Wes hurried outside.

The odors on his patio were a strange assortment: the sharp tang of explosive residues, and a sweet musk like that of pork, competed with the faint scents of excrement and vomit. *This was one party nobody will ever forget*, he thought with resignation. To the T-man he said, ''Don't tell me you found a head for me to identify. He wasn't part of the catering staff, I can tell you that.''

''Confirmed. The credit card was reported stolen. The prints on it match those on the suspect.''

Wes smiled faintly. ''Suspect. Boy, now there's caution for you.''

''You could use a little of it from here on out, Mr. Peel,'' said the T-man. Pause. "Ever hear the name Majid Hashemi before?"

Wes gnawed his mustache for a moment. Then, "Not that I recall. I'd hate to think he's—was—one of my employees."

"Nope; a foreign university student back east. I can't tell you more than that right now. Some of my guidelines get tangled when," his glance flicked toward the house, "the press is involved. Masefield is one of the best, but my guidelines are clear."

"What the hell are you trying to say?"

"As little as possible," said the T-man, with a wan smile, "while asking you to accept some Treasury men for . . . well, not bodyguards, officially. It's just temporary, in case this guy has local backups."

Wes thought about the implications. "This Hashemi has friends?"

"He didn't make that plastique out of match heads, Mr. Peel. We'd like to keep an eye on you while we run some checks. Our people won't cramp your style," he promised.

"But they'll follow me everywhere," Wes replied, and got a shrug. "I have a personal life."

"Everybody does. Actually, I didn't have to ask you. Uncle isn't new at this."

"But I am. Is this your way of telling me to look out for running waiters without, ah, bending a guideline?"

"Very perceptive," the T-man said with a solemn wink. "Waiters, or little old ladies hitching a ride up this hill, or anybody else you can't vouch for. If you always play cards on Tuesday, or buy booze at the same place, break up those patterns for a while. I don't suppose you practice with a sidearm?"

Wes shook his head and showed the man open palms. "Never thought it might be important."

"I invite you to suspect it is. The Sheriff of Alameda County, I can tell you with fair assurance, will not look askance if you ask for a permit. But if you do, join a shooting club and take advantage of it. We'll get back to you. Okay?''

Wes nodded absently, and shook the proffered hand. ''You're taking off now?''

''Right. The county stationed a man outside your gate. Our guy may be harder to spot, but if you see or hear anything you don't like, sing out. You might be surprised.'' The T-man's smile was more confident now.

As the three men turned away, Wes could not resist it. ''You forgot to tell me not to leave town,'' he called.

''We know who you are, Mr. Peel. You have more ways of leaving town than an AIDS virus, no slur intended.'' One of the other men laughed briefly, with attendant echoes that fragmented into the night from the almost-empty pool. Suddenly Wes felt the need of friends, and wheeled toward the house. The digital thermometer on his patio read 72 degrees. His skin said it was twenty degrees colder than that.

*   *   *   *

Waiting for coffee to perk, Wes glanced at his two confidantes who slumped on stools at his kitchen pass-through. ''Vangie, you need sleep, not caffeine,'' he urged.

''Can't sleep. I have to talk to you,'' she said. Her tone unnerved Wes a little. Her sidelong glance plainly said she did not want to talk in front of Masefield.

But if Wes could not trust the reporter, he could trust no one—Vangie herself excepted, he thought. ''Okay. It won't be long,'' he promised, which was hint enough to Masefield. ''Reese, this is all deep background. Okay?''

''Shit, excuse me, shitshitshit.'' This drew something that might almost have been a smile from Vangie. ''Cut my heart out while you're at it. But okay,'' he added.

Abandoning his search for clean cups, Wes began to wash three of the dirty ones. ''You tried to tie this to the senator and the director? Well, when you're right, I tell you; and maybe you're right this time. The waiter wasn't a waiter, he was a foreign student named Ra . . . no, Majid. Majid Hashemi.'' Masefield sat up straighter, the crinkles around his eyes suggesting that his formidable synapses were firing at double-speed. ''Even I can draw an inference from that,'' Wes added. ''Not proven, but a solid maybe.''

''Hashemi? Syrian, Iranian, Jordanian—too damned cosmopolitan to pinpoint, but it's all crazyland. By God, there *is* a pattern,'' Masefield said, looking at the wall. ''You're getting too bloody important. Patriots with a small *p* and a big effect, who aren't in anybody's pocket. Forty years ago, Bill Hewlett would've been on the same list.''

''Still is, for my money,'' said Wes, drying a cup.

''Oh, my God,'' Vangie breathed, and lowered her head on crossed arms. Her next words were muffled, her voice almost unrecognizable; but the words were clear enough. ''Reese, please go home.'' As the two men frowned their mutual amazement above her dark hair, now in pathetic disarray, she raised her head. Her eyes were red, her breasts rising as she tried to keep from bursting into tears. ''I can't say it with you here, and if I don't say it now, I will never have the courage again.''

Masefield made the kind of face a man makes when he is told by a gorgeous woman to go home. ''Why do I get this nagging suspicion that three is a crowd?'' he said, and stood up.

Vangie, her tears now beginning to flow, stood too, and wheeled toward Masefield. ''I . . . one more thing,'' she stammered. ''I saw you throw that chair, Reese.'' And with that, she stepped up to him, both hands cupping the back of his head, in an openmouthed kiss that would, under any other circumstances, have brought Wes to a towering fury. Masefield just stood there and enjoyed it. And, understanding her motive, so did Wes Peel. After a moment, Vangie moved back. ''That, suh, is the sincerest way I know to thank you for saving my boss's life.'' The tone was full of banter now, and she attempted a smile despite the tears. "I owe you. That's all I'm going to pay you; but I owe you. Clear?"

Masefield had to cough twice before he could say, "Clear." Heading toward the front door, he went on, "The Treasury man was right, Wes. It's hard to get help like that." Then he closed the door softly behind him.

Vangie turned, half-smiling, toward Wes, and then her face shattered again. "Oh, my God," she said, and covered her face with her hands.

He carried her to the master bedroom, ignoring her objection that she wanted to be sitting across the room from him. "Now," he said, when he had eased her onto the bed and waved the lights off, sitting beside her. "You can tell me—whatever."

She sat up; kicked her sandals off; hugged her knees, turning to look at him in faint moonlight. With her hair falling past her legs almost to the bedding, he thought she had never looked lovelier, nor half so vulnerable. "I brought that man here," she said.

She waited until he had stopped laughing. "I would rather you slapped me than laugh at me, because then I'd know you were taking me seriously," she said, fighting to control her breathing. And then he fell silent, and then she told him.

Her brother, Thibodeaux, driving a Calcasieu rig years before, had opted for long hours; the kind of hours that urge a man to take little pills to stay awake. He'd had an accident in Mississippi which could be traced to those pills. Tib might have been unemployable after that, if not for Joseph Alton Weatherby. Joey Weatherby had smoothed it out, caused the blood test to vanish. After that, the surest way to pick a fight with Tib Broussard was to bad-mouth Joey Weatherby.

Tib honorably went to Weatherby and bent his knee. And in time, performed certain little favors for Weatherby and the NTC. Vangie did not know what those favors were, but had little doubt they were shady. In time, Weatherby developed a sort of fatherly interest in Tib Broussard. "And that's how

Weatherby learned about my tawdry little dreams," she said, now reciting it in a deadly monotone. "He had someone spiff up my resume. I think he knew I'd set my cap for Peel Transit. You were already one of those firms university profs like to puzzle over."

For the first time in many minutes, Wes spoke: "You weren't *summa cum* at LSU? No master's at Loyola? No thesis on technology and transport in Acadia?"

"Oh, that was all true. I didn't even understand what Weatherby had done, Wes! But I began to get the picture three months after I signed up with you. He waited 'til I'd gushed to Tib about how happy I was here, and then he called me one night."

"He'd probably seen pictures of you."

"Will you just—just let me tell it? Please?" A pause with labored breathing. Then: "Joey Weatherby did not care if I looked like Mother Theresa. He cared very much that your short-haul rigs were, as he put it, 'creating a lot of interest' at the NTC. I guess he didn't realize I knew what kind of interest that was. Hostile interest. Well, in short, he wanted me to spy."

"I see."

"Not yet, you don't; I was furious with him, even more furious because of what he said he'd done to get me this job, when I thought it was my sterling character. I hung up on the man. Believe that, or don't. I hung up on him, no matter what I might have to say to Tib later. But Tib called me the next evening, Wes. He was worried. Not scared for his life: scared for his career. Tib has a wife and four kids. He reminded me of that. Told me that if I cared about the food in their mouths, I'd call Weatherby back. Collect, of course."

"So you did."

"Of course I did, Wes." In a very small voice, "I have spied on you from that day until . . . very recently."

Wes: "How recently?"

Vangie, staring into the darkness, shrugged as she thought

about it. "Until I began to worry about the way you drank, and realized I was probably in love with you. Weatherby has known about your vendetta for a long time. I quit feeding him tidbits a few months ago; claimed you were watching me."

"That was no lie." He reached out to stroke her hair.

"Don't—please, I don't want to be touched right now. If it wasn't for me, you wouldn't be on an NTC death list."

Wes stood up; began to pace the carpet soundlessly. Presently he paused before the room's moonlit window, wondering what the shadowed acreage hid, juggling scenarios. "So you don't think this Hashemi guy was a terrorist."

"You bet I do, but not from the Land of Oz. I think Joey Weatherby realizes that if you're not stopped soon, Peel Transit's big lifters will bankrupt the NTC."

He returned to sit beside her. "Only two problems with that, Vangie. One, it's already too late. Freightliner, Mack, and Ford are already on the market with short-haulers and efficient freight-routing programs. Too got-damn' good for comfort, and getting better. And Boeing knows we have Delta Two's girders in place, and they're not waiting any longer.

"Two, if the NTC goes under, it'll be their lousy management. Short-haulers still need teamsters, and much as I hate to say it, there'll always be a few special cases where a double-tandem will do the job better on a highway. The NTC will just have to fit itself into new kinds of transport. Even if that crazy little bastard had blown me to pieces, those two facts would still be the handwriting on Weatherby's wall."

"Somebody should say that to *him*."

Wes gave a one-syllable chuckle. "Not a bad idea. Face-to-face, maybe. Why not?"

"You? Sit down with the NTC? After what they've tried to do?"

"We don't know that. I'm inclined to doubt it, Vangie; but I'm not ruling the idea out." A long silence before he added, "Would you call him, set up a meeting?"

Quick, frightened: "Are you out of your mind?"

"It's been suggested. But I know a little about Weatherby, and I don't think he'd try to whack me while I showed him around my own plant. Let him bring a friend if he wants to. It'll be my turf, and he can publicize the visit beforehand. Bolster his image among his troops, and how will he know I don't have a super-duper laser cannon trained on him?"

"He'd never do it, if I'm right," she warned.

"Which will give us a hint, won't it? But we have a carrot as well as a stick, if you phrase it right. If Weatherby's inclined to give us a 'bye, just hint to him that I'm ready to blow some evidence to the media. You don't even have to know what kind of evidence, Vangie. Get it?"

"Poor Tib," she said softly. "I'm not worried for myself —yes, I am, Wes."

"Tell him you've left a confession in a safe-deposit box."

"That's not what I'm worried about. I'm scared about us. You can't possibly trust me after . . . all this."

Softly, tenderly, he leaned nearer. "Sure I can," he said, in a near whisper. "I just can't touch you."

"That's what I mean," she said.

" 'Cause you told me not to," he reminded her.

"Oh, you mean . . . dirty . . . bastard," she said. "Well, I think maybe I would like you to touch me now."

As she lay back on the pillow, he moved so that he was poised above her, his arms flanking her, not quite touching.

"You're absolutely sure about that," he teased. "I want you to be sure—whooo," he finished, startled, in response to her fingers at his groin.

"How sure is this?" she said.

"It's what I'd call a sure thing." Then, moving his mouth until it touched hers, no longer teasing, "I knew something was bothering you. Now I know what it was. It needn't bother you again."

"I love you, John Wesley Peel."

159

"Even if I'm really sleepy?"
A giggle. "No, not if you're sleepy. Anything but that."
He pursued the "anything" option.

NINETEEN

Network news provided its usual coverage with the apotheosis of Majid Hashemi. Without links to other known suspects, the event was merely a mystery which slid beneath the notice of broadcasters in three days. Newspapers, with more space to fill, carried follow-up stories for a week. Bruce Hassan Winthorp breathed more easily when, ten days after the blast near Crow Canyon Road, he finished scanning his day-old copy of the Oakland *Tribune*. Winthorp failed to find so much as a single column inch devoted to the Peel story.

Winthorp's clippings carried Hashemi's name, and varied guesses as to the assassin's motive. Inevitably, the attempt on Wes Peel was linked to other, more successful, hits. But no reporter had yet mentioned *Farda* or Kosrow Nurbashi, and according to the mullah no one had questioned any *Farda* member. Nurbashi was perfectly capable of lying about that, even to Winthorp; but because Nurbashi did not get cuter with his communication links, Winthorp felt that they had all dodged this ricochet of mischance. He even offered a new name of "necessity," a Johns Hopkins epidemiologist whose work might lead—within a year or so—to an oral AIDS vaccine.

It did not disturb Winthorp that such a vaccine could save lives in Iran as well as Omaha. The United States now admitted to half a million AIDS victims, and western youth seemed bent on screwing itself literally to death in anonymous couplings. Winthorp himself viewed sexual partners as messy, roundabout routes to self-gratification, but felt deeply reluctant to explain this part of his rationale to Nurbashi. The solution, when dealing with a man of such profoundly narrow interests as Nurbashi, was to claim the Johns Hopkins man was really working on biological weapons. In a way it was true, in the sense that a shield is a weapon.

Nurbashi did not seem particularly interested in the fresh name, and Winthorp guessed why: John Wesley Peel, alive, remained a deadly affront to Nurbashi and his two remaining berserkers. Winthorp needed several days to resolve the problem in his mind, and another week to choose his man. The National Transport Coalition *had* been mentioned in those newspaper clippings. A scholar with Winthorp's reputation might, in the course of some innocent research, personally contact NTC leadership.

Studying his files, Winthorp zeroed in on a man who would understand the feather touch of delicate nuance but, according to published rumor, might not shrink from a bloody necessity once it was pointed out to him. It was entirely possible that Antony Ciano might perform the Peel necessity in enlightened self-interest without ever hearing the name of *Farda*.

* * * *

Wes Peel breezed into his office by the back way and perched his flight helmet on the plaster head of Thomas Jefferson, one of Vangie's heroes. She turned from her terminal and smiled at the sacrilege. "How'd the training go?"

"By the time Delta Two is ready, the new crew will be," he promised, leaning over his desk to query his own terminal for unfinished business.

"I meant *your* training," she said. "Yesterday at lunch, Jim Christopher said you're logging more time than the new guys."

"Lunch with Chris, hm?" He studied his readout, then looked up. "He knows about you and me?"

"I suspect everyone does," she admitted. "They just don't talk to us about it." Leaning back, tapping a perfect fingernail as she considered an imperfect world, "In fact, nowadays they don't talk to me much about anything important. Kaplan, Tom Schultheis, Boff—not like they used to, at the commissary. Lunch can be a sort of informal progress report, you know. Or maybe you don't need those lunch soirees. But I get a," —she stroked the air with her free hand—"a feel for the tempo of things; what's going well, or what smells like a cost overrun before it shows on the bar charts. But I don't get that anymore. I'm getting something else, and I don't like it."

He snapped off his terminal, stood erect, and stretched. "You have jazzercise or guitar lessons this evening?" At her negative headshake he nodded toward the digital clock. "It's quitting time, ma'am, and I don't have to practice with this fool pistol every day. If we're going to talk business, let's do it over a pizza."

In nearly two weeks since the attempt on Wes's life, he had obtained a permit and a deceptively small, nine-millimeter Walther automatic, the most potent weapon that would properly fit in an Alessi ankle holster. It chafed his leg, and was no quick-draw arrangement, but it freed Wes from wearing sport coats and no one seemed to notice his new penchant for flare-leg slacks. He practiced with it three afternoons a week, hating the necessity, learning to like the tiny Walther. It might be useless at fifty yards, but so was a jacket lined with French plastique.

Wes and Vangie had avoided her condo by unspoken agreement. This was the fifth time they had eaten out together since the party, never twice at the same restaurant. It was Vangie, on their third evening together, who had spotted the neatly suited young man watching from the bar as they dined. When Wes made the immediate call, he learned that the man was *supposed* to be there, not to worry, but for God's sake not to engage the T-man in idle conversation. This concrete evidence of support buoyed Vangie's spirits, so Wes did not admit that it made him uneasy. The truth was, a man hated to know that even the friendliest eyes were on him when he wanted to caress a knee behind a damask tablecloth.

On this evening they met in their respective cars at Vangie's choice, a place in Hayward near Jackson and Hesperian. Vangie's tastes did not run to pizza. After ordering wine, his scampi and her antipasto, Wes glanced around idly and then, with a villainous squint and side-of-his-mouth delivery, rasped, "You spot our tail, Chickie?"

"No, but it's nice to know somebody's on your side," she replied, unwilling to play moll to his mobster. She waited until the wine was served, then toyed with her glass. At length she said, "Wes, what's going on at Barstow that I shouldn't know about?"

He flushed slightly, then hid his sheepish grin behind his glass. "What did Chris say?"

"Nothing! He doesn't want to talk about the maglev work. Maybe I should ask what's going on that *you* aren't supposed to know about."

"Oh, relax, Vangie. It's just some tests on the maglev. You remember when the Santa Fe man called last week?"

"Sage? Of course. I had to hunt you down in the plant."

"Well, they wanted me to verify some canard tests that Tom and Rogan scheduled. Rogan's cleared to run the unit now without those deadheading union people, so . . . well, I got the schedule and flew down Monday, and, well, uh . . ."

Her lovely mouth twitched and, for the first time that evening, Wes basked in her good humor. "You drove that stupid locomotive, is what you did. Illegally."

He made a parody of outraged innocence. "A man who'd do that would, uh—he'd play footsie in a fine restaurant."

"So you did," she nodded, now studying some vague point

in space near his head. "But Schultheis didn't check with you before he scheduled those tests?"

"No reason he would, necessarily. What's eating you?"

She shook her head. "I'm not sure, but—Schultheis and Kaplan both put in for a week's vacation. And then they canceled it. Why?"

"Ask them, Vangie. They've been trying to find time for a fishing trip ever since that close call with Delta One in Arizona. The canard tests just set 'em back again, I guess."

She nodded, and seemed satisfied, and then he asked her about her contact with Joey Weatherby. She was still awaiting a callback on her condo's answering machine, she said. Weatherby was not the easiest man to reach.

Wes realized that she was still gnawing on a suspicion only after they'd been served. Vangie usually had a longshoreman's appetite, but tonight even antipasto was more than she wanted. At last, watching him devour his scampi, "Here's the sequence," she said without preamble. "Kaplan and Schultheis ask for a week's vacation. Then the Santa Fe people ask you to verify the need for some more maglev tests. You give the okay, and *then* you check up on those runs. Who gave you the schedule?"

"Allington. The data reduction is his, so—"

"But you had to ask Boff for it?"

"Well, Tom and Dave weren't around Friday. Sure; Boff has to know what's up."

"I guess he does, doesn't he," Vangie said, her gaze turned inward. "But you don't."

She had never seen him look at her with such displeasure. "I don't hire men at that level who need close supervision, Vangie."

"I'm trying to do *my* job at the moment. Let me finish this sequence, and then I'll shut up."

"I'll hold you to that," he said, starting to chew again.

"Finally you fly down to Barstow on Monday. When did they know you were coming?"

"Mm, I guess on Monday morning, when I called to say I was coming before noon."

He thought she'd finished because she took so long before saying, "But Boff Allington knows your ways. He could have suspected on Friday that you'd take a quick run down there."

"I suppose. So what?"

"So Dave Kaplan called Personnel late Friday afternoon from Barstow to cancel the vacations for him and Schultheis. All top management duty changes get flagged to me, but Kaplan probably doesn't know that. Anyhow, I wasn't snooping. But whatever they had planned, they changed it fast when they realized you might be coming down for the new maglev runs."

He sighed. "Finished?"

"I hope so."

"So do I. It might look funny to you, Vangie. But in their shoes, I'd probably do the same thing if my boss made a sudden decision to look my project over. Remember, I was there, and the only one who did anything out of place was me! What the hell do you think they might do, sell the maintenance unit?"

"I don't know. Certainly not that, but—"

"You'd have Tom and Dave, Rogan and Allington and Christ knows who else, in some conspiracy. You know what I think?"

Her smile was bleak. "Yes, my love. You think I'm a nervous nag since I found out what Mr. Joey dirty-hands Weatherby wants to do to my lover."

"That's pretty close. But thank you," he added, stretching out his hand to hers.

"All the same," she began.

"I'll remember what you've said," he interrupted. "Kaplan and Schultheis will be back tomorrow anyhow, so you can watch 'em all you like."

. "Their secretaries have been putting off vendor appointments all week," she said. "What're they doing still in Barstow?"

"Resetting those canards, letting Rogan try short runs. And if you don't want that anchovy, how's about giving me a shot?"

"Lips that touch anchovies will never touch mine," she murmured. So Wes left a perfectly good anchovy on her plate and strolled outside to the parking lot with Vangie, where long shadows heralded the nearness of evening.

At that moment, three hundred and eighty miles to the southeast, Glenn Rogan tried to ignore lengthening fingers of shadow as he slid downward into the cockpit of Highjump.

*   *   *   *

The huge old truck that Kaplan drove onto Ivanpah Dry Lake in late afternoon had seen many a year of service before Exotic Salvage picked it up as surplus. It had once been Air Force blue, with twin spotlights the size of kettledrums mounted atop its towering cab. One of those big sizzlers still perched there, mounted backward, toward the flatbed. Above the flatbed trailer, a crane arm jounced lazily between limiter cables. A Porsche-engined dune buggy, Rogan's personal property, squatted on the flatbed, secured by cables. Flecks of yellow paint still adhered to the crane and to the stowed jack pads. Some men could still smile to recall when the C-2 wrecker was their burden-beast of choice, the biggest lifter on many an Air Force base. David Kaplan had smiled when writing out the laughably small check because, as the seller said, the whopping six-cylinder Hercules in that ol' hummer would run until the second coming, but the only thing on earth a C-2 was good for was hauling crashed aircraft.

With no load and twelve forward speeds, the C-2 could rumble down a highway at exactly thirty-seven miles an hour.

With a groaning load that bowed its flatbed, the C-2 would rumble down that same highway at exactly thirty-seven miles an hour. If the C-2 was good only for retrieving crashes, it might be superb for Exotic Salvage because Highjump, as Rogan put it, had all the earmarks of a dry-lake posthole digger.

Kaplan pulled to a stop on Ivanpah's hard flat alkali, a natural raceway lying in this vast depression between mountains of the high Mojave. Like other dry lakes it was resurfaced by seasonal runoff from nearby ridges, the nearest thing to a perfect landing field that Highjump's creators could have found. Somewhere across that vast open stretch lay Highjump's hangar, below Kaplan's line of sight.

Staring hard below the ridge of Clark Mountain some miles to the west, he could see the gleam of high-tension lines. From the miles-long depression of the dry lake bed he could not identify anything that far away in any detail. Neither could the occasional driver whose car might be crawling along the Interstate 15 corridor between the lake bed and Clark Mountain.

Kaplan checked his digital clock; turned off the Hercules ignition; flicked the tightband radio to their scrambled channel with fingers that trembled. They had lost an entire day because of Wes Peel's visit, rescheduling Highjump and losing considerable liquid hydrogen from the storage tanks, and without these long summer days they would have canceled the test. Only four men for the launch, one of them a septuagenarian! But one who had fueled vertical-flight interceptors with hydrogen peroxide in 1945, and who had fifty years of steadiness at control consoles.

They hadn't been sure they could fire Highjump until midafternoon with all four men sweating and straining, and while driving the C-2 across from Clark Mountain, Kaplan had cut his own timing nearly too fine, though his role would be only as observer and photographer until the test was complete. Afterward he would have one of two roles: retrieval of Highjump if it worked, or material witness if it didn't. Kaplan grabbed the video camera with one hand, his mike toggle in the other, and leaned from the cab.

He mentally paced the measured, accented bass of old Wolf Schultheis through the checkoff ritual, and knew that Highjump was already in motion somewhere on the backside of Clark Mountain. "First stage systems?"

Allington: "Go."

"Comm systems?"

His son's reply: "Go."

"Range operations?"

Kaplan toggled the mike button with his free hand: "Go."

"Highjump second stage?"

The rasp of Glenn Rogan: "Let's go."

Old Schultheis went on, implacable, perhaps with a rising tone of excitement. "All prestart power lights correct; ready light is on. Eject Highjump umbilical."

Rogan could not see the umbilical from the quartz windows of his tiny cockpit. It was Boff Allington, after the briefest of heart-stopping pauses, who exclaimed, "Highjump umbilical clear!"

"Recorders to fast, T minus twelve seconds and counting," said the old man. Now Kaplan strained to spot any sign of movement high on the northwestern flank of the mountain.

At T minus three, Wolf Schultheis said, "Second stage ignition." Still no visible movement against the mountain.

"I have ignition," Rogan confirmed a count later, and, "Separation," after two more seconds. Even with adaptive geometry, scramjets produced marginal thrust below Mach one.

Kaplan cursed, realizing that he had forgotten to aim the video camera, and found the eyepiece as he leaned far out of the C-2, bracing with his feet. And now, on full zoom, Kaplan could see a surge of flame lancing just above a miles-distant berm of alkali dirt, now two flames, as a tiny silver dart climbed against a slate-blue horizon. It slid upward, slanting across the sky, its velocity now more startling because it was approaching Ivanpah Dry Lake but also because Rogan had the little vehicle's throttle firewalled, and two scramjets running on liquid hydrogen could send the tiny craft bellowing across this broad desert bowl at twice the speed of sound within seconds. If they hadn't lost so much hydrogen in the boil-off, they might have hoped for Mach three.

"One point seven—one point niner," said the voice in Kaplan's speaker, intoning the machmeter's readout firmly, but with a buzzing vibrato. Oh yes, that little screamer would be shaking the pilot like a bird dog on point, not ruinous high-amplitude shakes but a hard vibration throughout the ship. Then, "Second-stage cutoff," Rogan said, as Kaplan followed the passage of Highjump no more than two thousand feet above the lake bed. The twin lances of flame winked out, and Rogan began to bank his tiny silver dart, testing its controls deadstick at thirteen hundred miles an hour.

Only then did the slam and roll of scramjet thunder reach Kaplan, who thought for one instant that Highjump had exploded in midair. He leaped from the wrecker's cab to keep the craft in sight; saw that it had slowed significantly. Rogan kept the vehicle in a shallow turn, never rising high enough in this natural bowl to make a blip on distant radar, and without the zoom lens Kaplan would not have seen Highjump, a silvery speck against distant peaks, begin to extend its wingtip panels.

It was one thing to boost upward on outsize scramjets and steeply angled delta wings, and quite another to land with those same flight surfaces. Highjump's delta wings were the same titanium surfaces that Peel Transit had tested for the maglev, then sold as scrap to Exotic Salvage. Tom Schultheis had, in fact, designed them for Highjump, knowing that the maglev would be far less sensitive to the precise shapes of its canards.

But those stubby surfaces that made Highjump resemble a tiny hypersonic cousin of Delta One would never give her the lift she needed to land at only two hundred knots. For that, she needed slender extensions to those wings, and the loads on those extensions had been a nightmare for David Kaplan. Static tests said they would survive. Rogan's flight test, after a Mach two ride, might say otherwise.

Kaplan saw the fat little craft oscillate slightly, then steady during its long descent toward the flattest, deepest part of Ivanpah Dry Lake. Through the faint whirr of desert wind, Kaplan heard the eerie whistle of a massive titanium dart approaching. "Sloppy response below three hundred knots," Rogan's voice echoed from the C-2 cab's speaker. "Pitch-up may be out of the . . ." But he tried; God knew he tried. As the tiny craft settled, Rogan seemed to be testing its stall sensitivity, and then its nose dropped sharply, at a lethal angle, while only five hundred feet above the alkali.

Tom Schultheis had explained his fears of a knife-edge stall before; had planned wing slots to lessen the danger. But there had been no time, and Rogan knew to expect trouble. He was getting it.

Dave Kaplan screamed, "Jesus; NO!" The little craft knifed steeply downward toward deadly unforgiving alkali and then, with the added velocity of its dive, obtained enough lift to flare out at fifty-foot altitude in a path that was almost horizontal at well over two hundred knots. Highjump was sinking fast, now, heading slightly crosswind, in a path that would bring her uncomfortably near the C-2, and her landing gear was still up because gear extension adds drag while it subtracts lift.

"Do it, Mr. Goodrich," boomed from the cab speaker, and Kaplan understood now why Schultheis had built pneumatic boosters into the "gear down" rams. All three wheels popped from their wells. "Gear down and locked," Rogan announced. Now it was up to those three little Goodrich twenty-ply, tubeless tires which Tom Schultheis had scrounged from a Rockwell salvage sale. The raised legend on each of those tires warned, "2 1 7 KNOTS, MAXIMUM SIX LANDINGS." They had been used by Rockwell, and one had been scuffed down to the first layer of cord, perhaps by one of Rockwell's little remotely piloted ramjet vehicles. David Kaplan bared his teeth as Highjump's rearmost two wheels slammed hard into alkali, leaving a glisten of salt dust trails and smoke in the sunlight.

Then, "Range ops, get on it," Rogan suggested, and Kaplan realized that the pilot could see him standing beside the C-2 when he should be up in that cab. Highjump had no power, and precious little in the way of brakes. If one of those tires caught fire, the nearest extinguisher would be on the C-2. Kaplan vaulted into the cab and felt the rumble of the Hercules just as Rogan passed, less than a quarter-mile away but still doing over a hundred miles an hour. Smoke was trailing the nearside wing, but that might have been only something inside the scramjet nacelle. It wasn't.

By the time the C-2 rumbled up with a sigh of its air brakes, Glenn Rogan was already out of the cockpit, kneeling to face the portside wheel. Kaplan leaped down, knelt, and stared.

"Yes, I'm pissin' on this tire," Rogan snapped. "Reckon you can find somethin' better?"

David Kaplan wheeled toward the big carbon dioxide extinguisher mounted behind the C-2's front fender well and brought it into play seconds later, laughing despite the stink of urine on smoking rubber.

"Thanks. I was just about all out," Rogan said over the rush of cold gas, and began to rearrange his fly. Five minutes later, they swung the dune buggy to the lake bed with the crane, then brought the sling hovering over Highjump's silver hide. They ignored the outrigger jacks because when empty the tiny craft weighed no more than a small sedan.

Rogan helped Kaplan position the little aircraft on the flatbed before reaching for his helmet. "I've got another ride," he said dourly, gazing westward into shadows that grew longer by the minute. "Can you get the tiedowns?"

"No problem," Kaplan grunted, wrestling the big hook from its sling. He watched Rogan warm up the old Porsche and set off across the lake bed with gear changes brisk as the song of a chain saw.

David Kaplan paused, smiled, and patted the still-warm tip of a scramjet tailpipe. It would be another ten minutes before he could haul a tarpaulin over this bird. Postflight inspection would tell the main story, but from a cursory look at the belly of Highjump with its Fresnel lens and thrust chamber, all systems appeared to be "go." "No problem," he echoed, his smile fading as slowly as the sun. But then, for Highjump, this had not been much of a jump. . . .

TWENTY

Wes called a staff meeting the following Monday, and found both Kaplan and Schultheis "cautiously optimistic" with the canard tests—which Allington had carefully faked. It did not occur to Wes that those computer simulations might be simulating events that never occurred, while hiding events that did. Kaplan claimed that a foam injection into the canards could solve the vibration problem; Schultheis insisted that this would require one more set of tests with the maglev. Since neither of them seemed willing to set a date, Wes agreed to that test and left the date open. One thing sure: It should be prior to the beginning of the Santa Fe's maglev service between

Los Angeles and Las Vegas, in mid-September. They assured Wes that it would be. Privately, they knew it had damned well better be.

If Wes did not question this vagueness, perhaps it was because he had another problem on his mind. He became more restive whenever he left the plant, impatient to face Joey Weatherby so that, one way or another, he could escape that friendly surveillance.

* * * *

After another fruitless call to Weatherby and ten more days of waiting, Vangie called her brother, Thibodeaux. The following morning at the office, she passed her findings on to Wes. "I," she announced grimly, "seem to be Cajun non grata in Weatherby's outfit. In any case, Tib claims Mr. Himself won't be receiving calls 'til he gets back from some trucker powwow in Dallas."

"Oh, yeah. I'd forgotten; we've got an exhibit there," he replied, pursuing other matters.

It was fifteen minutes later when Vangie, continuing her normal work, suddenly vented a "Huh! Glenn Rogan is taking two days of sick leave. Guess where he can be reached."

"Halfway up the outside of the World Trade Center," Wes joked.

"At the Market Center Marriott. In Dallas, Wes. I wonder just how much I believe in coincidence."

He looked up; put down his pen with a half-frown of surmise; and then burst out laughing. "I'll let you check this one for yourself. Get me Alma Schultheis, will you?"

Vangie tried. Ms. Schultheis, it transpired, was attending a convention. At the Dallas Market Center. "Ahh," said Vangie, when Wes clarified it for her. "She's supposed to be lacking our Shorthaulers in Dallas, where Weatherby just happens to be, but instead, she and that cowpoke—"

"She can do both," Wes cut in calmly. "Let me remind

you that it's not altogether coincidence because Weatherby and I are in the same business. And Alma had the idea for our display back in, um, April. Before she even met that cowpoke as you call him. They're just getting away for a few days, is all.''

"And rubbing shoulders with Joseph A. Weatherby," she riposted. "A pity you couldn't manage it yourself."

"Who says I can't," he said suddenly, reaching down to scratch abraded skin under that ankle holster. "Rogan will be there. It's neutral turf." Brightening, "For that matter, you can come with me."

Her face cleared for a moment, then fell. "I think Mr. Weatherby might not like that, on several counts. And don' kid yourself, he would soon know if I were there. That man has more tripwires than a bayou farmer."

"Book me on the next flight," he said, slapping his desktop, rising. "A room, too, all under the name of Lou Boyle." He spelled it out for her, an old racer's joke that Vangie missed completely. "I'll toss a few things in a suitcase. Call me at home with the flight booking."

He was at the door when she said, "Wes?" He turned. "Be sure and wear your little ankle bracelet."

"That's mainly what gets checked through with the suitcase," he replied, and returned to kiss her. Judging her expression, he added, "Relax, honey. It's going to be all right," and made sure he exited smiling.

The set of her jaw had said, clearer than words, that Vangie feared for him. *Whatthehell*, he thought, *Alma and Rogan have different reasons but they won't like it either. Add Weatherby into the equation and I'm the only one who does like it. Which is as good a reason as any to do it.*

* * * *

Once he found his way out of that county-sized airport near Dallas, Wes was almost to his destination. He felt the faintes pang of remorse when registering at the Marriott; Alma might never forgive him. But it was next to the action, all right. Weatherby was not registered there, but a man could tell just from watching the flow of clientele that the Market Center Marriott was, for the time being, the biggest dang truck stop in all creation. It was almost dinnertime, but Wes registered into the convention as Lou Boyle and checked the exhibit map.

Alma Schultheis, sitting near a sparkling Peel Shorthauler where she could change Peel Transit videotapes and exercise her best marketing smile, surprised him. "My Lord, look who's coming to dinner," she cried happily, and stood to embrace him. "You devil, I'll bet you're just checking up on me!" Then she saw his name tag. "Lube oil? I don't get it. I mean, I get it, but . . . " Her eyes widened. "You're meeting someone," she accused softly, with a half-smile that said, "naughty boy."

"Could be; not for the reason you think," he said, and explained, ending with, "I think a hotel lobby is about as good a place as any."

"Would you feel better with another good man beside you?" Her eyes sparkled with her secret, and Wes chose to let her enjoy the telling. "Glenn is here."

He registered surprise and nodded. "I'll bet he's at Six Flags, trying the thrill rides."

"Not him. He purely *hates* any ride where he's not at the controls." She waved around her where crowds were thinning for the evening, and cargo vehicles of many kinds squatted silently, gleaming with paint and pinstriping. "He's tried on most of these rigs by now. He'd be doing a slalom between the pillars if they'd let him."

Wes laughed and agreed, curiously lighthearted to find that Alma accepted his sudden appearance so easily. She was showing him the packet of cards signed by truckers interested in Peel Shorthaulers when Rogan appeared, at first with some reserve. It disappeared when Wes divulged his reason for anonymity.

Rogan asked, "You figure on just walking up to this guy, having it out in front of God and everybody?"

It might not be all that traumatic, Wes explained. Joey Weatherby could be very smooth, especially when he saw an advantage in smoothness. "But it might be nice if I had someone with me."

"Me, for instance."

"For instance," Wes nodded. "But it's barely possible there could be trouble."

"You're lookin' at the regional distributor," Rogan grinned. "Sure you're ready for it?"

"I have a Walther PPK strapped to my right ankle. I'll never get used to the thing," Wes said. "I don't suppose you're armed."

"Give me time to rustle up a long-neck bottle of Lone Star, and I will be," Rogan promised.

And then Alma made an observation about machismo, and then Wes took them both to see what the Marriott's menu boasted.

Wes was polishing off a Texas-style strawberry shortcake, with layers like stacked pancakes, when a smiling, fresh-faced young redhead in stylish lederhosen stopped by their table and, saying only "Ma'am," to Alma, presented Wes with a note on Marriott stationery. The young man waited, his smile innocuous and unwavering, while Wes read.

Vangie was right about NTC tripwires. Aloud he said to the young man, "I'd be delighted. Would fifteen minutes be all right?"

"Yessir, I think so."

"He may want to meet my chief test pilot, Mr. Rogan."

The smile broadened. "Two on two sounds good," he said politely, and strode off.

"It takes good legs to wear those things," Alma mused, watching him go.

"And better padding than he has, to hide that flat little piece he's wearing," Rogan remarked. "Should I order that beer now?"

Wes nodded. "Weatherby wants to see me at the Short-hauler. Good a place as any. News sure travels fast here."

Alma's eyes widened. "That darlin' young man is a Weatherby thug?"

"Takes one to know one," Rogan chuckled, and patted her shoulder, rising. "I'll go by the bar, Mr. Peel. Alma, I'll see you at the room."

"Just like that," she said to Wes in faintly outraged tones.

"You know he'll make it up to you," Wes said, signalling for a waiter.

"He'd better. You bring him back intact, John Wesley Peel."

Wes paid the bill and found Glenn Rogan, thinking, *But why does Joey Weatherby want to see me?*

*   *   *   *

Rogan had to make do with a bottle of Pearl, and kept it under his sport coat until they had reentered the display hall. The place was nearly innocent of passers-by at this hour, and as their heels generated hollow chirps of echo, Wes felt less secure. Then Rogan grinned at him, the same grin you trade with the guy strapped into the next car on the starting grid when you're both trying to deny the flutter of leathery wings in your bellies, and Wes grinned back. If and when that flag dropped, you both knew what to do. . . .

Joey Weatherby pushed up from Alma's folding chair, and his smile was strictly *pro forma*. "Been a long time," he said, reaching his immaculate manicure toward Wes. He introduced the redhead as Grover O'Grady; the deep-set eyes showed real interest when Wes introduced Rogan as the test pilot of Delta

One but, "The new breed of long-haulers looks pretty much like the old one," was all he said, perhaps in the sincerest of compliments. He turned to Wes. "Why the cute name tag, Peel?"

"Actually, I just dropped in to see you. Seemed more informal this way."

"Well, I'm damned," Weatherby rumbled, and one thatched eyebrow went up. "You been trying to reach me by a third party, by any chance?"

"My third party. Used to be yours," Wes said, with a faint smile.

Weatherby sucked a tooth, glanced up at the Shorthauler cab nearby, and jerked a thumb upward. "They tell me a Shorthauler's seats are easy on the butt. What say the two of us try 'em out?"

Wes realized that they could talk freely inside the cab and saw the faintest of nods from Rogan. Without a word, Wes hitched his gimpy leg up to the inset step, then swung into the driver's seat, opening the other for Weatherby, offering his hand to help the big man puff into the adjacent seat.

Joey Weatherby sighed and leaned back. "Last thing I ever expected was a helping hand from Peel Transit. Funny how things work out," he added, and bought thinking time by offering Wes his choice from a pocket humidor. Wes shook his head even before it occurred to him that poisoned cigars were not unheard of.

Weatherby chose one, lit up, adjusted his window. Then, "Sorry about the Broussard girl. It was just business."

"You've sent a lot of funny business my way," said Wes laconically. "It's not the kind that'll help us get together. Ever."

"Yeah, well—a lot has happened, the last couple of weeks. Enough to set me thinking. Maybe I can make it up to you."

Now Wes was smiling. "That doesn't sound like the Joey Weatherby I knew and loved."

The crow's-feet crinkled, nearly hiding the man's gaze. "You keep being cute, I'll get the idea you've got no respect."

Vigorous headshake from Wes, "Never think that, Weatherby. If I didn't respect the hell out of you, I wouldn't waste so much time wishing we were closer together." He paused, gazed directly at the big man. "But since an incident at my house a few weeks ago, I wonder if I should add fear to that respect."

Something unreadable passed across Weatherby's face. He toyed with his cigar ash, using a little finger with a one-carat stone on it, and nodded. "Don't believe everything you read in the scandal sheets, Peel. I've already had some federal cops around, oh, hat-in-hand, very polite and all, but they had the same idea. They don't worry me worth shit. You know why?"

"I'd like to."

"Because they're good, and they can sniff a clean smell as well as a dirty one. And the NTC is clean. Anyhow," he went on, the square mouth turning down at the edges in reminiscence, "that ain't my style, as Casey said. We don't hire anybody who'd stuff a load of dynamite up his ass."

At Wes's laugh, both Rogan and O'Grady looked up quickly, then returned to their careful, noncommittal discussion. Wes adjusted his own window a trifle to wave the smoke away, then said, "Well, the little fella sure knew how to break up a party."

"Uhm. And you figured the NTC might have some more party-poopers out there, somewhere, so you decided to sit down with me about it on my own turf."

"I thought of it as neutral," Wes said.

Weatherby's entire frame shook with mirth. "Peel, you straight-arrows get me, you really do. This place is as much my backyard as I want it to be. So are the interstate highways when it comes to the rough stuff, and if we want it to be. But leave it; you're safe as my own brother-in-law, God rot him."

"You do wonders for a man's confidence," Wes grumbled.

"Good. Because somewhere out there *are* some more people who want you in little pieces. You'll need more help than a sidekick with a beer bottle to stop 'em."

Wes sat up, repressing a shiver. "I'd like a few specifics."

Weatherby hung the cigar out the window; waved a clearer path through the blue-tinted air. "You wouldn't be running a chicken-wire, would you?" Then, seeing the blank look from Wes, "A wire; a microphone, Peel," he said, with elaborate patience.

In answer, Wes lifted his arms. The big man ran thick hands up and down his rib cage, his arms, then leaned back. "You could still be bugged, the feds have some great stuff these days. And so do we. That has a bearing on what I'm gonna tell you, and it's strictly to save your personal hide. So I'm counting on you to be clean of wires. You want to take a little walk? Come back in a few minutes, no questions asked?"

Weatherby's face was straight, but his eyes held mild amusement. There was none in Wes's as he said, "No wires. That's not why I came."

The big barrel chest was heaving again. "Oh, you straight-arrows. Well, no offense, Peel. I would've worn one, in your place." He let his chuckles subside, then went on earnestly. "You know why guys like you survive against guys like me? I'll tell you why: because of the fucking feds, is why!" With lowered voice, "And I was twenty years in this business before I realized that it was a good thing. Sure, there's cops on the take, and stupid cops, and bad laws. But by and large, the system works. I've got grandkids, Peel; if I thought there was a better system someplace else, I'd try to have 'em grow up there.

"Only I haven't found one as good. Canada? Pulling itself in two. Switzerland? Gimme a break. We're stuck with this system, and it's in deep shit and getting deeper, thanks to energy trouble and NASA trouble and just plain don't-give-a-damn trouble. I got a grandson, won't wipe his nose without he gets a quarter for it, and he better get the quarter *now*, for a goddamn video game, you know what I mean, Peel? We could be heading where England is, and by God I won't have it!''

Weatherby's big fist raised to strike the padded dash. He lowered it again, with a muttered, ''Remind me not to shout. O'Grady is the nervous type, you don't want to take his smile too seriously. Anyhow, it gravels the shit out of me to say it, but my priest claims it'll be good for my soul: *you're more important to the future of this country than anybody in the NTC*. Now,'' he growled, ''ask me how I know.''

''You have my full attention,'' Wes said. ''How?''

Long pause before, ''You ever hear of a little double-dome named Dr. Bruce Hassan Winthorp?''

Wes tried to keep everything in order; wished he did have a recorder to keep it all straight. It seemed that NTC board member Tony Ciano had given an interview to a man claiming a scholarly interest in the NTC, and it hadn't taken Ciano long to intuit a hidden agenda. The long and short of it was that *if* the economic future of the NTC was shaky because of Peel Transit, and *if* John Wesley Peel was such a thorn in the side of the NTC, well, perhaps that thorn should be plucked. Permanently. All very theoretical, very indirect, very innocent and full of questions instead of assertions. But Ciano thought the little bastard had ''Federal Sting Operation'' written all over him. It was entrapment, of course, but . . .

Tony Ciano had the elegant little scholar followed to a motel; got a friendly inquiry run on the name and number on the credit card he'd used for his room; and learned enough to approach Joey with some solid facts as well as a tape of the whole effing interview. Ciano smelled smoke and, after handing the facts to Joey, wanted nothing further to do with the whole mess.

With the utmost caution, Joey's own people, men with the innocent smiles of a Grover O'Grady, flitted mothlike around the neighborhood of Professor Winthorp, around Grayson University and, in point of fact, around Winthorp's anal-retentively neat bungalow. Unless the feds were utterly and terminally off their collective gourds with this choice of a stinger, this butter-wouldn't-melt-in-his-mouth midwest professor was a genuine loony with no connections to Uncle Whiskers. But maybe with a few connections to someplace else. The man had made two calls to public telephones in Michigan within a week, then had driven away from the bungalow in his Caddie with two big suitcases. Somehow they had botched his tail. The tapes were gibberish, but a tame NTC language hotshot identified it as a Middle East dialect. One word that kept recurring on the tapes was one you didn't have to be an Ayrab to understand: It was "Peel."

"So there you are," Weatherby finished, stubbing out his cigar in the Shorthauler's ashtray. "With the new laws against bugging, or use of credit cards, or hell, half the stuff our people did checking this fucker out, I'd just as soon not have to tell anybody what I know, much less *how* I know."

Wes, with wry good humor: "And you told me only because of your priest, and me not even Catholic?"

"Shit, I don't care if you're Mr. Harry Krishna, the principle's the same. Anyhow, I drew the old Confessor, and I knew what he'd say. I put it to him this way: I've got this business competitor who's bustin' my balls by doing things different. But now I find his way is right. I'm pretty sure it's right because some of the world's sneakiest people want me to pop this guy. They seem to be people who are out to put this country in the dumper, and so far, they're doing pretty well. They probably want this guy popped because his ways work better than mine for my country as a whole; and it looks like they've already tried to pop him themselves, and, uh, blew it. *Those foreign fuckers thought I was on their side, Peel!* That's not this country's side; I'm certain of that. Ciano might not think it through this way, but that's how I see it.

So I'm sure not gonna have this guy popped; this is my country, too.

"Some of these old priests can ask questions that make a man squirm, you know it? So then I ask mine. Question, Father: Can I sit back and watch, or must I tell this competitor where the heat is coming from?" Weatherby waved an idle hand as if considering a matter of little importance. "So I get this lecture about the higher good, just like I expected—and by the way, you don't want to go and quote me on any of this. Man in my position isn't smart to let on he makes real bottom-line decisions based on, uh, Providence."

"You can say 'God' without losing my respect, Weatherby. Or 'patriotism,' either; but I know what you mean."

"I wonder if you do; you Protestants have it easy, Peel. If I didn't tell you about that confession, well, you might not take this seriously enough. Telling you about it is enough to bag me some Hail Marys." Weatherby's laugh asked Wes not to.

"You can say 'sin' to me, too," Wes replied. "You don't think I get stuck between thou-shalt-nots?" Wes remembered old Nell Peel, perhaps not so old at that, now that Wes himself was nearing fifty, and thought of the old girl's role as his spiritual advisor and yes, sometimes his confessor. "I've made some sacred promises that give me more trouble, the longer I live to see how little sense they made. But I made 'em, and now it's too late to start over—what's funny?"

Weatherby mastered his chuckle to say, "Just thought of how it'd sound to give an NTC board report on this. 'Oh, we just climbed up in one of Peel's Shorthaulers, and spoke of God and country.' No, I don't think I will."

After a half-minute's silence, Wes asked, "Any reason I can't pass on the information about this Grayson professor, if I keep my source to myself?"

"I expect you'd better, unless Peel Transit's got more stand-up guys than I have," was Weatherby's reply. The big man reached for the door handle with the sigh of a man who has just surrendered a long-sought goal.

Wes laid a hand on Weatherby's arm. "Weatherby? I know I've been a problem."

"Damn' straight."

"I can—well, maybe not remove it, but I can help the NTC if you'll let me."

"Wonders never cease," said Weatherby, with new interest in the intelligent, calculating gaze.

"With the new intermodal stuff, those got-damned triple-trailer rigs will be rare on the highways in a few years. I admit it; hell, I planned it. But the new stuff will create new jobs, and the NTC will still be needed. Maybe a trucker won't like giving up his king-of-the-road crown to be just a prince in a Shorthauler, or a cargomaster in a delta. But who ever promised they'd never have to learn something new? You'll just have to stay ahead of the changes."

"Jesus *Christ*, don't I know it! That's why you find things slowing you down here and there, Peel. I can't read your mind, do you blame me for putting somebody where I can see what's in your crystal ball?"

"Yep. Because I can show you where we're headed. Time projections, regional gross loads, even some leaks from Boeing and LockLever; I'm not *that* straight an arrow. What you do about it is your business."

"Hell it is," the big man rumbled. "I get a lot of mileage out of saying this country's freight is everybody's business. Shit. Turns out it's true! Here's one that'll give you a laugh, Peel: I'm envious because those fucking Ayrabs want to pop you, and not me. Maybe I'll make the grade—if you meant what you said about those projections."

Wes nodded, thinking about blocks of spare time. "How'd you like to spend a day or two at the Hayward plant? Say, anytime after Labor Day? You can bring a friend—and a chickenwire, if it suits you."

"You'd do that?"

"I owe it to you," Wes said simply.

"No you don't, Peel. I told you," he said, one side of the big man's mouth rising in irony, "for the greater good."

Wes grinned. "No, I owe you for the best got-damn' executive assistant in the country."

With a faint flush on the heavy features: "You putting me on?"

"Putting you straight. I'm pretty fond of the lady."

"Well I'm a dirty—son—of— a—bitch."

"You ever meet a mover and shaker who wasn't?"

Laughing, they climbed down from the shorthauler. Joey Weatherby seemed satisfied that he might, in September, get as much as he had just given. The one thing Weatherby had not given Wes was the thing he did not know: Winthrop's CCI bug sensor had told him, when he finally thought to use it, that someone was monitoring that bungalow. And a loose tail is not hard to evade when you suspect it is wagging back there in traffic.

TWENTY-ONE

After a bottle of Pearl with Rogan and Alma, Wes decided against six pointless hours of sleep in a Marriott bed. Instead, he made a lighthearted purchase at the DalWorth terminal and caught two hours of sleep on the coast redeye, beating the sun back to Oakland International. Vangie Broussard found him in his office, slightly bleary-eyed, when she arrived for work.

After kissing him soundly, she also found a new life-size plaster bust on her desk.

It didn't look like one of her favorites, and neither its sweeping mustache nor the strong aquiline nose resembled Wes's, but the name incised on the pediment read "JOHN WESLEY." The last name was printed, in Wes's neat draftsman's hand, on tape: It said, "PEEL." She looked from the plaster to Wes. "That's not you, my dear."

"It is, and it isn't; it's really a pun. Do what it says."

So she peeled the tape away. Beneath it was the last incised name: "HARDIN." "You *are* impossible! Why would you imagine I'd want John Wesley Hardin leering at us all day?"

"Seemed fitting," he said. "I went to Texas and faced the badmen down with my trusty seven-shooter." Then he told her of his unexpected rapprochement with Weatherby, and of the NTC man's desire to visit the Hayward facility. "During the week after Labor Day," he said. "Call him for me this morning; tell him I can put him up, whatever. He'll take your call this time."

She "hmphed" in a way that told him she was secretly pleased, lugged the plaster head to a blueprint cabinet, and stuck her tongue out at it before returning to her work.

He was checking his appointment calendar when he realized she stood before him, arms akimbo. "May I suggest your first call this morning?"

"Sure," he said.

"Make it to the Treasury Department. The sooner they know about this Middle East connection, the sooner you and I can get away from prying eyes."

Wes agreed. Thirty seconds into his telephone call, the Treasury man stopped him with, "This isn't a secure line, Mr. Peel. Ah, you recall the time you called me about the gent watching you eat dinner? Hold it; calling up my notes. Yeah, that place serves lunch, too. If you have the time . . ."

Wes took the time, driving to the place near Foothill Boulevard, and found the Treasury man keeping company with a rangy, freckled blond specimen in a suit entirely too neat to belong to anybody but a fashion model or a fed. The man spoke in the twang of an Oregon farmer, using the phrases of an attorney. He was Agent Royston Kimmel from the Oakland Resident Agency of the FBI.

Kimmel's handshake was as cool and dry as Wes's lunch martini, and he asked questions in an unhurried, detached way over salads and luncheon steaks, clearing a place for his memcomp next to his iced tea. Why couldn't Mr. Peel tell them a little more about his source? Did Mr. Peel realize how much tax money it took to find answers Peel himself could furnish? Grayson U. was well-known but what, exactly, was the spelling of Bruce Hassan Winthrop, and did Peel realize that this inquiry might wind up as a joint endeavor, a Federal task force that went a lot farther than the San Francisco Field Office?

The Treasury man seemed satisfied to take a secondary role in the meeting. Kimmel's statements were as pointed and, in a few cases, as cryptic as his questions. The Oakland RA would pass a message on the suspect to Cleveland by teletype. No, it was definitely not the teletype of yore, but that's what they called it, and it was as secure as a battleship anchor. The Treasury Department handled explosions and such but terrorist groups on U. S. soil were the province of the Justice Department. Until now, no one had more than tentatively considered the idea that widely spaced suicide bombings of a few Americans in apparently unconnected walks of life were, in fact, pieces of one specific international conspiracy. You couldn't ram a task force down the pike on such slender evidence as Peel offered, not yet. But you could learn more about Winthrop than his own proctologist knew, and then maybe that joint endeavor could be mounted.

And by the way, the Treasury man put in, not a word of

any of this must reach Reese Masefield or anybody else, but especially not the press. And had Peel decided not to carry a piece? It sure wasn't tucked into his waist or armpit.

Wes told them about the Walther on his ankle and earned something like approval only because he swore he was practicing.

"I'm not all that sanguine about your piece," Kimmel admitted, "because you don't always know who your friends are. I'll put it this way: Never draw it until you see a target who is trying to put you down. And don't brandish it." He followed this with a faintly disgusted look toward the Treasury man. Federal agents, Wes decided, did not always agree on advice to the innocent.

They strolled into a warm overcast after Wes refused again to divulge the source of his information. "The man knows he exercised more than the legal amount of, ah, patriotic zeal," was all Wes would admit.

"One man's patriot is another man's terrorist," Kimmel replied drily.

Wes thought of Joey Weatherby and the massive NTC muscle that rolled in tandem rigs across the breadth of the nation, and smiled. "There's something to that," he said, offering his hand and his thanks with it, then heading back to his Chevy Blazer that loomed, the playground bully, over other vehicles in the parking lot.

* * * *

Only a man who personally ran his empire, or thought he did, would hold a staff meeting while inspecting a delta dirigible. Wes kept the audio tape running on his memocomp that afternoon as he mounted the unfinished cargo platform of Delta Two. Now and then, Kaplan or Schultheis punched notations into their memocomps as the three men reached decisions. Vast as it was, that assembly hangar would have to be expanded before Peel Transit could start turning out those big lifters at he rate of one a month. And the first order was already in. "Or better still, duplicate this hangar," Wes went on; "run parallel assembly operations. Sometimes smaller is better."

"I'll remind you that you said that, one of these days," Kaplan murmured, drawing a grim glance from Schultheis. "Smaller and better" were the heart, liver and lungs of the Highjump concept.

"You two generally think farther ahead than this," Wes complained, pausing on an internal catwalk to study Delta Two's huge, filament-wound helium recovery sphere. "Our expansion this year is only the beginning."

The other two shared a glance, and Kaplan passed it off with, "That usually means an ending of something else."

Schultheis: "I think Dave feels what I do; we're leaving a phase that was a lot of fun, Wes." He laid a hand on Wes's arm and said, a little sadly, "Sometimes, moving ahead can hurt."

Kaplan, quickly: "I vote we take it out on some Kern River trout while there's still a bit of summer left. I'll be worn down to five-foot-three if I don't get that vacation pretty soon, Wes."

"Well, we're pretty much between phases," Wes mused, moving forward toward the cabin of Delta Two, his voice echoing through the great envelope surrounding them. "Just say when, so long as you're both here for the Santa Fe's inaugural runs."

Schultheis consulted his memocomp's calendar file as though he had not committed it to memory. "That means, oh, say the week after Labor Day. That way," he said, "we take Labor Day weekend and the next one too. Ten days."

"On the Kern," Kaplan added. "You'll just have to learn to get along without us, Wes."

"I'll manage," said Wes, thinking of a mere week without his boffins, missing the faint ring of apology and of permanence in Kaplan's voice. "Labor Day week it is. I've got half a mind to sneak off with you." He did not see Schultheis look toward

Heaven for help, but recalled something as he entered the delta's cabin. Some of its console systems were already in place, identical to Delta One's. A memocomp's intercom function worked poorly through the hangar walls, but, "If the comm system's in, I can patch Vangie in from here. Wait one," he added, flicking switches. By now, Wes knew his delta consoles well enough to pilot one of the great brutes in decent weather.

Vangie answered. Yes, invoking Wes's name she'd got through to the NTC, and was Wes alone?

"Tom and Dave are here," he told her.

"A man who wants to be registered as Lou Boyle says he'll take care of his bookings. He'll be here with a Mr. O'Grady for a tour on Wednesday to Friday, September six through eight, as agreed. I said you'd confirm. Problem?"

He said he didn't know, thanked her, and flicked off the set. He turned to find Kaplan and Schultheis leaning against seats in the broad aisle, looking around them with something akin to longing. It was the gaze of Oppenheimers, men who had created wonders but whose decisions could make those same wonders forbidden to them, perhaps forever.

Wes imagined that they were worrying about a fishing trip. "Just when you two want to be off somewhere falling in cold water, we've got a . . ." *No, got-damnit, I won't ask them to postpone it again for Joey Weatherby. That's not why Weatherby's coming anyhow. And these two would be arguing over every damn' projection I made.* Wes sighed and stood up. "The hell with it, gentlemen. Enjoy your trout. We've got a visit from an NTC man scheduled while you're gone, and if you can live without him, he can live without you."

The two seemed almost faint-headed with . . . pleasure? relief? . . . as they passed from the cabin and back into the superstructure of the big lifter. Delta Two would be flight-tested before November if the Bay Area weather held. The bare keel members of Delta Three were almost ready in an assembly shed.

Schultheis passed also to what seemed a casual mention of the maglev canard tests. True to their words, they had injected a special filament-loaded foam into those canards. And, unknown to Wes, they had used the same equipment to apply a thin spray-coating to ceramic tiles of Highjump's forward surfaces. "Wes, whoever the NTC guy is, promise me one thing," Schultheis pleaded. "Don't haul him down to see those canard tests Rogan will be doing with Boff. I don't see what could go wrong but it's not over 'til it's over, and if there's any problem with the system, you don't want some outsider blatting it out to the world. Okay?"

"Makes sense," Wes agreed. *I hadn't thought about it, but yeah, that's probably what I'd have done. And they're right.* "You two know me too well," he grinned. "Okay; no visiting firemen at Barstow 'til you sign off for the mods."

They shook on it, then completed their tour through the vast empty spaces of Delta Two, which would soon have her helium cells installed. The delta was slightly ahead of schedule, and that pleased them all. Highjump was slightly behind schedule because the liquid hydrogen storage tanks, during their cleanup in the warehouse of Exotic Salvage in San Leandro, were not easy items to secure on the flatbed of an old C-2 wrecker.

*   *   *   *

On Friday night preceding Labor Day, Wes sat propped on pillows in his big bed trying to watch old Benny Hill reruns. He was having trouble concentrating because he could see Vangie, counting slow brush strokes through that long mane of hers, as she donated occasional glances at him in the floor-to-ceiling bedroom mirror. When their glances finally locked, he grinned. "Did you know I had an X-rated mirror?"

"It's all in your mind, suh," she purred, shaking her tresses out, then paused, cocking her head. Two faint pops, no louder than backfires, echoed nearby. In the late summer evening, half of the windows in the house were open because Wes preferred honest-to-God breeze over air-conditioning. Somewhere in the near distance, tires were squealing and an engine rasped in a rising note.

"He's gonna blow that little engine," Wes remarked as the sounds faded down Crow Canyon. "Fool kids . . ."

He fumbled for the video controls, disintegrated Benny Hill in mid-innuendo, and flung a corner of his sheet back in invitation as Vangie stood, head flung back, hair swinging as she smiled back at him.

She was sliding into bed as they heard footsteps pounding up the front walk. "Wonderful," Vangie groaned, over the chime and the hammering at the front door.

With a curse, Wes heaved himself from the bed; grabbed a robe on his way, then paused to pull the Walther from its holster which hung at his shoe rack. "Keep your shirt on," he called, because the chime kept sounding and someone with the world's worst case of asthma kept trying to shout.

Wes, snapping on his porch lights, could not recall seeing the man before. He fought for breath, eyes tightly shut, tears streaming as he leaned against a planter box. "ID—coat pocket," he said, coughing, then, agonized, "Mace—gotta wash."

Wes could smell the acidic tang of something that made his own eyes water. "I'm armed," he said, still cautious of this stranger, and helped the man tear his light windbreaker off as they lurched into the living room.

Wes managed a staggering procession to the guest bath, then got the man into its shower, fully clothed. The stranger seemed in danger of total collapse until, after five minutes sitting in the shower stall under a tepid spray, he could make himself understood, blue eyes still streaming. By then, Wes had seen the Treasury Department shield, had tossed the windbreaker into his washer while Vangie busied herself brewing coffee.

Twenty-five minutes later, their familiar Treasury agent stood at the front door. "Got two men covering the grounds," he said without preamble, striding inside, then saw the stakeout man nursing coffee at the kitchen pass-through, enfolded in a spare bathrobe while his clothes tumble-dried. "Mister, are you ever out of uniform," he remarked drily, and then heard the stakeout's story.

The little pop-top van had pulled off the road at ten past eleven, a hundred yards from Wes's front gate, at an elevation that looked down toward the rear of the Peel home. The stakeout man had hauled his infrared video camera to his cheek and recorded a young woman as she raised the van's hood before returning inside again with no lights showing. "I've seen that van pass before, but so what," said the stakeout. "Point is, I swear I've seen it cruise Peel's plant, too. So I walk over to offer assistance, getting a shot of the license plate, stashing the IR rig in the bushes.

"She answers my hail; foreign accent, says everything's okay. I move back and identify myself, ask her to please turn on her headlights and step outside. She hits the lights, I come to the edge of the beams. It's one of those iffy situations; I don't know who else is in there but I don't want to give her cardiac arrest if she's clean. She comes out with a cigarette and a lighter, very nervous, drops the hood, asks to see my ID. She's a great-looking little number, by the way. So I've got one hand at my holster and one hand on my wallet when she brings up that lighter, and it's a Mace canister the size of a roll of dimes, not worth spit at twenty feet but I was closer than that. I failed a routine precaution, it was that simple."

Quickly, from the Treasury agent: "Where's that IR video?"

The stakeout: "Mr. Peel went out and got it. I told him not to, before we got some help here. The Sheriff's people pulled out a week ago."

"Christ, Peel, you just beg for it." The agent sighed and turned back to his stakeout. "Put you down pretty hard?"

"Not that hard; I went down and rolled while I drew. Got two rounds off while she piled into the van but I was firing at the tires. It's still possible she was just scared, maybe getting ready to bed down with some guy inside. She almost ran me down and I had a boa constrictor around my chest. I finally got here to the house, but I wasn't good for much, I can tell you."

"We'll discuss it later," the Treasury agent said, in tones that added, ". . . and you won't enjoy it much."

"We heard the ruckus," Wes put in, "and somehow he got to my front door in two minutes flat."

"Well, our suspect is long gone," said the T-man. "We can run a make on her plates right now. Where's the video camera? We can plug into your VCR, see if you recognize her."

Vangie brought the little camera with its big battery pack and IR beam tube, and moments later they had rewound the cassette. On Wes's big color-projection screen in the living room, they sat through perhaps a minute of a previous surveillance, as two young men walked down the road, hands in pockets. Then a cut to a Toyota panel van, parked beside the road, with a patch of brightness where its hot tailpipe signaled hard infrared emissions. A youthful figure with medium-length hair, wearing a blouse, skirt, and flat heels of an old-fashioned girl, emerged quickly and raised the vehicle's engine hood before disappearing again into the van. The next, and last, shot was a close-up of a license plate. Not the plate of a commercial van.

"Maybe a rental," said the Treasury man, tapping at his memocomp. "Let's hope not. Go back to where she raises the hood."

Wes did so, and stopped when he was told. Moving forward a few frames at a time, he reached a point where the dark-haired young woman with the huge soulful eyes was turning back toward the driver's door. Unwittingly, she stared straight toward the IR emitter for an instant. She was a looker, all right.

The Treasury man grunted. "I've got a plate to check. You folks sit here and study that face. If this was a comedy of errors, she's probably called the police by now. But I'll bet you've seen her somewhere, and a hundred to one she's been seeing you."

Wes played the scene backward and forward, now and then looking toward Vangie, halting the cassette repeatedly to stare at the impassive face of the young woman. They had to admit, finally, that so far as they knew they had never seen her before. For all her youth, Zahra Aram had managed her mission very well until this night.

*   *   *   *

Zahra fought down her panic long enough to realize that she would need hours to lug that expensive equipment from the van, wipe every surface clean of her prints, and get the tires changed to throw off pursuit. Zahra did not have hours, in her own mind. She'd heard the *whap* of a slug into the van, somewhere near her feet, and that would be an instant tip-off if it was visible. She took Castro Valley Boulevard to Lake Chabot Road and flicked her high beams wildly, searching for a spot from where the van could be driven into the lake. By the time she found an access with a suitable downslope, it was midnight and Zahra was mewling with such fear and frustration that she almost forgot to haul her bicycle from the van.

The van went in with appalling slowness, as if forging into a lake of moonlit molasses, but it floated awhile, and because it went down by the nose it moved farther forward, into deeper water. Zahra prayed it deeper, mounted the bike, and pedaled for an hour before she found an unmutilated public telephone outside a Castro Valley 7-Eleven.

In Lansing, it was nearly four o'clock in the morning when Golam Razmara answered his phone. He replied in surliness which quickly progressed through rage to horror as Zahra poured out her tale. The van, its equipment, and her usefulness: All vanished now. Golam furiously denounced her for incompetence, then impressed upon her how absolutely imperative it was that she put many miles between herself and the Bay Area, immediately, and without attracting attention. Above all, she was not to seek Golam out by any means whatever. He would, imsh'Allah, contact her at school in the fullness of time—*Farda*.

By dawn, Golam was en route to the three-room digs of Kosrow Nurbashi. Since the brief call from Winthorp, warning only of electronic surveillance, Nurbashi had begun preaching still more caution to Golam and Ali Zahedi, his last two minions. Golam Razmara did not know what Nurbashi would command next, but he guessed that they would not long remain in these comfortable haunts. Golam knew, however, that the mullah's response would, as always, invoke some grotesque revenge.

TWENTY-TWO

The role of the mullah, as repeated endlessly by Khomeini, was as clerical ruler: *velayet-e-faqih*. This being so, Kosrow Nurbashi had been schooled deeply and dogmatically in a few things, and very sketchily in most others. Nurbashi knew so little of some humdrum facts of American life that he did not even maintain a bank account, preferring instead to rely on his followers to exchange smuggled emeralds for cash.

This weakness delayed Farda's revenge for several days, because even purchasers of jewels were hard to contact during a Labor Day weekend; yet ultimately it had its peculiar strengths. For one thing, it forced Golam Razmara and the lank, taciturn Ali Zahedi to fence their unset jewels in different cities: Golam in Detroit, Ali over two hundred miles away in Chicago. This lessened the scuttlebutt about the sudden influx of fine stones into the market. And because Nurbashi was at best a poor driver, it fell to Ali, in Chicago, to purchase the kind of vehicle Nurbashi wanted; something fast, built like a tank, and with a huge capacity to store the tools of their trade where they could be reached instantly. Ali bought the stretch Cadillac limo in Evanston for cash; not much cash at that, thanks to its thirst for gasoline which Khomeini himself had made exceedingly dear.

On Wednesday, Nurbashi and his two dedicated crazies struck Interstate 80, bound for Omaha and ultimately for Hayward. While Golam and Ali took turns at the wheel, Nurbashi took his ease behind them, one elbow on the airline bagful of twenty-dollar bills, resting his feet on the voluptuous roundels of a bass viol case. The viol lay inside, in case it became necessary to open the case. But if anyone demanded to see the instrument, the ruse would be obvious, for its back had been pillaged so that the two Uzi submachine guns and the sawed-off Browning shotgun would fit inside. The two explosive vests hung neatly among the spare clothing that swung from a strap whenever the limo lurched during its long pilgrimage to Hayward, and to Armageddon.

*   *   *   *

On that same Wednesday, David Kaplan reached Los Angeles in the C-2, silently grateful for the attention Tom Schultheis devoted to long-range planning. Kaplan's Class A license to haul hazardous cryogenic liquids had involved a few lies two years before, but his specialized training since then had been legitimate. The C-2 was up to spec, with no steel cord in its tires and a fully-grounded cryo trailer for those monstrous Thermos bottles of stainless alloy. His permit, too, was legitimate, linked to Exotic Salvage. The chief problem was that, while "roading" the ferociously cold and explosive liquid hydrogen, internal fluid movement caused the boil-off of some two percent of the stuff each hour.

The conspirators knew that arrival at Highjump's hangar with one ounce less hydrogen than they needed was the same as having no fuel at all. It had been Schultheis who thought of their cellular radiophones, too; so Kaplan knew when the schedule slipped, even for an hour, back at the hangar. By now it looked like he must fire up the C-2 around six on Thursday evening to arrive near the hangar during the early hours of Friday.

Rogan had refused the pills that would have kept him working, as Schultheis worked, virtually around the clock with old Wolf Schultheis forever checking and rechecking details a tired man might miss. As Rogan put it, "No chemicals in my pipes, man; when I crank this sucker up it's got to be in realtime."

* * * *

Wednesday was realtime for Wes, too, though it began to seem a little unreal soon after lunch. He personally handed visitor badges to Joey Weatherby and a curiously subdued Grover O'Grady before escorting them down mahogany row to his office where, for the first time, Weatherby and Vangie met face-to-face.

"I hope you can let this old sleeping dog lie," Weatherby said to her. "By the way, Tib sends his regards. Grover, wipe that letch off your face, this lady is spoken for."

O'Grady, whose face mirrored no such thing, had nonetheless been thinking it. He only said, "Yessir," understanding very well that Mr. W. was wearing his jocular attitude. And

Mr. W. did that only on those rare occasions when he felt uneasy.

Vangie hid behind her southern belle facade, producing a schedule printout for them. "I'm not sure what you want to see, but there's a new Shorthauler cab on the shaker table this afternoon, and Delta Two's helium cells are going in."

"Told you she was sharp," Wes winked at the burly NTC chairman. "Or we could just have a drink and crowd around my desk screen and talk graphs."

"Plenty of time for that," Weatherby rumbled expansively. "I'll have that drink and then somebody can show me around your plant. Mind if Grover videotapes the tour?"

Wes gave them the killer smile as he opened the liquor cabinet. "I've got nothing to hide outside the delta hangar, and I'll be with you anyhow."

The bushy brows went up. "For three days?"

"A pleasure," Wes nodded, splashing scotch over ice. "Vangie has left a Weatherby-sized hole in my schedule, and if any brushfires break out, they should be easy to handle. Even that would be a snap if my design and stress heads weren't on vacation. You won't miss 'em, if you like sight-seeing in a delta dirigible," he added slyly as they set the glasses down.

O'Grady perked up at this. "That guy Rogan, will he take us up?"

Wes, ushering the two men to the door, told them Rogan was working on another project with their top instrumentation man, but Jim Christopher was a fine pilot and a first-rate flight instructor. Wes was too busy to ask himself why so many of his best people had arranged to be out of touch at the same time.

*   *   *   *

And on the outskirts of Council Bluffs, wheeling back toward the interstate from the truck stop, old Manson Perkins cursed as he twisted violently on the wheel of his Freightliner. His hitcher, the little Indian broad sitting across from Perkins, squealed in fright, watching that speeding black limo swerve back into place inches before Perkins would've clipped it. At least Perkins figured she was Indian; lots of Sioux and Osage hotsies in these parts, and some of 'em not too choosy to climb into the rack with a stove-up old veteran of the highway wars. 'Specially if she wanted a free ride and meals clean to Motown, though nothing was really free. What was it he'd seen on that bumper sticker? "Gas, grass, or ass: nobody rides for free."

"Stupid asshole found out who's boss," he remarked calmly, looking across at the Osage girl, whose frown suggested she was still thinking about their close call.

Zahra Aram looked at him and quickly produced a smile. For one instant, staring into the windshield of that black limousine, she had imagined the face of Golam Razmara, a Golam whose face was pinched in fright. But Golam, of course, would be back on the campus when classes began in a few weeks, so he was somewhere around Lansing. Imsh'Allah . . .

* * * *

And on Thursday, as Zahra boarded a Greyhound for her last leg to Lansing; and Golam surrendered the wheel to Ali near Ogden, Utah; and Joey Weatherby watched a video in Wes's office of Delta One snatching a fifty-ton load from a flatcar; Wolf Schultheis, in the Highjump hangar, spoke with Kaplan on their cellular radio link. "Dey are all on cots, snoring like drunken men," he observed gently. "But Allington swears dey will be ready for you early in the morning."

"And how about you?" asked Kaplan, beginning for the first time to wonder, in a subdued panic, what in the *hell* they had committed themselves to, and what tiniest, fatal detail one of them might have forgotten. "Does it look like a 'go'?"

"I cannot possibly be certain," the old man admitted. "My preliminary work was so long ago, and you and Thomas have made so many changes—good changes, yes, I believe." He paused for the duration of a breath. "But it must be done."

"Even if it doesn't work," Kaplan replied, and neither of them could be sure whether it was question or assertion.

"Even den. It could work, and dat will be seen afterward, no matter what does happen. Like de Natter project in 1945."

"God! I hope not, Mr. Schultheis. Most aeronautical historians claim the Natter was abandoned after the first manned launch killed the pilot."

"I know. We will simply have to set dem straight on it. And on dis, if it does not go well. Yet I have faith."

"How's Rogan?"

"As I told you: snoring. But as to what you mean to ask; he, too, has faith."

"That we'll do it?"

"Dat we must try," said the old man, cautious to the last.

*   *   *   *

And on Friday. . .

TWENTY-THREE

On Friday, 8 September 1995, a low-pressure region lurked off the coast of Baja California at dawn, and Boff Allington chewed a thumbnail to ribbons as he watched early-morning weather reports in Highjump's hangar. Above the Mojave they had only a smear of stratocirrus and, toward the southeast, nothing but the purest blue. That, and the sight of the C-2 grinding its way up the access road in early light.

Kaplan, the only one who had not slept the previous night, dropped like a stricken man on a cot for a brief rest, his feet protruding beyond the coverlet. Glenn Rogan, on his Yamaha, covered the hundred miles from Highjump's hangar on Clark Mountain to Barstow in an hour and a quarter. Minutes after eight, he signed the usual papers as if bored with the day's task, then climbed into the maglev maintenance unit alone. He held its pace down to two hundred during the trip back, aware that the refreshed Kaplan would need more time to ease the C-2 over rutted dirt paths to their staging area, towing a quiet volcano behind him.

It was no secret to anyone involved with the maglev route that the track followed old power lines because it was a cheap solution. The route ran southwest to northeast but, four years previously, Tom Schultheis had seen from the air that one—and only one—stretch of that route ran for ten miles due west to due east. Actually, he would have been happier to see that stretch aimed in a southeasterly direction, but it didn't take much fuel to translate an initial flight path twenty degrees or so, and a man can't have everything.

That stretch had everything else, though. It was even downhill off the flank of Clark Mountain, where gravity could aid acceleration. And finally, it was at the highest point on the maglev's route through the high, dry wastes of the Mojave. For Highjump, the higher and thinner the air, the better.

At the time, before his first designs of that maglev maintenance unit, Schultheis had felt gooseflesh thinking that no one had ever proposed a better scheme for a laughably cheap, *electric, fully recoverable* first-stage booster that never left its rails. Except that John Wesley Peel did not even want to discuss such things, quite content to pursue his own agenda for America's cargoes.

At first with great caution, then with mounting enthusiasm as Wolf Schultheis approved the numbers and David Kaplan hired on with Peel Transit, Tom Schultheis had begun to plan the project they finally dubbed Highjump. It meant abandoning other pastimes; largely ignoring a wife who demanded attention; conspiring with a man who, innocent or not, had given Tom's wife some of that attention.

It also meant cheating Wes Peel, designing components for other projects that were really perfect only for Highjump, and diverting the test hardware to Exotic Salvage. Almost certainly it would mean a handful of ruined careers, once their fraud was unmasked. To a man, they agreed; it was worth the penalty.

As Rogan tested the maglev's remote controls during its passage up to the flank of Clark Mountain, David Kaplan palmed a lever on the C-2's cable winch, lifting the still-unfueled Highjump vehicle from its cradle. Moments later, with the younger Schultheis and Boff Allington steadying stubby wingtips that were prototypes of the maglev canards, Highjump nestled among air bags that spanned the rear half of the C-2's long flatbed, behind the cryogenic tanks.

For a C-2, the load was no sweat. Hydrogen was, after all, the lightest substance in the universe—and one of the cheapest, as well as one of the most explosive. A half-hour later, with Tom Schultheis beside him sweating every jounce over that hardpan path, Kaplan drove beneath soaring power lines and chuffed his air brakes beside the maglev.

*　　*　　*　　*

Rogan deployed the crane of the maintenance unit, moving with great economy, saying little as they wrestled Highjump's small aluminum launch cradle—for the second time—into place atop the maglev's sleek hull. They used bronze tools, now, for bronze would not create sparks, and they could hear the hiss of hydrogen outgassing from those stainless steel containers nearby. They worried about those occasional spits and spats above them, as dust particles fried high up in the power lines; but the breeze had never failed them here, and the outgassing hydrogen wafted aside as it climbed, an invisible column of lethal stuff begging to be touched off. Lying on their backs, Rogan and Schultheis carefully wiped down the Fresnel beam-catcher lens that spread across Highjump's belly, flanked by retractable panels and an arm's length ahead of that sapphire port. This time, no magnesium struts lay anywhere near the port.

Allington and Wolf Schultheis were not needed for the mating and fueling steps; for one thing, because even with her half-ton of water as cargo, Highjump weighed scarcely more than a family sedan before fueling, and could be manhandled into her launch cradle by three men. For another, a mistake while fueling the tiny brute would consume everyone present in the kind of firebloom made infamous first by the *Hindenburg*, then by the *Challenger*.

Kaplan had dismissed the risk with, "A leak in your boat, an arrow, or a hydrogen explosion; no frontier was ever safe."

So they took every precaution. An hour before noon, Kaplan passed static ground lines to Schultheis; slung the insulated "python," their fuel feed line, from the C-2 crane arm; swung it so that it hung beside Highjump's tiny cockpit for the necessary bottom-fill, venting inert gas above. "Go for helium purge, Glenn," he called. It had been old Wolf who pointed out how Highjump's tanks should be chilled before introducing liquid hydrogen into them, and the maglev had its own helium tank for its supercooled magnets. But only after Rogan had pushed the maglev to near-sonic speeds with its crucial canard controls were they sure they had a system that could work.

Schultheis maneuvered the feed line into place, encumbered in clothing that might save him if, despite all precautions, any of the stuff leaked. He tested the probe connections and heard Rogan announce completion of the purge. Frost began to cake the fittings as the fuel transfer began.

Kaplan vaulted to the C-2 cab and spoke with Allington, two miles off at the hangar. Yes, Allington said, he'd confirmed the laser feed from the lads at Arizona State, though they were one mystified bunch when they got the precise coordinates. Rogan could file his own flight plan from Highjump's radio, at the last minute, just to make sure they didn't spook NORAD's radar people into a militant response. In three hours or so, it would be time for Allington to start the maglev's remotely programmed race down that long incline, with no one inside the maglev and one risk-junkie riding above it, and then for Glenn Rogan's one-oh-two-degree heading toward his rendezvous with a ravening beam of light, twenty-three miles above a wilderness in Arizona where chunks of sapphire already lay gleaming from the last trial.

*   *   *   *

And as the noon hour approached, and the dusty black Cadillac limo cruised the parking lots of Peel Transit in Hayward, Ali Zahedi struggled into his six-pound vest while Golam Razmara drove. "The license plates on that Blazer are Peel's," Ali argued, "so we need only be nearby when he comes out for a noon meal he will never enjoy. And I am ready to embrace him."

"You are the better driver," Golam protested, then beseeched Nurbashi through the rearview mirror. "Honored mullah, it is my turn; my honor. You will need Ali to speed you away in this ponderous machine."

Nurbashi bade them be silent, fingering the Uzi in his lap, filled with excitement now that he had seen their quarry's vehicle and knew that, somewhere behind that high fencing, the Peel necessity was very near. Razmara was in line for it, to be sure; yet through him, Nurbashi had control of that girl, Zahra. Still, the girl had finally made a serious error and, even if she was not already in the hands of Great Satan, she would probably be traced when the van was found. The girl, therefore, was of no further use. And Golam Razmara, therefore, would get his most fervent wish. Besides, he was a rotten driver. "It is Allah's wish that the eldest be most honored," Nurbashi intoned.

Ali Zahedi sighed and began to remove his vest. "Stop this contraption so that I can drive," he muttered to Golam, who quickly complied. From Zahra Aram's copious notes, Golam knew that Peel's habits were irregular. The man might issue from the building at any time.

*   *   *   *

But Wes, proud of the plant cafeteria's food, had already suggested that Weatherby try it. They were exiting from mahogany row toward the cafeteria when Vangie emerged into the hallway behind them, heels clicking like castanets. "It's Sage, the Santa Fe man, from L.A.; and he says it's urgent," she called.

Wes grimaced, then pointed toward the outside tables and sunshades. "Go ahead, I'll be along soon," he said to Weatherby, and turned back.

Two minutes later he was doodling on a pad as he spoke with Patrick Sage. "Sure I'm recording; you're a prime contractor," Wes said, and waited. "Of course I okayed it. Just a few final tests on the canards. . . . Out where we made those acceptance tests, I guess, where else? . . . Well, I'm sure they've got a good reason to be up there, but damn' if I know what it is," he admitted, with a chuckle that did not sound very convincing even to himself. Then, "A *what*? . . . Come on, Pat! Your guy in the Beechcraft was seeing things." And then, despite all logic, Wes's imagination began to see some things. "No, don't pull the plug on them. You know as well as I do, that could be dangerous and besides, I think somebody mistook a gleam on our canards for an aircraft. Tell you what: I can be there in two hours. . . . In Delta One, that's how! Just sit on this, Pat. You're recording too? Okay, record this: I'll take responsibility, and I'll do it in person. How's that?"

Before the earpiece was back in its recess, Wes was giving orders. Vangie tapped at her terminal without looking as Wes spoke, then waved her palm at her screen. "Is that it?"

He scanned it quickly. "That's it. And divert the delta training crew to the simulator but don't tell 'em why. I don't want this whole got-damn' plant buzzing with rumors."

"What about Weatherby?"

"*Hell!* He leaves tonight, but I can't take him with me."

"Why not?"

"I . . . because Rogan may be up to something weird, and . . ." He threw his hands in the air; let them fall to his sides. "I don't know why not. Weatherby expected a ride with the training crew anyhow. Lady, if this doesn't show the bastard I'm up-front with him, nothing will! Okay, go for it. I want Chris windmilling those props when we get to Delta One."

As he reached the door, Vangie called, while dialing, "Wes, is there any way we could reach Schultheis and Kaplan?"

Face set, he paused in the doorway. "There'd better not be," he said grimly, and hurried out.

* * * *

"You won't miss a meal," Wes promised as he ushered the puffing Weatherby onto Delta One's cargo platform. O'Grady hopped onto it, not entirely trusting all this sudden flurry of haste, sweeping the cargo hold above him with a professional gaze.

As the platform scissored up into the vast ship, Weatherby shook his head in disbelief. "I never figured it was so big."

"They were bigger sixty years ago," Wes assured him, and pointed forward. "We've got a freezer onboard, microwave, all the comforts. You'll see."

Wes pointed out the best seats, taking the copilot's seat so that he could brief Jim Christopher, quietly, using their headsets, their exchange lost in the rushing drone of Delta One's multiblade props. Christopher was nosing the big lifter above the plant as Wes finished with, "You have your heading?"

Christopher nodded. "Already called a flight plan on Ms. Broussard's say-so. We can't go over the Sierra's spine, and Uncle says we can't fly over China Lake, but I've filed over Tehachapi Pass. I make it two and a half hours, maybe less with a tail wind."

O'Grady, craning his neck at the plant buildings below, jerked around as Delta One turned toward the south. "Hey, Mr. W., who's driving our limo?"

Weatherby, following O'Grady's point, swept his gaze across the vehicles below, first with a frown, then a relieved headshake. "You'll be the death of me, Grover. Ours is parked over yonder," he said, pointing. "That's a stretch you're lookin' at."

O'Grady "hmphed" and relaxed, waving at the head he saw leaning from the window of the dusty Cadillac.

There was no return wave, though Ali Zahedi saw the hand passing back and forth across one window of the behemoth as it climbed. Ali had more important things on his mind as he drove slowly through the parking lot.

Joey Weatherby leaned back and enjoyed his microwaved Chicken Tetrazzini on the Bakersfield leg, content to watch the tandem rigs crawl down Interstate 5, almost content with Wes Peel's assurances about the future of the NTC. He realized that this walloping brute of a dirigible was part of his own future, like it or not. He did not ask many questions about this aerial junket because it was obvious that Peel had a sure 'nough brushfire in his outfit that he plainly didn't want to discuss yet. Well, you sure learned about a man's management style at times like this, if he didn't mind you watching. Peel's style was personal, idiosyncratic, hands-on. Like Joey's own, come to think of it. Maybe they by-God *could* work together.

They picked up the tail wind as they banked eastward toward

Tehachapi Pass, with distant peaks of the Sierra and Coast ranges rising on both sides of Delta One. Wes spied the Kern River canyon, wondering if Kaplan or Schultheis might glance up and see the delta cruising overhead, wondering just exactly where the hell those two really were. They had seemed more at ease with Rogan, the past month, and so had Allington, the whole got-damn' bunch of them thick as thieves, and they'd made him swear he'd stay away from the maglev this week. *Somehow, it's all tied together, and looking at all these loose ends will drive me nuts if I don't think about something else.*

So he moved back to sit near Weatherby, pointing out Edwards Air Force Base to the south. "That's where the shuttles land," he said. "They're big lifters too, but they need a lot of runway." He leaned nearer, pointing to the horizon. "Those low mountains ahead are the Clark Range. Not much for height, but that's where we're headed."

"You wanta tell me why all the rush?"

"Not 'til I'm sure," Wes admitted. "I got a wild-ass report that our maglev has some kind of a got-damn' airplane perched on its back up there. And Glenn Rogan has the maglev, and, well, I don't really know what to think. But I'm going to, in a few minutes."

Weatherby squelched the smile that he felt, but said, "Weatherby's umpteenth law: Never hire a man who's too much like yourself."

Wes studied the big man for a long moment. "I probably break that law a lot," he replied at last.

"I just said it was a law. I didn't say we never break it," Weatherby said, letting the smile come.

Presently, Christopher banked the big craft to follow the power lines and the twin sets of maglev rail, and Wes went forward again. "I'll take her," he said, donning the headset, swinging the delta northward, watching his sink rate as Delta One slowed. The tip of Clark Mountain rose 7,900 feet, but the maglev track did not rise much above its flank. The bare sunburnt mountaintop was to starboard now, as high as the delta, and Wes watched Delta One's shadow flit across the mountain as the gentle curve of rail came into view, and that long straight stretch he remembered . . .

"Good God Almighty," he shouted, and pulled the stick into his gut, reversing his props with his free hand.

TWENTY-FOUR

Even from his foreshortened view in Delta One, looking down that arrow-straight slope off the mountain's flank, Wes could see that the orange maglev was moving away from him at a speed all out of proportion to anything else on any railway, twin cyclones of desert dust unfurling in its wake and an extra set of canards protruding from something atop its cowl. Wes judged that the maglev must be nearing the speed of sound, and then saw that it was only the first stage of the system.

By the time Wes hauled the delta back to an even keel, two lances of flame had shot from the gleaming silvery thing that rode the maglev's back, and an instant later the silver dart hurtled forward, climbing slowly at first, passing over Interstate 15 at a height of perhaps a thousand feet. Wes estimated its speed at Mach two, but instantly realized that it was accelerating hard even as it banked over a dry lake and straightened again, now climbing at a steeper angle, matching and then surpassing the velocity of an artillery shell, propelled on smokeless, blue-white tongues of flame almost as long as the tiny craft itself. The maglev slowed quickly, its dust-devils disappearing as if by magic.

As Wes cut his power, they all heard a muted thunder rolling in across the high desert, already fading as that tiny dart dwindled to a speck between two pinpoints of light in its long climb toward the southeast. No one spoke for moments, and then Wes looked across at Jim Christopher. "Did I really see that thing lift off of my maintenance unit? Did you see it too?"

Christopher only nodded. Weatherby, who had rushed to a better vantage for viewing, said in a voice softened by awe, "Holy shit, how it does flee the scene. You mean that . . . that little shuttle thing isn't yours?"

"Did look kind of like a space shuttle, didn't it," Wes mused. "Without all those boosters or external tanks—but it's no shuttle, it was too got-damn' small." A two-beat pause while Wes leaped to a conclusion. Then, "Got-*damn* that got-damn' Glenn Rogan, he's test-hopping somebody else's got-damn' prototype fighter planes! I've got witnesses and that little hellion won't have a license for a tricycle when I get through with him. And Boff Allington's in on this, too," he grated, palming Delta One's throttles as he brought the great craft sliding down toward the maglev that was now moving backward.

Then, "What's all that?" asked O'Grady, pointing slightly to portside. The ugly bluff shape of the C-2 wrecker, with a pair of huge spheres behind its crane on the flatbed, stood out clearly against the buff and pink of desert hills. The C-2 was parked beside a small hangar, and Wes could faintly make out the track of an access road leading up the slope to parallel the maglev rails.

Breathing heavily, Wes replied, "It's got to be . . . shit, I don't know: Boeing, Northrop, somebody. I can tell you one thing, it's not mine! I'm gonna see whose it is right now," he added, nosing Delta One lower, letting her weathercock into the breeze. "Take her, Chris. We're going down there."

As Wes hurried down the passageway toward the cargo platform, Grover O'Grady saw a slight jerk of Weatherby's head and interpreted it correctly. He followed Wes back into the airship's bowels and stopped when Wes did. "Mr. Peel, ah . . ." He passed a hand under his casual jacket near a kidney, and magicked out a charcoal-gray automatic. "Everybody needs a backup sometime, and you say you don't know who those guys are."

Wes paused an instant, then waved O'Grady onto the platform with him. "Good enough, but put it away. I notice you can haul it out fast enough."

"Fast enough," O'Grady agreed, putting the thing away, and Wes saw the same smile O'Grady had worn in Dallas. It was the ready smile of a readier man.

Wes stepped to the uneven desert hardpan a hundred yards from Highjump's hangar, and the first man he saw through the open hangar doors was David Kaplan, who was already striding to meet him. Whatever Kaplan said, Wes did not hear, determined as he was to march into that hangar as Kaplan paced him. "Uh-huh! Ri-i-ight, fishing on the Kern, and where's that other sportsman? Ah, there he is," Wes went on, hardly noticing the spread of air navigation charts that covered three sides of the hangar like wallpaper. He was glaring at the back of a head he recognized from its shock of bronze hair, even with the headset clamped across Tom Schultheis's skull. "And what the ever-present hell are *you* doing here?" He said it to Wolf Schultheis, who was similarly seated with a comm set, now turning to see the source of the commotion.

The old man simply shook his head as if at some insistent insect, turning back and murmuring into his mike, the stubby old fingers flying before a computer screen.

"Coming up on t'ree t'ree zero seconds, injection burn in ten seconds; mark," said Wolf Schultheis.

Wes, breathing like a man who had held his breath for at least three hundred and thirty seconds, spun back to Kaplan, who had followed him in and was offering his hand to O'-Grady. Though he was smiling, O'Grady seemed not terribly anxious to grasp that hand. "Where the got-damn' hell is Glenn Rogan," Wes raged. "Up there in that airplane?"

"He is near Globe, Arizona, about six hundred miles from here, due to take the Arizona laser feed right . . . *now*," Kaplan said, listening to the countdown of Wolf Schultheis. "And I'll tell you about it in a few minutes but not, for God's sake, until he's finished the jump!"

At this point, Boff Allington trotted into the hangar lugging a jury-rig device with three joysticks and a hefty battery pack. "Saw your runabout, Wesley," he said with every evidence of good cheer, setting the pack down. "Congrats, your maglev's a smashing first-stage booster and good as new. Or did you see it?"

Wes considered his reply, and the fact that Allington always acted this way when there was not one damned thing he could do about a situation. "I saw it. Have you ever seen the inside of a federal prison?"

"Not yet, but we all expect to." Suddenly, behind them, a brief statement from Wolf Schultheis and a cheer from his son and David Kaplan. Allington spun around. "Injection?"

"On the fucking money," Tom Schultheis said, choked with emotion, and suddenly Wes saw that the towering Kaplan was trying to speak while tears coursed down his cheeks.

Moving toward one of the wall maps, Kaplan said huskily, "Glenn Rogan is on his way to orbit, Wes. We put him there. You made it possible; you just didn't know it." And then he turned away, sighing heavily, wiping at his eyes as he tried to contain long-pent emotion, leaning with his forehead against that sectional chart. "*Yisgadal v'yiskadash sh'may rabo*," he began, intoning the Kaddish, by tradition a mourner's prayer. But it could also be employed to acknowledge that the issue was squarely in the hands of God, and this was David Kaplan's employment of it, an invocation from man's distant past in aid of his beleaguered future.

"Orbit." Wes said it in absolute disbelief.

Allington, standing behind the elder Schultheis, leaned over to flick a switch, and then an overhead speaker cut in. ". . . And from now on I'm mostly spam in a can," said Glenn Rogan, tiny pieces of his words lost in the transmission. "Gee-meter showing just over five-point-five at cutoff. My integrator says we won't get that orbit you predicted. Talk to me."

Tom Schultheis, checking readouts fed back from High-jumps's telemeters to the hangar's integrating equipment, confirmed it: "We're almost a thousand feet low on burnt velocity, Highjump. Now predict orbit of one-two-eight miles, plus or minus three. Don't use those control jets any more than you have to. They're all you've got left."

"Not much vision unless I do. Rolling to starboard anyhow. Will try to stabilize at six-oh degrees."

Wes tried to visualize Rogan in the tiny dart, rising ever more slowly to an orbit nearly a hundred and thirty miles up, trying to hold it at a sixty-degree bank. But the roll attitude would make no difference, once he was in airless space. Wes looked at Allington and snarled, "He won't make it?"

Allington's headshake preceded his answer by scant seconds, but in those seconds Wes Peel cut through his own confusion and anger with a phrase that was, like Kaplan's, a heartfelt prayer: "God in Heaven, help him!" His fury seemed a petty response as he began to accept the idea that somehow, without major resources of any government or corporation, these few men had fired an aircraft into low earth orbit. He could strangle them all later, *but right now, God, help Glenn Rogan.*

"Not as bad as it might be, Wesley," Allington said softly, both of them listening to the comm set as Rogan switched to a cellular radio relay near El Paso. It appeared that Boff Allington had made the best possible use of commercial channels, so that Rogan would remain in radio contact for the longest possible time. This was no NASA job with tracking stations around the world, but they had communication during those first crucial minutes after lift-off.

Allington motioned Wes to an inflated plastic globe that hung, swaying, from a tawdry piece of cord. O'Grady followed, saying nothing, ready for anything. "See this yellow tape? Rogan's orbital path. The maglev was his first stage, up to transsonic where he could cut in the scramjets. The jets were the second stage; took him up twenty miles and about six hundred miles downrange. That's about as high as he'd ever get because the scramjets can't gulp enough air above that, even though they're doing over Mach twenty-five. But remember those laserboost units we tried on Delta One?"

"You were testing 'em for this," Wes accused.

"Guilty as sin," Allington agreed cheerfully. "With liquid hydrogen feed switched to a thrust chamber, and Arizona State's laser feed for sixteen seconds, Rogan doesn't need anything more. That sixteen seconds of laserboost injected Rogan and Highjump into orbit."

"Not the one you wanted."

"No, there's still a few molecules of air where he is, and it'd bring him down within a few orbits whether he wanted or no." Allington turned the big globe in his hands, following the yellow line of tape with a fingertip. "He passes near El Paso, then Corpus Christi, and then across a swath of South America. Then across the South Atlantic, off Cape Town and into the Indian Ocean. Then he swings past the northern tip of Australia, over the Pacific." The fingertip stopped. "He's got two options to land: La Paz, in Baja California, or Mazatlan, on the Mexican mainland. They're both airports of entry for Mexico, and we've already filed his flight plan. He won't even break any Mexican laws, Wesley."

"But a pisspot full of 'em here."

"Not as many as you think; mostly fraud, and he was only following orders. He's even cleared with NORAD, even though I would dearly love to see their faces when they check flight plans against their radar plot.'' Allington was beaming with the glee of a man who has brought off the all-time, gold-plated, Nobel-prizewinning practical joke.

Wes grasped the globe; began to turn it in his hands, noting with astonishment that this orbital path lay almost entirely over the world's oceans, and nowhere near any nation that might view the flight as hostile. Then he released the globe and strode to the sectional charts on the hangar walls.

Here, too, a yellow line of tape stretched across the charts, proceeding from one he knew well. Wes studied the Los Angeles sectional chart, one he had spread across his lap a hundred times in cross-country flights. Someone had penciled in the maglev rail's path along the power line route which was already marked, in standard cartography practice, on the chart. And yes, at exactly the highest elevation on that route lay that long, downhill west-to-east stretch where an earthbound maglev could piggyback a small vehicle to near-sonic velocity. *Almost as if God and man had conspired to produce an orbital system. No! As if God had nudged man into it. And this path over the Phoenix sectional chart, perfectly situated to take a huge laser feed, a path almost exclusively over wilderness to the Gulf of Mexico.*

Wes shook his head in wonder. ''It can't all be just by chance, Gram,'' he muttered.

''Beg pardon?'' It was Allington, standing by.

Wes snapped back to the present. ''Never mind. I swore I'd never work on this kind of thing,'' he said.

''God knows, you didn't, Wesley.'' Allington's expression lodged somewhere between accusation and compassion. ''But you paid for most of it. We kept a set of books on it so you'd know. Seemed like the least we could do for you.''

''You got that right,'' Wes replied, then jerked his head up. Kaplan, after finishing his Kaddish, had moved nearer the two who were monitoring Rogan's transmissions. Wes called, ''What's the status of Rogan's whatchacallit?''

216

"Highjump," Kaplan corrected. "The last cellular link was Merida, and he's already jettisoned the bracelet. Probably taking pictures of the Amazon basin right now."

Tom Schultheis stood up, rubbing his neck, and met the gaze of his employer. "I can't tell you how sorry I am that we had to do it this way, Wes," he said softly. "But we *did* have to do it."

Wes studied the little designer silently, and decided that Tom Schultheis did not look like a man filled with sorrow; he looked like Horatio at the got-damn' bridge. "You want to tell me why? When you knew how I felt?"

"Because dis country is so full of people who will not look at de obvious," said old Wolf Schultheis, pushing himself up from his seat. "Big shuttles do big jobs, but dey are much too large to be helped by a laser feed. De maglev sent Highjump off with cheap electricity, and orbital injection was with more electricity, Mr. Peel."

Wes thought about that for a moment. "How much cheaper?"

The old man looked toward his son. Tom said, "Payloads cost two thousand dollars a pound by shuttle, Wes. That's why it's taking so long to build our space stations. Using electricity and liquid hydrogen, Rogan has just released half a metric ton of water, tethered in bags like a bracelet so it'll freeze into ice. We'd intended to get it into an orbit that wouldn't decay for a few months. Anybody who wanted that water could go and get it. And pay Exotic Salvage forty dollars a pound. *Fifty times cheaper*. Now it looks like the stuff will vaporize during reentry pretty soon. But it's out there, and radars all over this world will track it. Our point is made. Smaller can be better."

"So in sixty flights this Highjump thing will equal one shuttle."

"Or sixty Highjumps will carry the same tonnage," Kaplan put in. "Maybe ten or twenty a day, maybe automated. How big a production line you think it'd take, Wes?"

"Oh, . . ." Wes paused, and leveled a long stare at Kaplan. "I'm sure you could tell *me*."

"That he could," said Allington. "Peel Transit's Line Two could build a hundred Highjumps in three years." The Brit's voice quickened, "Whatever happens to us, Wesley, we will use the trial to publicize our figures."

By now, Wes had moved toward another chart he had known better in the days when he drove hell-for-leather down the length of Baja California. "I flew out of the Cabo San Lucas strip once," he said. "Seems to me it would be a straight-in approach."

"Too short," said Kaplan. "Mazatlan's Buelna is nearly straight-in, too, and it has almost nine thousand feet of runway; takes commercial jets. But DeLeon, in La Paz, is almost as long, and Rogan said you can generally depend on a brisk head wind. It was his choice."

Wes gnawed his lip, eyeballing Rogan's options which were separated by two hundred and fifty miles of the Sea of Cortez. "When does he come into radio contact again?"

Kaplan squinted at the console's clock. "About ninety-five minutes from lift-off; an hour from now. He won't be in contact until he's scrubbed off some velocity, and you can't transmit through that ionized stuff. He'll make one skip off the upper atmosphere, right about here." Kaplan's long finger moved from Hawaii slanting toward the Baja peninsula's Pacific coast. For the first time, Kaplan's demeanor was uncertain as he added, "We weren't absolutely sure our leading-edge coatings could take reentry thermal shock in one lump, so Glenn will watch his thermocouple readings."

"So what? There's nothing he can do about it."

"He can stretch his reentry if he has to."

Wes eyed the tall man. Tom Schultheis had moved near them, sipping a glass of iced tea, perspiration now drying at his temples. "So Rogan's got Mazatlan if he has to overshoot,'' Wes said, and saw Kaplan nod. "But what if he *under*shoots?''

"He can't,'' Tom Schultheis said quickly.

Wes turned, fixing his gaze on Schultheis. "You mean, he'd better not.''

Schultheis looked away. "Yeah, that's what I mean.''

Allington, from behind him: "Wesley, could you wait for your recriminations until Highjump is down—one way or another? This isn't Peel Transit's problem, it belongs to Exotic Salvage. Yes, it's our company. This gentleman with you can witness what I say: No one can blame you for—''

"Shut up, Boff,'' Wes snapped. "I can have your collective asses on a shaker table anytime I like. Let's get on with the agenda: Would this Highjump vehicle fit into a delta cargo hatch?''

"With its wingtips retracted, yes,'' Schultheis replied. "I made sure of that a long time ago.'' He saw the unasked question in Wes's face and went on, "If someone were boosting a dozen Highjump cargoes a day to orbit, you'd expect an abort now and then, landing on strips in New Mexico and Texas. You'd have to retrieve 'em to stay on schedule.''

"You bastards had it all worked out, didn't you?''

"God, I hope so,'' said Schultheis, glancing back at that digital clock, then at the silent O'Grady. "I take it this guy will want to read us our rights.''

"I've heard 'em a few times,'' O'Grady said. "Mr. Peel, if you're sure about this crowd, I'd like to go tell Mr. W. If the rest of this went down while he was sitting in a dirigible, he'd have my liver on a plate.''

"Go get him,'' Wes replied. "Everybody in the got-damn' country will know about this by tomorrow, and I don't intend to face the press like a man who's been hoodwinked on his own turf!''

TWENTY-FIVE

Joey Weatherby was perfectly capable of believing that Rogan's tiny craft could achieve orbit, having seen it disappear so abruptly into the blue. What he could not reconcile was Wes Peel's grudging acceptance of insurrection within his ranks. "So," he said, not caring who heard him in that scruffy little hanger, "you're gonna kiss and make up with a bunch of bozos stealing you blind?"

"Not stealing; just borrowing," Wes growled, still wrestling with a sense of betrayal nonetheless, rubbing his throat with a hunk of ice from his tea under the roof of that broiling shed. "Look, Weatherby: The truth is, these guys have revolutionized cargo-lifting to orbit right under my nose. I'm not against it being done, I just . . . it's a personal thing; I swore I wouldn't do it.

"And I didn't exactly, but *they* damn' well did. Even if Glenn Rogan doesn't make it down, he's already *up*, fifty times cheaper than it's ever been done before. That's the breakthrough, man; they've just put this country into the commercial space business! How's it going to look if I bring charges against my own people after they used my hardware to do it?"

"Like you run a sloppy shop, is how." Weatherby watched Schultheis father and son as they arranged screens and charts for an event that could be no more than ten minutes away, now. "And you do, for a fact." The heavy chest rumbled with mirth. "Just goes to show you. A man who's always runnin'

220

this far ahead of everybody else can find his pants at half-mast. So what's your next move?''

"Depends on Rogan's luck," Wes admitted. "If he makes it, we bring the vehicle back in Delta One, at our leisure. If he doesn't, I guess we go to Rockwell or somebody for better reentry hardware. Either way, I'm backing this effort as of now. Those grandkids of yours will be got-damn' glad of it!''

* * * *

Rogan wondered why his jaws ached until he realized it was from grinning for so long. Somehow it had little to do with the achievement, or the fame it might bring; it had everything to do with the reason why he had doled out precious gouts of peroxide to roll Highjump onto her back. Here, vision was everything, worth whatever it took. He marveled at the lights of Rio De Janeiro from one hundred and thirty miles up and, soon after (too soon, much too soon, but once he saw it, he knew this glory could not appear soon enough) the slow emergence of Indonesia on his horizon at dawn, with a cloud scatter of flat cotton batting across Micronesia, and the sun, oh God, the great flare of red changing slowly to yellow and rising to meet him over the Pacific where the only sounds in the universe were his own breathing, so that he held his breath to make the silence perfect.

Many times, spread-eagled in a controlled free-fall before grasping the D-ring of his chute, Glenn Rogan had imagined that he was truly flying, his arms mighty pinions that might carry him soaring, not merely into the clouds, but up and up, into the vast reaches of the high beyond, where nothing was imposed between him and those pinpoints of starlight that composed the rest of all Creation.

Well, now he was doing it, blinking away the tears of joy that blurred his instruments, those reminders that he must roll back into the proper attitude for his first deceleration over

Midway Island in mid-Pacific. Though Highjump's taped announcement played on several channels, only once had Glenn Rogan answered a response, from Darwin in Australia, perhaps because the accent was American. "That's a roger, Darwin," he'd said, "Commercial vessel Highjump, an hour out of Barstow with a cargo of water for the natives up here. Bound for Mazatlan, Glenn Rogan commanding." And then he'd done some more grinning. It didn't matter much what he said now, they were either gonna gold plate his ass or skin it when he got back. If he got back. As cargo vessels went, he commanded only a kayak but it was, by God, the only truly commercial vessel in *this* corner of the galaxy. Now, according to the digitals, it was time to make good that boast about Mazatlan, with the La Paz option still open.

He spent more peroxide than he'd like, overcoming Highjump's inertia to start that slow roll maneuver, overcoming it again when the gyros told him his roll attitude would be on the money. The microwave DF locator placed him some twenty miles north of dead-solid perfect, too much for safety, with Midway off his starboard bow though he could no longer see it, seeing instead the star-pricked not-quite-black of space interrupted by shining arcs of lighter blue on each side of his bow through the tiny quartz windows. He might have used more peroxide to improve his vector a bit, but he needed it to orient Highjump properly. Then, when he employed those control jets for retro fire, she would ease downward against that shining shell of air beneath, presenting her insulated belly with her nose proud.

He spoke his intent, not only for the onboard recorder but for anyone who might be listening in case this was his last mortal act, and with the long retro burn felt the straps bite into his body in prolonged discomfort. It seemed to take forever before he felt the first faint shudder sixty miles up, and he resisted the temptation to urge her down faster because, now that her surfaces were scrubbing off more of that orbital velocity, Highjump would be coming down soon enough, maybe sooner than was healthy for a country boy from Okie State. He watched his thermocouple readouts leap, saw a flare of ionized particles bleeding back from Highjump's bow. The deceleration grew from a suggestion to a definite surge of Rogan's body against the straps. As the shudder grew to a hum through the structure, he stole one glance at the DF locator before pulling back on the control stick gently, ever so gently, and then a bit harder, twitching it to the right, then left again, as he did so. It was a gamble. Hell, so was picking your nose . . .

The bow flare dwindled near Hawaii, and Rogan imagined that he felt through his educated rump that the craft was rising slightly now, but not for long, in a shallow skip off of the feather edge of atmosphere. The locator, computing his position from one millisecond to the next, yielded a plot of his progress, and that smidgin of pressure on the control stick while slamming into air molecules at miles per second had brought Highjump within twelve miles of her ideal path, maybe good enough and maybe not. There wasn't a damned thing he could do about it in any case, because his peroxide tank light was on, and what was left must be available to keep the gyros happy.

Highjump was still over forty miles high, committed absolutely and inevitably to reentry now that she had bled off ten percent of her velocity in air friction. Thermocouples said that she was also bleeding off some of that heat, but Schultheis had told him straight-out that no one could say for sure whether that spray-coat insulation would protect the bird.

But that tricky maneuver to adjust his descent path had slowed Highjump a little more than he'd intended, and now he saw that there was no longer any Mazatlan option because Highjump would reenter well off the Pacific coast of Baja, and as the shudder grew to a hum, and the hum to a battering roar, a wall of flaming ionized air and particles of insulation began to wash back from Highjump's bow. He described it profanely, the only way he knew, aware that the recorder was taping his instrument readings and that no one could hear his transmissions through that fireball with Highjump behind her bow wave and Glenn Rogan in the center.

The G-meter reading rose past six and was climbing rapidly before the hammering shudder blurred images too much to read, and his eyeballs were trying to pop out and the same deceleration force was hauling at his guts, but now he had turned Highjump over to the gyros and to God, letting the harness reels haul him cruelly back against the seat. Spam in a can again, just hapless meat in a roaring inferno committed to the automatic flight attitude program. Glenn Rogan did not know whether he really lost consciousness, but if it was a dream, the pounding of his heart was still hellish enough to punish him for ninety minutes in Heaven.

He knew that the fireball was diminishing because his chief visual sensation, the dazzle of that fireball, was dimming. *Can't blackout or redout or any other kind of out, now*, he thought desperately as that dazzle faded. But there was still some ambient light, and still the bite of straps into his body and that thunderous vibration, so he wasn't entirely out of it.

And then the vibration and the ferocious bite of straps abated, more quickly than he expected, and his mind was clearing at a fantastic rate. Highjump hurtled toward the west coast of Baja with less than twenty miles of altitude, and as soon as air friction slowed her enough, Rogan could extend those little wingtips and glide the sucker for many a mile.

Simultaneously he was trying to raise the DeLeon tower at La Paz, a hundred miles to the southeast. No more of that salty talk of commercial vessels on the high seas, this was strictly SOP except that landing Highjump at over two hundred knots was, by definition, a declared emergency. Rogan raised DeLeon, and declared it. It escalated to a world-class fuckup almost instantly.

They had him on DeLeon's radar but could not believe their own readings of his approach speed. Runway One-Eight had traffic stacked with a Mexican jumbo jet on final approach, and they would need time for the straight-in approach he proposed on that same runway. It meant an S bank, which Rogan had planned to line him up, but now he was dropping fast over the Magdalena Plain and knew that he could not just hang up there forever. It was then that he spotted the light of his cellular comm link and flicked the toggle. He was already shrugging from straps, mentally reviewing the procedure to stall the bird and try to fight his way out with the chute on his chest, when the familiar voice spoke.

It was Wolf Schultheis. "Highjump base to Highjump One, over."

Rogan presented the situation in seconds. He was dropping to twenty thousand feet, dead-stick at four hundred knots, hoping somehow to stretch that glide or luck into some impossible updraft. He was not going to risk whacking a commercial airliner and that was that.

"How's your hydrogen?"

"Thought of that. Fifty pounds left, vents off, pressure up, but I'm too slow to light these scramjets now." The inlet geometry of a ramjet was critical, and they all knew it, so why bug him with an impossibility?

"You could dive for that delta vee," said the old man.

"Thought of that too. Not enough altitude left."

The voice of Tom Schultheis: "Not even with your wingtips folded?"

Why not? Because he was thinking of those extended tips as his only hope, that's why. Folded? He might push the envelope an inch beyond the possible, might wind up plowing a few miles of Mexican hardpan, but my God, how she would plummet. "Retracting," he said, pushing the stick over, seeing the wingtips retract, watching those flat hills develop contours and distinct features as he flicked protect covers from the shotgun-start toggles. He'd had the tips extended when he maneuvered on that test hop. Well, he'd just have to be damned spry if the shotgun start failed.

Loafing at three hundred and seventy knots, Highjump began to drop like a stone, her arc steepening, and now the airspeed indicator was climbing, but not fast enough if he intended to pull this sucker up without her wingtip extensions, and then he realized that any thrust at all, no matter how inefficient, was better than none, and cracked his throttles, the pyrotechnic starters flashing sparks from beneath the scramjet nacelles.

He was still losing altitude when the machmeter took off, and hugged the stick to him, now dead level but inching downward still, whipping fronds from the tips of a line of coconut palms some idiot had planted on the outskirts of La Paz as Highjump began her shallow climb.

Glenn Rogan kept those scramjets bellowing well out over the Bay of La Paz, the simultaneous flameouts producing a deafening silence in the cockpit, and extended the wingtips again for a long and, it seemed to him, almost languorous circle beyond islands in the bay as he called in his new position. The DeLeon tower had seen and heard him, all right; *Por Dios*, who in all Baja del Sur had not? Rogan had done more than declare an emergency: his treetop pass near the city had caused a few . . .

Rogan touched down almost at a stall, with only a hundred feet of runway eighteen behind him and a mile and a half of rollout ahead. He used it all, running off the end at a trifling pace into sand that engulfed his landing gear. Because, as he said on his cellular comm link, if a man can cover a burning tire with sand, he isn't obliged to piss on it.

TWENTY-SIX

As Jim Christopher banked Delta One north toward Hayward in late afternoon sun, Wes rubbed his back across the copilot's seat to ease the residual stings of celebration and grinned ruefully while talking to Vangie Broussard on their scrambler circuit. "I'll be sore for a week from hugs and back slaps, honey. If there was a dry eye in the hangar, it belonged to Weatherby."

"I can imagine," she replied. "I'm ashamed of myself, Wes; I should have spotted something of what your boffins were up to. Now I'm glad I didn't," she reflected. "Exotic Salvage, my Aunt Rodie! Why didn't someone drop into San Leandro and see about that little operation?"

"I left that to Tom; he said they were small but fair."

"I'll *bet* he did! Oh, you want Alma Schultheis to make up a media release right away?"

"You help her with it. And stress the point that Peel Transit could never have done it without the farsighted Santa Fe, blah blah blah. We've gotta co-opt those folks, Vangie! We'll be at the plant by seven, and Weatherby has some luggage to grab and a plane to catch. I'll go with him, but I'll be back later. Do you mind working through the evening, honey?"

"What I do on Friday nights for love! Well, I don't mind if I can pack a swimsuit and go to Baja with you tomorrow," she replied, laughing. "I gather you'll be picking up your wayward boys on the way down, tomorrow. What should I tell their wives?"

"As little as possible until we've got our stories together. Rogan's camped out with our vehicle so nobody tinkers with it, and we'll be back by Monday, God willing. That should cover it. Any calls that won't wait?"

"No. Somebody tried to reach you a couple of times. The receptionist said you were in Delta One and wouldn't be back before five."

"Media, maybe?"

"I didn't handle the calls, but they didn't ask for a call-back," she said, adding quickly, "I've got a lot to do before you touch down here, my love. Got to run."

Wes doffed his headset and moved back with Weatherby, who had spent much of the past hour dictating into O'Grady's memocomp. "We'll have you in your limo by seven. I, ah, hope we can count on complete discretion, Weatherby."

The big man waved his cigar in dismissal. "Hell, why add to your troubles? You know something, Peel? If you start tooling up for those little Highjump gadgets, all those projections I've been looking at are up in smoke. They would'a been a big help, but not now."

Wes tossed him a killer smile. "You mean, what can I do for you lately?"

"Well, shit, you gave me a bucket with a hole in it."

"Yeah; well, something came up," Wes said laconically. "Turn off that memocomp and we'll talk all the way to the limo and then to your hotel. Or do you have a radio in that rental barge?"

"I do, but I like to watch a man's face while he diddles me," said Weatherby, his eyes sliding sideways at O'Grady's chuckle.

"Suits me," Wes replied. "I know what you're after; how Highjump will affect the NTC."

"You got it," Weatherby nodded, snapping the machine off.

*　　*　　*　　*

After Golam's call to the plant from a nearby phone booth in early afternoon, it became clear that Farda had lost one chance as that vast delta droned away overhead. "But these new dirigibles do not burn," Ali had said, with better than average understanding of Great Satan's machines. "We probably would only have warned him. If he returns anytime today, our original plan will still work."

"We have squatted in the dust outside his palace long enough to be noticed," said Nurbashi.

It was Golam Razmara who observed that they might drive miles away and wait, because that airship was simply too large to be missed as long as they had an unimpeded view of the skyline.

So the stretch limo slid up toward Castro Valley Road, where the view was adequate, and to a vendor of fish and chips for the midday meal. Nurbashi vetoed Golam's suggestion of a nearby McDonald's because, he said, Great Satan's ground meat was without doubt deliberately contaminated with pork. Allah did not provoke Nurbashi to ask himself about the fat in which that fish was fried, because Allah is merciful.

But because Nurbashi was anxious, Ali made a second call in midafternoon, verifying only that John Wesley Peel was expected after the close of the day shift, and could anyone else be of help, or would he like to leave a message. Ali's response was a broken connection. The message, for Peel alone, sat fidgeting and sweating in the front seat of the stretch limo.

Toward the end of the Friday afternoon rush, Golam finally saw it, leaning from his open window and squinting toward the southern skyline. "There! It must be he, that thing is far too huge to be anything else." And Ali saw and agreed, putting the limo into motion, bullying his way through traffic toward the valley floor and Hesperian Boulevard.

Waiting for the last traffic light, watching Delta One sink behind buildings of the Peel plant, Ali looked over and saw Golam drumming his fingers on the windowsill. "There is no reason for anxiety," Ali said with some anxiety, wondering if that light would ever change. "You shall be on the spot appointed to you before he is, brother Golam."

The appointed martyr smiled, his eyes now alight, and then he said a curious thing. "You remember the route, brother, from Foothill to the Five-Eighty Freeway?"

"Perfectly," Ali replied. It struck Ali as curious because, by the time Ali had the limo speeding out of Hayward, Golam Razmara would be eating peeled grapes in paradise. Ali wondered if he, too, would care that much about the mullah's welfare when Ali himself was moments from martyrdom. Then Ali sent the limo spurting ahead, and asked for one of the Uzi weapons, just in case. Peel, he explained, might not be alone and they did not want witnesses.

*   *   *   *

Royston Kimmel checked his watch and sighed, tooling his unmarked brown Ford around to the main entrance of the Peel plant. The Oakland office couldn't afford several agents for surveillance around the plant perimeter, not on something as nebulous as the Peel case; but one good man on the job was infinitely better than none. Kimmel had agreed to pick up the slack for his relief man, who had something going with his lady in The City on this Friday night. He hadn't figured on Peel staying this long at the plant. Maybe Peel was in that walloping great airship that had ghosted down to its hangar a few minutes back. Kimmel had chosen not to put in a call to find out earlier because it was poor practice to keep reminding a man that he was watched, even by friends.

From long expertise, Kimmel took note of the swing shift cars in those parking lots; the patterns they made, the singletons that liked to park off by themselves like that twit who had his red 'Vette straddling two parking places so no one would chip the pinstriping on his three-thousand-pound red plastic cock. Sometimes, when it was a van off by itself, somebody was humping somebody inside. And sometimes somebody was just waiting with a clear field of fire, waiting to hump somebody good. This evening, as Kimmel cruised toward the exec building to reassure himself that Peel's Blazer was still out front, he saw no suspicious loners.

But he did see a stretch Caddie limo with smoked glass, gliding along like a rubber-tired locomotive as it approached the building's front. Only three vehicles squatted in the line of exec spaces: Peel's Blazer, his assistant's little Fiero, and twenty yards from Peel's boxy machine, that other Caddie limo with the visitor's sticker. The black stretch trundled past, too distant for Kimmel to make those plates, disappearing between ranks of swing shift cars. Kimmel had seen two thousand cars that day, a thousand of them parked around Peel's plant, but only one black stretch limo with smoked glass. He had seen it cruising past the plant's front entrance about lunchtime. Kimmel saw no good reason why anyone who rode around in a beast like that would do much of it in Peel's lot. But there could be a bad reason, and as Kimmel turned the Ford around, he made a fateful decision and reached for the hand mike at the dash, glancing into his rearview toward the front doors of the exec building.

He saw a big duffer emerge, the door held for him by a younger, husky redhead, and the last man out the door was tall and blond, hurrying enough to limp. That had to be Peel, and then something in the edge of Kimmel's vision made him look straight ahead, and now that stretch limo was squalling around in the big lot heading in his direction but with a line of cars between, and Kimmel made the connection without even thinking about it. He dropped the mike, crammed the lever into reverse, and burned rubber as he shot backward.

Wes, carrying enough papers to keep him busy half the

night, stopped at his Blazer and unlocked it long enough to toss his armload inside. "Start it up, O'Grady," he called as the others moved toward the rental nearby. "I'll be right with—"

He stopped, seeing a brown Ford sedan careening backward from the nearby parking lot, suddenly furious that one of his swing shift people was hot-dogging it in his *parking* lot, for God's sake, and Wes moved into the open waving one fist and shaking the other.

The Ford's front wheels cocked sharply, whirling its rump end so that it projected across the mouth of the next lane, and then Wes saw the chrome and black of the stretch limo barrel into that opening, and the limo's front bumper slammed the rear of the Ford so hard the smaller car spun, walloping the limo which was now turning left toward Wes, fifty yards away. The one-two punch of that grinding collision echoed shockingly loud off the front of the exec building, and Wes flinched from it, and when he opened his eyes a second later, one hell of a lot of new things were corking off.

At his right, on the edge of his vision, Wes saw O'Grady's head and shoulders pop from Weatherby's limo. The Ford driver was still trying to peel rubber to prevent that limo from proceeding, the limo now making a T with the Ford and not making much headway, and the front passenger door of the limo was open and someone was sprinting like hell toward Wes as if running for eternal life. Then the limo stopped with a sharp dip of its prow, and the driver's door flew open, and a rattling burst of gunfire erupted from inside, shattering glass into the passenger's side of the Ford.

Wes went down, impeded by his bad hip, fumbling for the Walther on his ankle. Someone was shouting, "*Stay down, Mr. Peel,*" and as Wes brought the Walther up, several reports issued from O'Grady's direction. The fellow sprinting toward Wes was still twenty yards away, and at the third of those rapid-pace shots from O'Grady the runner's right leg flew outward as if jerked by an invisible wire, spinning him hard onto his left shoulder against macadam.

Then the limo driver, a tall swarthy man, burst from the limo, whipping the short wooden stock of a weapon to his shoulder as he leaned toward O'Grady. Wes's first round holed the driver's door as the driver loosed a half-dozen rounds; his second, after a careful adjustment of sight, slapped the man's weapon sideways and sent splinters flying into the face of the gunner, but not before the man had fired another rapid burst. O'Grady shouted like a boy on a playground and fell against the far side of Weatherby's limo, and as the limo driver dived back into his vehicle, Wes starred the windshield exactly where a driver's head ought to be.

And then Wes saw that the felled runner had come to his feet, staggering toward Wes with one hand fumbling into a bulky vest and the other arm out as if to embrace Wes himself, and Golam Razmara saw pity wash across Peel's face, and knew that the American would not prevent his coming nearer, and Golam offered a brief prayer of thanks as he forced himself forward against the pain in his right leg.

The injured runner, whose hands held no weapon, was yelling something in a language Wes did not understand but it looked like that limo might run the poor guy down, and Wes moved forward fast to drag the man out of the limo's path. But the limo shot backward as the wounded man staggered within a fishing pole's reach of Wes, and Wes thought those next shots were intended for the limo driver until he saw the right side of the injured man's face shatter into a blossom of pink and gray.

Golam Razmara, with his forefinger on the button in his vest, had one final instant of awareness. *So this is what an exploding vest feels like*, he thought, believing that the brutal shock of a nine-millimeter hollow point was the result of his detonator. He fell like a bag of shot, face up, arms flung wide.

By the time Wes rounded the rear of Weatherby's limo, the

big man was on his knees on macadam, trying to lift a gasping Grover O'Grady whose eyes were open as his mouth worked almost silently. "Nailed him, Joey," he said, and tried to smile.

"I love you for it, kid," Weatherby managed to choke out, letting Wes help as they heaved the hideously gut-shot O'Grady to his feet. "We'll get you fixed up."

Incredibly, the driver of the brown Ford was again in control of his savaged vehicle, accelerating forward down the two-lane entry to the Peel plant with eight-foot chain link fence on each side, narrowing the gap between himself and the stretch limo just ahead.

Wes snapped, "My Blazer's got blankets and room for him to lie down, and I know where the hospital is. Let's go!" He saw O'Grady's face as they rolled him into the rear of the Blazer, ashen, eyes shut, his lower lip bleeding between his teeth.

The distant concussion of brown Ford against black Caddie, as the limo tried to make its left turn onto Hesperian, sounded like a tower of garbage cans collapsing. "I got the license number," said Joey Weatherby over his shoulder as he lumbered toward his limo. "What hospital?"

Wes shouted, "Kaiser, to the right," as he hit the Blazer's ignition, angry that Weatherby was not with him to secure a dreadfully wounded man for a two-minute scramble to the hospital. Carefully, because he could hear the thumps of O'-Grady in his cargo section, Wes wheeled out and then urged the Blazer to Hesperian. He was only half-aware that the Ford was beginning to block traffic, its horn a constant complaint, or that the black stretch limo was just getting underway after tearing loose from the Ford's front bumper. He did see Joey Weatherby booting his own limo down the macadam behind him, and wondered why Weatherby did not follow his right turn but, instead, thrummed his limo left after that battered stretch.

In less than two minutes Wes careened into the Kaiser's tall shadow, horn blaring over the hammer of his engine. He shouted for help but did not get it from either of the two citizens standing by the emergency entrance, but one had the decency to swing a door open as Wes, carrying Grover O'Grady as a man crosses a threshold with his bride, swung inside bellowing for help.

* * * *

Ali Zahedi thought he was clear, once he had ripped free of the Ford's fishhook bumper, and in his inside rearview saw the ferocious teeth-bared visage of Nurbashi as the mullah, terrified among the clatter of loose weapons at his feet, snatched for purchase at anything he could grasp. "Safety belt," Ali shouted. He ran one red light, narrowly missing pedestrians, and then slowed to avoid any further display. He found the turn to Foothill, collected his wits, and then called, "I heard no explosion. It is my turn, now!"

"Get us out of here," the mullah screamed, "that cursed black car will catch me!"

And then Ali saw the other car, much like his own, narrowing the gap behind them, and recognized it but could not believe the man he had shot was capable of driving. Ali floored the pedal, all four tires howling like *djinn* as he began the long turn onto Freeway 580. "Shoot the demon," Ali cried, no longer caring about the bizarre roles a mullah would, or would not, choose.

But the car behind was curiously loath to approach closer than fifty yards as they sped eastward toward Interstate 5. Ali knew about this California autobahn because Zahra Aram had briefed them; forbidden to use radar, the state police often let traffic find its own pace. Well, Ali would set a hot one. In the slanting rays of a dying sun, Ali thought he could see massive shoulders hunched in the chase car. The man seemed content to lie back, and then Ali noticed the whip antenna on that chase limo, and realized what that meant, and without concern for Nurbashi he slammed his brake savagely, hoping the chase car would rear-end him.

Weatherby swerved to the shoulder, braking adeptly, and then Ali was well and truly onto it again, swerving around a big double-tandem Peterbilt, hoping he could hide in traffic. Another big rig ahead began an abrupt move into the fast lane, a third rig some distance ahead slowing so that Ali had to careen around those wheeled buildings. Ali saw the driver of the chase car with his window down, apparently shouting to someone in the cab of a big rig, and when that hefty arm swung out of the window, it pointed toward Ali. For some reason, on the two-mile stretch he could see ahead, most of the huge cargo rigs seemed to be hanging back, and those behind seemed to be gaining, a staggered wall that eliminated other passenger cars, discounting the immaculately restored Porsche roadster that snarled past them all on the outer shoulder like a scalded wolverine.

Ali, his suspicion growing, thought he would take the Dublin exit but an enormous triple-tandem rig was parked there, and its driver doffed his long-billed cap as Ali passed. Now Ali could not see the chase car, no other cars at all, but over the wails of the praying mullah he heard the buzz-saw whirr of huge tires ahead, and behind, and now beside him, and when honking did no good he decided that anything a Porsche Spyder could do, a stretch Caddie limousine could do as well. Ali's understanding of machines was, after all, not perfect.

Ali did not actually elect to go for the shoulder until he had been nudged up to eighty miles an hour and the rig to his left made an abrupt lurch in his direction. Then Ali swerved, and the rig ahead braked just enough to close the hole, and then, only then, did Ali Zahedi spy his immediate future. It did not look much like paradise.

It looked exactly like a culvert flanked by a shallow sculptured fan of concrete. Ali's reflexes were excellent, and he hit the brake instantly, so that the Caddie hit the foot-high lip of concrete at only sixty miles an hour, carrying away the entire front suspension and catapulting twenty-three feet of limo into a series of end-over-end flips shedding pieces of metal, glass, flesh, and twenty-dollar bills at each impact.

TWENTY-SEVEN

Joey Weatherby, puffing from his exertions to locate the waiting room outside Surgery, did not have the look of an NTC Board Chairman; here he was only a harried, overweight man in rumpled clothes hoping for some barest scintilla of good news in the kind of place that wholesaled bad news by necessity.

Vangie, who had arrived minutes before, saw the big man first and dropped the dog-eared copy of *Sunset* she'd been leafing through without seeing it, nudging Wes as she arose. 'He's still in surgery,'' she said.

"They made optimistic noises,'' Wes added as he stood up, 'but between the lines it sounded like touch and go.'' He raised one hand, fingers crossed.

Weatherby's heavy shoulders slumped. ''The guy in the Ford. Who the hell was he?''

"A federal agent named Kimmel. I saw him down in Emergency a half hour back, with a couple of his friends from the Department of Justice.'' He waited to see that register on Weatherby's face. ''They say the man O'Grady shot was toting several pounds of plastique around his ribs, just like that weirdo at my party.''

Weatherby blinked, taking it in, saying only, "Imagine that. Now I owe *them* one. How is he?"

"Mad as hell. Broken nose, glass cuts, and a gunshot crease across his back. But he was on the scene because you told me about that Winthrop guy. Just think about it, Weatherby: Where would we be right now if you hadn't?"

"Too goddamn many 'ifs.' " Weatherby closed his eyes, rocking slightly, and let Wes's hand guide him to a seat. Hugging himself with crossed arms, the big man rocked back, then forward, staring at his shoes. "Joey," he said softly, and sighed, and then looked with dry and feverish eyes toward Wes. "He never called me that before. I think he knew he'd bought it, and for once I was helpless as a baby."

"You could do what I'm doing. You can pray," Wes replied, and lowered his head again.

They were still sitting with bowed heads when a woman in hospital greens approached from down the hall, mask hanging like a necklace, pinching the bridge of her nose. The trio stood for this ritual. "Are you Mr. O'Grady's family?"

"My son-in-law," Weatherby said softly. "My dau . . . his wife is in Pennsylvania." He did not notice the effect of this revelation on Wes, but stood as if expecting a physical blow from the surgeon.

"He is not out of danger, but we think he's going to make it. Helps to have a middleweight's physique," she said, and gave details only after a careful scrutiny of the three who stood before her. One slug had slit the peritoneum, laying open the abdominal cavity like a razor. Another had glanced off a hipbone, damaging a kidney and displacing several organs. "I suspect he had some rough handling on the way here," she finished, shaking her head.

Wes, a little defensively, "What if we'd been a minute later?"

The surgeon donated a wry smile. "There would be no good news tonight. A lot of arterial bleeding, and—let's just say we stabilized him at the last possible moment. We'll know more in a few hours. Now if you'll excuse me.'' She accepted their handshakes and returned down the hall, scuffing in her paper sandals.

"So much for weekend plans," Weatherby said, but looking like a man reprieved. "Thanks for . . . for Grover," he added, with a rough hug for Wes. "I know you've got that Mex round-trip to make, and I'll be okay here. Listen, don't pass it around that Grover is family. First he was the best damn' soldier I've ever had. God! I saw his innards sagging out like that, and told myself he was a dead man."

"Is that why you took off after that guy?"

A nod.

"What makes me suspect you caught him." It was not a question.

Now a muscle twitched in Weatherby's face, and Wes saw a glitter in the deep-set eyes. "No. But I did see the damnedest wreck east of here on Interstate Five-Eighty, a half-mile ahead of me, just about sundown." A considered pause before, "I even stopped to render assistance, of sorts. Two guys, both in satisfactory condition." He drew a finger across his throat.

Wes studied the big man's face a moment. "Guy you were chasing?"

"Him and another one in that Caddie. I don't know why their limo didn't burn, it sure had some interesting hardware spread along the shoulder. Like a sawed-off Browning. Anyway, the guy tried to bluff a big rig; well, several of 'em, actually." Now Weatherby's teeth were showing faintly through a tight smile.

"You said you had a two-way in your limo," said Wes. "Did you use it?"

"I might have. There's a lot of CeeBee talk with codes your average driver doesn't understand. You know, for emergencies, and like that," Weatherby said, waving his hand vaguely.

"And you had an emergency," Wes said in bogus innocence. "Did you get any help?"

"The other guy sure as hell didn't get any," Weatherby said. "I told you before; the freeways are still my turf."

"I didn't hear any of this," Wes said. "But thanks. Is there any likelihood that . . . accident . . . will be studied?"

"Doubtful. Nobody pranged anybody, and nobody told anybody what to do, exactly."

"Not exactly," Wes echoed, with his first smile in hours. He bent to retrieve his coat, motioning toward Vangie's handbag, then stopped. "Just out of curiosity: How would someone with a lot of NTC clout make an, ah, *in*exact suggestion of that sort?"

"You got me," said Weatherby. "I suppose he'd just point out the problem, and tell the kings of the road to do what they do best."

*　　*　　*　　*

Delta One reached La Paz late on Saturday afternoon, with a spirited crew including Wolf Schultheis and both his children, because Alma and Rogan raised hell from both ends until Wes agreed to take Alma along. Something about long waits and Mexican civil law; and besides, Alma wanted her father to give her away in a romantic tropical setting, now that Rogan had popped the Question by long-distance cellular link. Jim Christopher kept referring to the trip as the Honeymoon Special.

Mexican weddings, as Boff Allington remarked while watching La Paz beach palms sway through the bubbles of a champagne glass, must be infectious. "It has to be pathological," he said to Vangie, who beamed resplendent with a hibiscus in her dark hair and a simple gold band on her left ring-finger. "No woman in her right mind would have married Wes Peel," he charged.

Vangie laid her cheek on the shoulder of her new husband.

240

"It seemed like the wrong thing to do at the time, so I did it," she said, straight-faced.

"And I was afraid she might not ask me again," said Wes slyly, earning a bite on his earlobe for his calumny.

Without taking his arm from Vangie's waist, Wes used the other hand to toast the grown children who were gamboling on a beach backlit with the last ruby glow of a La Paz sunset. Alma Rogan's formal dress bunched around her thighs as she rode the back of Glenn Rogan, arms hugging his neck, her squeals punctuating his progress through deep sand. Tom Schultheis and David Kaplan, like Rogan himself, frisked barefooted with trousers rolled to their knees, with shouts appropriate to men whose bellies were full of Margaritas and Coco Locos.

"Dey will be sorry tomorrow," remarked Wolf Schultheis, his elbows resting on a tile balcony. "It is hard on de leg muscles. I would be with dem otherwise." He smiled reflectively toward the beach.

"Let 'em play," Wes replied, inhaling the spicy breeze. "They'll be working their buns off soon enough, converting our plant lines for Highjump assembly."

"It is what dey wanted," the old man reminded him.

"I expect I'll have to remind 'em now and then," Wes said, and kissed his bride.

*   *   *   *

Winthorp appeared on the Grayson campus on the first day of the Fall Semester, subdued as always, his emotional antennae quivering for any sign of surveillance. The fireplace of his bungalow was full of pulverized ash now, and his files were half empty. In any case he certainly would not need clippings to remember the news articles on Kosrow Nurbashi and his minions. Fingerprinting had crystallized the identities of Razmara and Zahedi, though Nurbashi's illegal entry into the country had kept him an anonymous smear of meat on a California

freeway. With luck, Winthorp himself would never be impli-
cated.

And in six months or so, perhaps Winthorp could extrude
fresh tendrils of interest into the undercurrents of Shiite di-
plomacy. If the media could be believed, John Wesley Peel
must be stopped before he consolidated the cargo systems of
Great Satan from highway to orbit.

Winthorp was a week into his fall schedule when an agent
from the Cleveland FBI office paid him a visit. Winthorp had
memorized the news releases of that Hayward fiasco, and knew
that the NTC's Joseph Alton Weatherby was with Peel at the
time. Therefore, Winthorp admitted his interview with Antony
Ciano. It was legitimate scholarly research, he insisted, ex-
ternally calm, internally vibrating. Winthorp had only asked
questions, he said.

And yes, he was the son of Sultana, his entire life was an
open book; and no, he did not recall the names Razmara or
Zahedi. Students, perhaps?

Winthorp met his classes that day because he knew that he
must, though his guts continued to vibrate like a bowstring.
Valium helped a little. Three more days of placid campus life
helped a lot, especially after he disposed of those pulverized
ashes.

Winthorp knew that he had dodged that FBI bullet and his
heart pounded only for a moment when his door chime sounded
one evening. It was one of his new students, a young woman
whose eyes reminded him of his mother's though her accent
was more southern.

Zahra Aram had needed only an hour to decide her course
of action after seeing Golam's fate on television and in newspapers. She knew, of course, that the unidentified man had
been Nurbashi. It had taken her a week to find a Midwest
academic named Hassan Winthorp; two more days to move
from one university to another.

Now she simpered and stammered until the professor invited

her in, and showed her class notes to him obsequiously, apologizing for the intrusion. Could he, perhaps, explain how a young Sunni Moslem woman might pursue a career in his exalted footsteps?

When he heard her Sunni claim, Winthorp relaxed further. He became somewhat more alert and cordial when the girl, intent on her notes, kicked off her shoes and showed him a flash of thigh.

Her hair reminded him of Sultana's. He told her so. She pulled the ornate pins from the loose bun of hair and preened for him, and as they sat facing one another she asked if her figure also reminded him of anyone, and leaned so that he could see between her breasts, and Winthorp leaned forward too, dry-mouthed, knowing he must not touch this luscious creature but knowing also that he did not really need to.

Focusing on her cleavage, he did not see her hands sweep toward him as if to box his ears, but he felt an instant of agonizing pain, leaping forward, forcing her to scramble aside.

Zahra left soon after, polishing the door handle, leaving the place dimly lit and walking quickly to the campus. It was three days before they found Winthorp, as dead as *Farda*, lying in a pool of his own blood. The most careful search of the man's effects, including those file cabinets and his library of tacky old movies, failed to turn up the faintest hint of an enemy, or of *Farda*. Police forensic specialists said he was done in by an ice pick of needle sharpness; maybe more than one. Sixty years previously they might have suspected hat pins, or those heavy-shafted, ornate carved hair pins of yore. But these days, who would suspect the vengeance of an old-fashioned girl?

THE BEST IN SCIENCE FICTION

THE BEST IN FANTASY

☐	53147-7	DRINK THE FIRE FROM THE FLAMES	$3.95
☐	53148-5	by Scott Baker	Canada $4.95
☐	53396-8	THE MASTER by Louise Cooper	$3.50
☐	53950-8	THE BURNING STONE by Deborah Turner Harris	Trade $7.95
☐	53951-6		Canada $9.95
☐	54721-7	FLIGHT IN YIKTOR by Andre Norton	$2.95
☐	54722-5		Canada $3.95
☐	54719-5	MAGIC IN ITHKAR 4	$3.50
☐	54720-9	edited by Andre Norton and Robert Adams	Canada $4.50
☐	55114-1	STALKING THE UNICORN by Mike Resnick	$3.50
☐	55115-X		Canada $4.50
☐	55486-8	MADBOND by Nancy Springer	$2.95
☐	55487-6		Canada $3.95
☐	55605-4	THE HOUNDS OF GOD by Judith Tarr	$3.50
☐	55606-2		Canada $4.50